TRAINER
THE BEGINNING

TRAINER
THE BEGINNING

JAMES CATES

TATE PUBLISHING
AND **ENTERPRISES**, LLC

Published by Tate Publishing & Enterprises, LLC
127 E. Trade Center Terrace | Mustang, Oklahoma 73064 USA
1.888.361.9473 | www.tatepublishing.com

Tate Publishing is committed to excellence in the publishing industry. The company reflects the philosophy established by the founders, based on Psalm 68:11,
"The Lord gave the word and great was the company of those who published it."

Book design copyright © 2016 by Tate Publishing, LLC. All rights reserved.
Cover design by Samson Lim
Interior design by Mary Jean Archival

Published in the United States of America

ISBN: 978-1-68254-501-0
Fiction / Christian / General
15.10.27

CONTENTS

PROLOGUE

Bill and Saundra sat in the living room looking at the sonogram. "It's a boy. From the looks of it, he's going to be a big boy."

"Yes, Saundra, I'm so proud. Our son. In about nine months, we'll have all the joys of a new baby."

"I'm excited. We'll grow so much through this. Bill, I love you so much."

"I love you more, Saundra." He took her into his arms and kissed her, wanting to never let her go.

For a long time, they sat there just holding each other, enjoying the closeness.

———

Trainer felt the successful plant of the genetic transfer of the demon. *Now is not the time to come out. I'll be better off waiting for the time of the birth.* "Master, the first boy is on the way. The plan has started. Your victory is near."

—✦—

Fred sat with Harry, John, and Peter at the Bible study. "Can you believe that just two years ago, it was only you and I, Harry?"

"God has blessed us in many ways. Peter and John are certainly proof of that."

Peter said, "We need to thank you for being willing to work with us when we didn't understand."

Fred looked to Peter. "It is an honor to take a new disciple under your wing and help them through their weaknesses. We need no thanks. We are simply following God's instructions. We want you to be a Christian that takes others under their wings and guides them too."

1 THE FURY BEGINS

Standing from the night's sleep, Bill stretched his five-foot-eight (5'8") body to get his muscles warmed up for the day ahead of him. The heavy thud of his footfall on the wood floor led him to glance back to make sure his beautiful wife still lay asleep on the bed. All his eyes could make out in the dark was her long hair lying across her pillow. The stillness of his wife told him all he needed to know. For over five years, he's never wakened her when he gets up, and he hadn't really felt a need to look back in all that time, but this morning was different.

One glance in the mirror told him something was really wrong. It wasn't the three-day shadow that caused the alert or even the blank stare. What shocked him was the sight of dried blood across his forehead and around his eye. His thoughts roamed through the events that took place before bed; but he found nothing unusual to cause what he saw in the mirror. What had he done that would have caused that?

The faucet refused to open. One hand on the hot water knob and a quick twist always got it before. Now it was like he had no strength in his hand at all. Securing both hands with a firm grip around the faucet handle, he twisted it all the way on to send water splashing in the sink. Quickly, he turned the water halfway down with the feeling of confusion and anger raging through him; he had not experienced this before. Was he really that angry and didn't know it?

His mind reeled. *Certainly I can get through this morning without this. I can't remember the last time I was angry, and now I get angry because a little water splashed in the sink. Bill, what is wrong with you? Why are you so angry?*

His fingers rolled into tight fists, his elbows curled to ninety-degree angle, and his shoulder muscles tightened, ready to strike on a whim. *Relax, Bill.* His mind slowed into control again. *Don't do something stupid that you will regret.* "I'll just get this blood off my face and let it go." He reached his hand into the running water to check the temp; the washcloth was right beside the sink. He lightly tossed the washcloth into the sink for it to soak up the water. A few seconds later, he grasped the faucet to turn it off and remembered what happened when he turned it on. With slow steady control, it turned easily. He took the washcloth out of the sink to wipe his face. *I've got to shave anyway.*

He slowly wiped the washcloth across his face and around his eyes. With most of the blood wiped away, he saw no physical scrape that would have caused such bleeding. He wiped off the rest of the blood with amazement that there was no cut on his face. Where did all that blood come from? What did I do last night?

Bill shook it off with a shiver and picked up the shaving cream. The shaving cream felt cool on his face and relaxed his nerves. Finally, something that went right this morning. This was going to be a good day. With a deep breath, he repeated, "This is going to be a good day."

The razor glided down his face, removing the three-day shadow with the greatest of ease. Bill's mind went immediately to the many razor cuts that he got most mornings and wondered why his super beard, that never gave up easily, would surrender so quickly today, and why had it grown so thick in just one night? With everything else that had gone on this morning, he didn't argue the point anymore.

The rest of the morning went easily enough. By the time his briefcase was in his hand, lunch ready to go, and ready to give his wife a morning I-love-you kiss, he saw the clock on the wall. It was as if it jumped off the wall and yelled, "You're late! Get in gear and go now!"

Bill flew out the door, not getting it closed completely. He jumped off the full-length porch and landed squarely on the walkway to the drive. His hands in his pocket for the keys, he spun right to shoot directly to the Mercedes Benz.

A strange voice came from somewhere inside him and said, "Don't take the Benz, the truck would be better."

"The truck?" Bill looked at the '70s model F-150 that he used only once or twice a month. He hated the truck for the rough ride and body-beating torture that it created. He had no intention of taking that truck unless he had no other option. Whoever came up with that idea was a lunatic, and he would not accept that he came up with that as an idea.

"I know you don't like the truck, but I do. Take the truck." This strange voice insisted, and Bill was confused where the voice was coming from.

"I like the Benz. The ride is incredibly smooth and has the power to get me anywhere with speed and control, unlike that ugly truck." Bill knew the truck had an old, faded paint job that would not look good in any situation on his job. This meeting was very important, and he couldn't look bad in any way to make this deal work.

"None of that is the point. The point is you need the truck today because I want you to need the truck." The strange voice still insisted and was making a case for taking the truck.

Bill had not stopped moving as he turned the corner to the driver's door of the Benz. Fluidity in motion had always been his strong point, and his expectation was the same today. His hand reached for the door handle and froze.

"I told you to take the truck. You don't want me to force on this issue. Go to the truck, get in, and take the truck. End of story!" This voice was sounding tense and angry; whoever it was that was saying all this stuff or junk, as Bill thought of it, was not going to win this fight.

In an act of defiance against whoever or whatever, he opened the door to the Benz, got inside, and slammed it. "Now what are you going to do?"

"I told you not to make me force the issue. Now you will know the price I make people pay that resist me." The voice was not calm but rather fierce, at the edge of uncontrolled anger.

Bill attempted to put the key in the ignition but failed. He removed the key and scowled at it, noticing that he had the Ford key instead of the Benz key. He knew those keys by feel, and it had been ages since he had mistaken them.

"I told you not to make me force the issue," the voice said, with a bit of a teasing tone in the background.

Bill refused to acknowledge the voice, switched the key to the Benz key, and swiftly placed it in the ignition. The Benz turned over but refused to fire. So he tried again. His anger began to boil up from his toes. "What are you up to, and who are you?"

Bill could feel sweat forming on his forehead and the veins in his neck throbbed on the surface.

"Never mind about that now, you will know that soon enough," the voice recanted with satisfaction. "You are learning. Now will you listen to me?"

In his anger, he threw the door open, stomped over to the truck, and mumbled, "I don't know who you are, and I don't have time to deal with you now. I'll take the truck."

"Thank you." The voice had an attitude. "You will learn."

The door of the Ford opened more swiftly than expected and banged into the Benz passenger door. "No, not the Benz. I hate this truck!" Bill's anger escalated into fury. "I'll worry about the Benz later. I have more important things to do now."

Bill's face was red; fire burned in his eyes, and his palms ached from his fingernails pressing into them. *What is wrong with me today?*

Bill flung himself into the truck, yanked the door shut, "AGH!" The door slammed into his shin with all the force he could put into it. Immediately, he felt his shin swell. He lowered his head into his hands as the pain shot from his leg through his body into his head. When the pain subsided, he slowly raised his head. His eyes fell to his hands, and they were covered with blood.

———

Saundra was still resting quietly in bed half asleep. The baby kicked hard, curling her into a ball. Intense pain shot up her shin to her knee. A squeak escaped her lips and turned into whimpers. Still curled into a small ball, the baby kicked again, sending a new round of pain in her womb. Struggling against the pain to get out of bed, she got both feet on the floor and rose up. Immediately her left leg collapsed, and she crumpled to the floor. A whimper and moan of pain cried softly from her lips. The tears flowed from her eyes.

———

The voice inside Bill cried out, "No, Saundra is in trouble now."

Her name filled Bill's mind and brought an immediate reaction, "Where?"

The voice filled Bill with fear, "The bedroom. Get her to the hospital now."

Bill jumped from the truck and fell to the ground, rolled first to his knees, his side, and finally to a prostrate position. What in the world? He glanced down and, for the first time, noticed his left leg was soaked with blood. Fear and panic filled him.

Get up, you got to keep moving. He got his good leg under him and rose up on it. He hobbled as quickly as he could to the front door. Forgetting the pain in his leg, he reached for the doorknob. As the door opened, he fell over the threshold into the living room. Bill winced as the pain increased with the blow; he forced himself to his feet, putting the least amount of pressure on his left leg. "Saundra!"

"Bill, help me." Saundra's cries fired a spark into Bill.

Bill hobbled up the stairs with the help of the railing. He went as fast as he could down the hall and into their bedroom.

As Bill entered the room, he saw Saundra lying on the floor in a heap. He rushed over as fast as his legs would allow. Kneeling beside her, he picked up her hand. "Honey, what's the matter?"

"The baby is coming now," she cried in pain.

The voice took over, "Get her into the Benz. The ride is smoother and faster. She needs to get to the hospital now! The baby must live!"

Bill slowly raised Saundra into a sitting position before lifting her up. He held tightly to her five-foot-five frame, supporting most of her weight. Bill helped her into her bathrobe, grabbed a pair of shoes, and carried her to the top of the stairs. Cautiously, he walked down the stairs, one step at a time. The new weight added pressure to an already tired leg, and now, at the bottom of the steps, it started to tremble.

The voice kept encouraging, "Keep moving, Bill. I will make sure everything is okay."

Bill guided them to the car. Bill could feel Saundra's body cringe with each contraction. Their heartbeats increased, beating as one. Bill felt the blood drip down his leg, and Saundra grew heavier in his arms. He glanced down into her pale face. Bill found it hard to maneuver them both with the constant pain shooting up his leg.

"Move, Bill. Now!" the voice cried out.

Bill forced every step to the car through the pain; every whimper from Saundra felt like a cattle prod to his heart. Every step revealed that too much time had passed and the emergency level had risen greatly. Saundra was tucked safely in the passenger seat of the Benz. Bill hobbled to the driver's side. Finally in the driver's seat, Bill started the car with the backup key secured in his wallet.

"It's time to go." Bill's foot slammed down the accelerator, causing the car to jerk back out of the drive. A simple turn of the wheel caused the car to slide around the corner on the road. The brakes stopped the car, the shifter jammed down to drive, and the accelerator slammed back down to the floor, sending the car weaving and fishtailing out of control down the road.

"Ooohh." The soft moan from Saundra made Bill slow the car down to a controllable level. Bill could still hear the tires squealing and see the smoke from the tires.

"Bill, speed is everything. We have to get to the hospital now." The voice knew the consequences of not getting there fast would mean death for Saundra and possibly the baby.

"Going, going, not stopping now."

"AGH!" Saundra screamed with another painful contraction.

"Forget control." Bill was steadfast in his decision. "It's time to move. Benz, let's roll." His foot pushed the accelerator, which didn't stop until it hit the floor. Bill felt the engine respond, sending torque to the transmission then the wheels. The Benz snapped forward, turning so fast that all Bill could see was the blue haze of the rubber burning off the tires.

Bill focused only on getting to the emergency room. He knew every sway and twist the Benz would make and how to keep it in the general direction.

His pulse quickened with each second of motion. The pain in his leg intensified with his pulse. Brake lights and the lines painted on the road were where his mind registered. It is enough. We are almost there.

The car swerved and squealed to a stop by the large hospital sign. He knew the look of the emergency room doors well enough to at least guess these were.

Two shadows ran for the car doors. Bill, exhausted and sore, groped for the door handle and missed. His shoulder hit the door and stopped cold. The thud sounded like a hammer pounding on a block of wood in his ear.

The passenger door opened, and hospital staff was already helping Saundra out of the car. Saundra whimpered then cried out with a contraction. Quickly, they wheeled her into maternity.

As Bill leaned against the door, it popped open. With nothing to hold him up, he spilled out of the car, caught by a guard. The lights went dark, and the voices muffled out. His heart slowed, nearly stopping. He could sense movement, but it drifted away, as a wave rolling off the beach back to the ocean.

"Bill," the voice inside him spoke up, "are you there?"

Beyond his belief, Bill could comprehend the voice and hear it when no one else did. "I am here."

"Good. I am here to help you. I need you to listen to me."

"Listen to whom? I stopped listening to voices in the night when I grew up and became a man. You're not an exception." Whatever was going on? Bill was not going to accept a voice not coming from a body.

"They call me Trainer. I have been with you from your birth, and there is nothing that I do not know about you," Trainer sounded prideful.

"If you have been with me since my birth as you say, how come I have not heard from you before?" Bill was challenging Trainer and didn't know what to expect.

"Search your memories. Can you think of a time in your childhood that you wanted to go out to the country to a street called Power Lane?"

Bill looked back to a time when he was only eight. He was a bright kid and had felt a strong urge to go to a house on Power Lane. The fight that had ensued burned vividly in his mind.

—∽∽—

"Where are you going, Dad?"

"I am going to the house on Power Lane."

"Can I go with you?"

"No, Bill. I don't think that would be good. How about we go out to the Tasty Spot for a bite to eat when I get back?"

"Dad, I want to go with you."

"No, Bill, I am just going to drop this off and leave anyway. It isn't anywhere you want to see."

"Yes, I do. It sounds exciting." Bill was getting excited and jumpy at the thought of going.

"Bill, sit down here. You are not going with me, and that is final. Stay here, and we will go to the Tasty Spot for some supper later."

"No, I need to go with you!"

"Bill," his father forcefully said, "you are not going with me, and that is final."

The more he cried and fought, the worse it got. His forehead grew damp with sweat. His blood vessels pulsed and pounded harder as the fight continued. His hands swiped at the air across his head. They pulled into eye view: whatever was on his hands was pink.

The color gradually changed brighter and brighter with the volume and intensity of the battle. Bill's father's eyes showed the desperation to get out without any more confrontation. The sternness in his voice said his patience came to an end.

Bill's forehead streamed bright red streaks of sweat as his father left the house. The blood continued for a short time after his father left. He settled down, and the bleeding stopped.

The babysitter never kept him again after that day. In his short life, he had never seen such shock and what he could only relate to terror before.

"I remember that. What was that to you?"

"I got impatient and wanted to start working before you were ready to understand." The calmness Trainer spoke in was more than he could believe. "The dinner at the restaurant afterward was a training session for me. It was then I learned when to activate, and you are finally ready."

Bill thought about that and remembered a time just two years later. He had gotten into a fight in school. It wasn't anything unusual, just the standard schoolboy junk, but this was no ordinary fight. The other boy was taller, bigger, and two years older. When the boy told Bill he was going to give him his lunch, Bill unleashed a fury that shocked even the teachers. The boy was in the hospital for a week with extensive broken bones and bruising all over. The teacher said that the boy had never touched him in any way. The strange thing was the emotionless way he sat down and ate his lunch, like a predator enjoying his kill. "How much of that was you?"

"More than you want to know. That was another experience that I learned much from."

Bill thought, *Trainer has to learn, how much has he not learned? How much could I keep him from learning?*

Trainer came back, "Everyone learns. I've learned more than enough to make your life miserable. No, you can't stop me from learning. You have many things to learn from me. Are you still with me?"

Bill replied, "I'm still here just thinking. I am prepared to learn everything you want to teach me."

"Good, first thing's first. You have to get to 5757 Power Lane. There will be many lessons learned there."

"That was the house that Dad would not take me to, wasn't it?"

"Yes. That was the problem. I could have learned a lot before this day came."

"Like what?" Bill's curiosity rose with that.

"Don't go there. You will learn what I need you to and no more. Besides, you will not and should not cry over spilled milk." Bill made mental note of that and continued to listen.

"You will learn so much from the logs in the basement. A fair warning: you will read some stuff that you should not believe. You can ask me if it is true, and I will tell you. Acting on something without my permission will cost you."

"Will cost me? What is there for me to act on?" Bill was looking for anything that would reveal how to deal with Trainer.

"You are not going to go there with me, ever. If you know what is good for you, you will look, ask, and respond as I say."

Bill could hear frustration and tension in Trainer's voice.

Bill, still searching for a clue but finding none, continued to pry. "Can I play Twenty Questions with you?"

"No, I will not answer questions from you."

Bill held any questions that he had for the logs. He knew that there would be time later.

—◦—

Trainer knew the training he missed was already costing him more than he wanted to pay. Already he was being challenged with questions that he was uncomfortable answering.

I know that I need to get to the house fast. The help I need is waiting there. What will it take to get out of this place? The thought completely captivated his attention as he floated freely through the vein.

Suddenly, Trainer felt a needle enter into the vein. He started watching and looking. Working to stay on the backside of the needle and against the flow of the blood, Trainer searched for fluid entering the vein. Seeing nothing, he worked hard to stay on the backside of the needle, yet he was drawn closer to the needle. Trainer immediately pulled away with all he had. He thrust rapidly against the pull, moving away. With all the resistance Trainer could force, he fought to get distance between him and the needle.

The needle's pull reduced and then stopped. The needle left the vein, and Trainer fell stiff with exhaustion, allowing the blood circulation to carry him on the current through the body.

Bill's steady breathing and relaxed muscles allowed for an easy time of drawing the blood for the test. Bill never knew the needle was coming. Any sounds from the outside world were no more comprehensible than a faint whisper coming from the far corner of a room. The only conversation he understood came from inside his body.

His whole body began to convulse. More hands applied pressure over his body to keep it still. Sweat started beading on his forehead. His muscles trembled with fear as his eyes rolled to the back of his head. As the convulsions grew more severe, the sweat became red and began to drip down the side of his head. Once the needle was removed from his arm, he relaxed and settled down into the bed again.

Bill asked "What was all that for?"

"That is the reason I don't like going to hospitals. I hate needles."

"What is wrong with needles? They are only used to draw blood and inject needed medication." Bill tried to relax Trainer about the needles.

Trainer retorted, "You don't understand all of the circumstances involved. I will never like needles."

—◈—

The panic returned when a needle returned into the vein. Though Trainer's travels had taken him far away from the needle, his insecurity led him to shiver as a nervous response. Like radar, he tracked his location to the position of the needle. Settling into a small vessel in the chest, he waited and watched for more needles or anything else that might be important to know.

Trainer instantly realized that the only eyes he could use were dark, revealing nothing of the outside world. He had to wait to see where the problem may come from. He was left with no other option but to hide for the time being in a place of safety.

—◈—

The needle easily penetrated the skin, found the vein, and slid inside it. Bill's pulse rose at the onset of the IV needle. Tension applied over every muscle, stiffening his body and shaking every muscle like a minor earthquake. Sweat started at the forehead, dripped down and around to his ears, then the clear sweat turned pink to red.

The flow of blood oozed out of his leg, saturating the sheet below it. The bruising that was once light in color and green shifted to a bright blue and purple and expanded up to his knee. The shaking worsened, blood dripped steadily out of his nose, everything steadily increased to a high rate and appeared to lock there.

The doctors and nurses worked persistently on Bill, but everything remained the same. Then as suddenly as his heart changed, it dropped and stabilized at a normal rate. All the bleeding stopped, and there were no cuts to account for the blood loss.

—∽∾—

"Bill," Trainer prompted, "are you still with me?"

Bill replied, "Yes, I am. What are all these medical problems that keep coming up?"

"That was one issue that I, nor any of my ancestors, have ever learned to control, or I was never was taught by my father. The importance of this training is the key to the success of the mission."

"Mission?" Bill thought he had another valuable piece of information. "What exactly is this mission? Is there something I can do to help?" Bill was looking more for information than he was an opportunity to be of help.

"Yes, there is. Get to 5757 Power Lane and learn what I need you to learn."

Bill could hear the irritation in Trainer's voice. *This must be something that I am not to know.* Bill collected the information for future reference.

—⁓—

Trainer shivered in realization that Cadet was born and alive. He could feel Cadet's call and knew the need. Though he desired to get to him and teach him, he could not get Bill conscious, and up to get to him. With all the trouble the medical staff was already having, he knew it would be a while before he was free to see him. The decision was final. Just sit back, let Bill rest, and work with him as much as possible and wait on the rest.

2   THE SIDES DRAWN

Fred looked to the wall clock realizing that time was slipping away, and he still needed to prepare spiritually and physically for the Bible study. His five-foot, four-inch frame was handsome, he was smart, and he had easily mastered his Bible studies. Though he had a strong desire, he had minimal skill and less natural talent for physically active sports. His 140-pound frame made him even less apt to fit in this world.

Now he was preparing to lead a small Bible study of just three other men. John, Harry, and Peter were all that had ever come. They had become a strong prayer team that, through Jesus's strength, had seen many more miracles than they deserved. They could do nothing but thank Jesus for the victories, and the group became known locally for their answered prayers and the power they were answered in.

Fred remembered the three men he met with every week. Though John was slow in speech, hard to understand, and had a lot of questions, he had become the one to spread God's wisdom to the group through a supernatural prophetic ministry that only God could provide.

Harry was a believer for a long time and knew Jesus deeply. He had wisdom and understanding that went beyond most scholars, though he had spent not one day in college. He had the notation from the group that he and his gift from God was the reason for the group's success in answered prayers. When he prayed, it seemed heaven's gates opened and the floods poured out.

Peter was new to the group. He had accepted Christ just last month and was learning a lot from the other three. They were continually patient with his questions that must have seemed below them, but they kept assuring him that he was to ask them. Though he thought them as stupid, they kept telling him that all their knowledge was learned too and they would always show him what he wanted to know. In fact, he had chosen the last three books of the Bible to study.

Fred was sliding into his jeans when the thought had struck him that he had been meeting with these men for three years now. They had changed homes to meet in three times. Each time they did, it was to make it as convenient as possible for the newest member of the group. Now he had an hour drive outside of the city into farmland to meet in a house that was half the size of the barn with more animals than one person should have taken on in three lifetimes.

His plain blue T-shirt slid down his chest as he fell to his knees, raised his hands, thanking and praising God for His mercy and grace. He knew he would never understand them but could not help but feel like he didn't deserve them. These moments had come often and, as of late, a habit. It wasn't until he got up to put on his shoes that he realized the time to be leaving had come and gone.

His slip-ons would be enough for now. With all he needed already in the Gremlin, he was out the door and into the car in a flash. The dependability of the car was great. It shuddered off, taking him away from his home to the Bible study as fast as its small engine would allow. Sometimes he wondered if it had ever gone seventy-five miles an hour before in its life. It jumped up to fifty-five in two and a half minutes. With this car, you had to have patience, but it always got you where you were going.

God always provided for his needs, and this old car was just another answer to prayer. It was cheap on gas, could get as dirty as all the dust and bugs could get it, and ran like a top even though it has over one hundred thousand miles. His mechanic had kept it in good shape and kept parts stashed for it. This was just another blessing that God had given. With it, he was able to be with the people God put in his life to keep the ministry going to the few.

Steadily he rolled down the road. He thought about how he was going to approach the lesson and some of the prayer requests that came up last week. As he drove out of the city, he approached the T-intersection that took him to the long, straight stretch of road. Turning left on the road, he assured himself he was going the correct way by the houses and fields he used as landmarks so many other times. The landmarks appeared and vanished behind him as he instinctively turned by the big red barn with the John Deere green tractor and continued on. He turned on to the next road. The only thing that broke the fields with growing crops were a house or barn dotted here and there along the way. He had seen all the dots before, but now he noticed something about one dot in particular. The mailbox said 5757 Power Lane.

The lawn had been well kept, not a blade of grass a millimeter taller than any other. The For Sale sign in the yard stood straight, telling everyone that drove by to "Buy Me." The outside of the house looked immaculately polished, shining so bright in the sun that it was almost blinding. His eye did not stay on that though; there was something out of place, even scary, about the house.

———✦———

Trainer let himself run through the bloodstream freely. All of a sudden he felt it, the needle alert, and it was closing in fast. "No, no, no, no!" The needle was pulling at him again. With everything he could muster, he pushed away from the needle, trying hard to outrun the draw. As the pull stopped, he was flung away from the needle like he had been shot out of a rocket. He never slowed down until he got back into the hiding hole to observe.

—◦◦◦—

As the nurse placed the needle into Bill's arm, she remembered the last time, and pulled to fill the tube quickly. With the one tube full, she removed it to load the second tube. She filled the second tube for the necessary lab work and prepared to leave the room. Talking to him had proved useless; he was still out and had been since he entered the hospital.

Instantly, sweat pooled and ran from his forehead. She saw the team grab a hold, restricting the movement from Bill's quivering body. She could hear the man holding his legs saying, "His leg is bleeding badly. Hurry."

She secured the blood for the test, went immediately to his leg, and saw the bruise grow bigger, brighter, and started bleeding. As she continued to watch, the bleeding stopped, the bruise lightened and shrunk before she had time to retrieve any medical supplies.

Not knowing what to think, she looked at the rest of the team as if to say, "Did you see that?"

No one else responded. She saw the big open eyes of shock and possible terror over all their faces. She watched the patient lying still and calm while the rest of the team walked out of the room. When she walked out of the room, she felt as if something in the room had taken her body control away from her. She walked down the hall slowly, ignoring her surroundings, as she reflected over what she had just witnessed.

—✿—

"I am not leaving this place again until you leave this place."

Bill recognized fear in Trainer's decision. "Can you be pulled out of me with a needle?"

"I am a living being and reside in a host. If I am separated from my host, I cannot live long. I have many hiding places in here. If you are conscious, I can tell where the needle is coming from before it comes in and can escape. Since you are unconscious, I am having trouble making that determination. I need your eyes to see, your ears to hear, and your mouth to speak."

Bill thought about that, loading that into his memory for later use.

"Bill, your son has been born. He is getting stronger every minute. That is step one of the plan. We need to talk about step two. I need three sons to carry on with the mission."

"Why three sons? Wouldn't girls work as well?"

"Bill, for generations, girls have been tried. We are DNA-driven creatures, and something about a girl's DNA doesn't allow us to live within their system. Otherwise, we would not be a 'single to double' living creature. There have never been more than two of us at a time."

"So you need me to have two more boys," Bill concluded.

"Yes, the problem is I made the same mistake my ancestors made. The more stress I have on me, the more stress Cadet has. The more stress Cadet has, the greater the chances are that the wife of the host dies."

"What? Is Saundra dead?"

"I can't be sure. Once the baby is born, I can no longer read the wife. Since I can't read the wife, I can't save the wife."

"You're telling me that Saundra could be dead and you are unable to do anything about it? Are you still asking me to help you after saying—"The anger boiled up from the depths of Bill's soul.

"Bill, I need her as bad as you do. Every one of my ancestors has no other children after their first wife died."

"If you need her so badly, why didn't you put forth some effort to save her? You can't rip a man's heart in half and expect him to volunteer to help you again, can you?" Bill's words ripping like little knives into his own heart.

"Look, don't assume anything. She could be alive. You must have faith that the doctors have done all they can to save her."

"The faith I have tells me that if she died, you will have a huge fight on you hands. I will do everything I can to get you out of me and my son."

"Fighting me has always been a mistake. It has resulted in the death of every man that has tried. I don't want to get into a fight with you."

"Then hope that Saundra is alive and well. I promise you this: if she is dead, you will be dead too!"

———

The nurse taking his blood pressure saw sweat forming on his forehead, heard his pulse quickening, and saw the red color of anger tinting into his cheek. The blood pressure reading could not have been accurate, and a repeat check for verification showed totally different results. She noticed that the sweat had turned to blood, and it was now rolling out with every beat of his heart.

———

"Bill, I understand, but you need to calm down." Trainer fought to keep him calm so the reaction didn't get worse. "I'm sure everything will be all right. Your son is healthy and strong. There is no use worrying about the unknown."

Bill must have considered what Trainer thought as Trainer felt Bill's body relax.

———

Just as suddenly as the symptoms came, they reversed. The nurse reported all she saw on her chart. *How am I going to explain this to the doctors?*

———

Trainer didn't want to get into anything here and now. He had enough to deal with, without added pressure from Bill.

"Not now, Bill. We don't know what has happened. Let's deal with that when we know more facts."

"Agreed, we still have hope that she lives."

Trainer could feel that Bill was not ready to get into more now. He agreed with the feeling and let it go.

Bill restarted the conversation with another subject, "What does 5757 Power Lane mean to you?"

Trainer answered carefully but decisively, "It means everything to me. My instructor is in that house. The Master Trainer is an accumulation of all the Trainers for generations in which their hosts have died. Every bit of knowledge ever acquired by any Trainer is contained within the walls of that house. The instruction I need as to when, where, and how to do anything that I will need will be learned in that house."

"What is in that house for me?"

Trainer felt that Bill's concern was more toward what was in this for Bill but needed what was in it for him. "You will learn the personal experiences of all the previous family members and what they did with their Trainer. You can learn how to make my mission a success, that will make your life easier."

—◁∿▷—

It seemed to Bill that this was going to be a one-sided battle, or was it? Didn't his father tell him that something inside him was going to fight him and he had the power inside to beat him?

Then the memory flashed back to him.

Bill was about seven years old when he walked into his Dad's study. His dad was writing in a book that he called Trainer's Log. He had heard him say as he wrote, "Joseph found a secret inside him that may enable him to become more powerful than I am in this moment. If this keeps up, the pressure will get too much for his heart, and as all the rest, I will die early of a heart attack. I still only have one child, and he won't even approach another woman to think about having another son." The log closed, and his eyes came to life. It wasn't until then that Bill noticed his dad's eyes would go blank and just stare at nothing.

That was when he was concentrating on Trainer or trying to blind Trainer from seeing what he was doing. Did he blind Trainer? Was that in 5757 Power Lane? That alone would make going there worthwhile. The risk is that I might not always have control of when I go blank. There was motivation now to go that house. Yes, Trainer gets what he wants, but I will get what I need too.

———∿∿———

Suddenly, small beams of light entering into his blinking eyes broke up the darkness. The feeling of awakening started with the fingers and toes, moving slowly into the main body. A groggy, "half in, half out" feeling possessed his entire body. Voices in the room became unclear but were there. Muscles twitching and moving throughout his body made him realize he was waking up.

—⁓—

Bill lay perfectly still for so long that Mary and Henry had just sat in the room, talking to each other. Glancing at Bill every so often to make sure he wasn't moving. The monitors told them his pulse, oxygenation, and his breathing were all good. The blood pressure checks showed a stable, good blood pressure all the way. There was no reason he should not wake up.

Bill's fingers and toes started moving; his arms and legs started rustling and shifting; his hips started shifting as if looking for a more comfortable place; his chest started rising and falling; and most importantly, his eyes opened to slivers and closed. Each time they opened, they opened a greater distance.

Mary noticed the blinking first. She looked intently at Bill and said, "He's trying to wake up."

Henry turned his attention to Bill and noticed all the body shifting and the monitors beeping faster, steady but faster. "He's coming to. It looks like he is going to make it."

"Bill, are you with us yet?" Mary asked.

"Ugh," was the only kind of response that he could come out with.

"Not yet," Henry said, looking at his wife. "But he is coming around."

The door opened to his room, and Sarah came in. "Is there any change yet?"

Mary said, "He's waking up."

Sarah looked at the monitors and said, "It looks like he is." She turned her attention to Bill. "Bill, how do you feel?"

Silence for a short while, but then, "I don't know."

"Do you feel any pain?"

"No, there's no pain." It was more of not knowing what was going on with the baby and Saundra. "How is Saundra?"

Mary said, "We have seen Saundra and the baby. We will tell you about them when you get done with Sarah. Does that sound okay?"

"Yes," Bill was satisfied with that and turned to Sarah and said, "What do you want to know?"

Sarah looked at Bill without saying anything, but her look said, "Are you sure you want to deal with this?"

Bill just nodded his head and said, "It's okay."

Sarah turned back to Bill. "Have you ever had a racing or fluttering in your chest before?"

"No."

"Pain, tightness, or pressure in the chest?"

"No."

"Light-headedness or dizziness?"

"No."

"Fainting or shortness of breath?"

"No."

"Excessive sweating?"

"No."

"Tightness or fullness in the throat?"

"No."

"Tightness or excessive urine production?"

"No."

"Do you or any member of your family have any heart problems?"

"My father, grandfather, and every known man down for an unknown generational line."

She made the note on the records. "Have any of those experienced the above listed systems?"

"All of them."

"Which of those above systems have they experienced?"

"All of them."

She noted that on the records and made sure all the vitals were good, his medications taken, and slipped out to talk with the doctor.

Bill turned to look at Mary. "Tell me the truth. How is the baby?"

After looking at Henry, she said, "The baby is just fine. You have a healthy baby boy. He was ten pounds even, twenty inches long, and doing very well. The nurses are taking real good care of him."

"That was encouraging," Bill was still hoping for the best with the next question. "How is Saundra?"

Again, Mary looked to Henry before looking to Bill to answer, "Bill, the doctors di—"

Bill cut her off, "All they could, but they couldn't save her."

Mary watched the anger boil in his face, but surprisingly the monitors remained steady. "Bill, you have a healthy baby to look after and help to get you through this hard time."

———~~~———

Henry reached out and hugged his wife close, letting her weight collapse on him. She was an attractive woman even at her age; she held on to her petite frame well through the years and kept herself with meticulous care.

Henry was a large, healthy, strong man. He was taller than Bill and looked down on most men regardless of age. His confidence exuded from him, and there were very few problems he could not face. The emotional tears of his wife had all been shed on his shoulder, and he would have it no other way.

No one had seen the time that Henry broke down and cried. His love for his daughter was great, and Bill knew it brought great pain to experience her loss. Now, in the presence of others, he would stand firm and keep anything from going wrong if it was possible.

———~~~———

Bill had rolled over, his face had gone blank. He knew what was coming and allowed himself to drift into the place he knew where he could find Trainer.

———✦———

Trainer retorted with concern, "I can't help her after I am forced out of her by birth. This has always been a flaw that no one in the past has dealt with successfully. I wish she had lived."

Bill said, "You said that right. You wanted and lost control. Now the control is going to turn. I promise you that the fight has just begun."

3 THE WARRIORS

The full-length porch across the front of the house looked strong, well designed, and well built. The porch swing and furniture on it placed immaculately for comfort and warmth to just sit and soak up the sun. The strange glow from the crack between the doorframe and door seemed to be a light source of some sort moving on the other side of the door. As he stared at the movement of the light, he noticed the same fluorescent green glow coming from all the windows on the front and sides of the house. The light shifted in direction and placement as if a man was walking around the house in all the rooms at the same time.

Fred's heart began to race. It was almost as if he could hear the house telling him to leave the premises. He couldn't get the accelerator down on the Gremlin; his legs were not moving as he stared at the light. The light grew brighter, expanding. Suddenly, from inside the house, a fluorescent-green, glowing round orb floated through the door. A spiderweb formed all the way across the front porch, rolling down like a screen that read, "Fred, leave."

Fred's foot, which was locked on the brake, broke free and slammed hard on the accelerator. The Gremlin eased off and down the road. In his rearview mirror, he saw another sign in the yard. "Fred, you will own this house one day." He wanted to push the accelerator through the floor. Light beams were reaching out and licking at the Gremlin, never seeming to get a grip on the car.

His mind reeled with fear of whatever was in that house and wished for a fast sports car to get away as fast as possible from the evil force he felt. The light fingers backed away and receded into the house. He was on his way, praying to God while he was driving. "Father, You know what just happened. Protect me and guide me, instruct me in Your ways that I could walk in Your power and freedom. Amen."

He relaxed under the protection of his Heavenly Father and proceeded on to the Bible study, singing his favorite praise song from the worship service.

—◈—

Master Trainer sensed the enemy stopped near the property line. He knew he had to get rid of him and get it done fast. The light grew brighter throughout the house the longer the stranger sat there. Whoever it was didn't seem to be in a hurry to leave. Was the enemy not scared of anything? Now, even Master Trainer was getting rattled; he brought himself through the door and sensed a spiritual power that he had never felt before. Using light beams as fingers, he reached for the car, but before he got to it, he felt something grab the light beam and hold it back away from the car. No matter how hard he reached and groped, he could not get a grip on it.

He heard a voice say, "Go back."

"This is my place," he replied with anger.

"You are trying to hurt my servant. I said leave him alone," the voice retaliated with force beyond what Master Trainer knew.

"Who are you?" he asked with fear in his voice this time.

"I AM."

He receded in surrender to the voice and went back into the house. As soon as Master Trainer was in the house, he sensed nothing. The force that had held him back had left as quickly as it came.

———⁓———

Trainer could sense the house calling louder than it was when he first got to the hospital. He still could not understand what it was saying or how far it was calling from. He just knew from the tone that it was an emergency. His current problem was that his host was not getting out of this place anytime soon and was going to resist any action he wanted him to take because of the loss of his wife.

Trainer had to think, and think hard to bring about a solution that would work. Bill needs to think that what I am asking is for his good and not mine. What would benefit Bill and not me that would get him out of the hospital?

"Bill, are you still with me?" Trainer attempted to get a conversation started.

Trainer didn't know how much of his thoughts Bill could read, but he knew not thinking things through was not an option. Bill's response interrupted his train of thought. "Yes, I am. What are you thinking about?"

Trainer knew that was a loaded question and was unsure how to answer it but knew he had to. "I think you know that I don't like this place. I'm sure you don't want to be here either. What can we do to get out of here?"

Bill answered, "I am not leaving this place any time soon. I am not staying awake long enough to make a difference, and they are concerned about the bleeding problem. Those are the two key reasons they won't let me out."

"The bleeding problem is something I have not been able to control. There has been no Trainer that controlled it in the past. It is something that I will work on at the house." Trainer was trying but failed to control the situation.

"Your failure is costing you by delaying my release. I also want out of this hospital, but I know that my only chance is to rest, stay calm, and keep the problems, like excessive bleeding, under control, and the excessive sleeping must stop. I can sell the doctors on so much, but I must tell them the truth to an extent."

Trainer fell silent in thought. I have to control the stress-related systems. Did my father teach me anything about that?

Trainer's memories danced through his head. He could feel the older, more experienced Trainer trying to teach his son something that was not getting through. The phrase "stress-related systems" came up over and over again. The details just didn't compute the way they should. The hit-and-miss training that he did receive was costing him his ability to get out of here and to the house.

The silence went on for a while, and then Bill broke it with a question, "Are you thinking of what you have to do so I can heal up enough to get out of here?"

Trainer knew what he was asking and had to keep calm with an answer. "Yes, I am. If I sit and wait this out, you can keep control of yourself and get out of here sooner." He said no more, for he knew Bill needed to heal in order to get well. He could not share too much with Bill for fear of Bill's further reaction hindering his healing process.

—◦◦◦—

Peter walked through the house to the stairs leading to the attic. This house had always been for the farmhands as long as Peter could remember. His father, who lived in the main farmhouse, worked more acres than he owned and hired farmhands every year to help with the workload. Peter was a volunteer but was expected to work as hard as every one else there.

Peter's office was in the attic area because it was the one space that he could hide from everyone else. He could remember the year he moved out of the main house. He chose the room in the attic for the privacy that it provided. Even after the farmhands moved out, that room remained his favorite place to meet God alone.

Now, he was unwilling to move back in to the house where his mother and father resided. He claimed his independence that day and wasn't going to give it up. He was close enough to his parents. They knew the help they needed was next door on their property but respected his freedom and privacy.

With a simple note on the door, his private quarters with God were going to be filled with people. All the people coming in were friends and willing to give their undivided attention to their studies and prayer time.

He could hear the door open and the footfalls moving toward the stairs. The first member of the prayer squad is here already. How long have I been praying?

His red and swollen eyes were drenched in tears. The hurt went deep into his being. The marks and scars left by the hurt were going to take time to heal, but he knew God was more than able to take care of them.

His mind drifted back in time to a place far away where happy times abound and fun rolled away the hours. The excitement of seeing Grandma and Grandpa was going to lead him to trouble again. It led to trouble every year on the drive, and he was learning to control it slowly—too slowly for his mother's sake. He could see her shoulders and knew he was nearing the limit he could push in the car. He would see her face soon: red, stern, with the silent warning saying, "You will straighten up or face the consequences."

This year, he behaved better partly because of the new radio-controlled tractor to occupy his mind and the homework that needed doing. They turned aside the excitement until he heard, "We're here."

The memory faded with him reading the obituary of his grandma. The good memory felt relieving, but the pain was so sharp. He deeply missed her and couldn't imagine a hole so large left by her death.

John walked through the house, seeing much more than he understood. Something happened that had deeply hurt Peter. Step by step, John walked through the house looking for clues in the surroundings. The house gave no clues until he opened the office door. The paper lay open to the obituaries, the picture said it all. He saw Peter holding the picture that normally sat on his desk. The words John heard gave it all away. "Grandma, I love you, and I always will."

He walked up behind Peter, took his shoulders in his hands, and prayed silently. His speech impediment made verbal prayer hard, and his continued practice was slowly working; but in deep stress, he couldn't get a word out at all.

4 THE MEMORIES

Bill continued to sleep, his mind roaming down his past to several times Trainer showed himself active in the life of Bill.

He was three years old. Already active like a child two years older, he was watched closely like a mother hen watches her young chicks. Bill could see his father, Joseph, at all times. He felt Joseph's watchful eye on him. Security and safety was always known and felt by Bill because his dad never let him get out of sight.

This day was one that Bill challenged his father's eye. He looked around to see where everyone was. He saw them all talking and not concentrating on him. He focused on his target. All he had to do was get to the bushes, and he was out of sight and gone. He got his legs moving as fast as they could carry him. He knew nothing of distance, but the bushes got bigger, and that was good.

He could hear big footsteps closing in from behind, but he was still moving. His ears rang with his name, but he had never responded before in this type of situation and wasn't about to now. Just before he got to the bushes, two strong hands grabbed him at the armpits and lifted as his pumping legs moved through the air. Swiftly, Bill was safe in the arms of his father, being taken back to play where he had started the run. He was still laughing and talking while his father communicated more through the physical contact than through words.

He was still locked away in his past. His mind skipped ahead a couple of years to his first real friend that he met outside his home.

He was six years old when he met the young boy who called himself Harry. Bill was playing in his fenced-in backyard, jumping and laughing through the puddles left from the past few days of rain. He glanced into the backyard next door and noticed a boy a little older, playing with a ball, trying to hit it with the baseball bat in his other hand, without any luck.

"Hey, do you want me to throw the ball for you?" Within a matter of minutes, the boys were playing in Harry's backyard.

That was the beginning of a lifelong friendship. Harry had always been taller, but Bill had amazing speed that his dad often referred to as "adrenaline plus." Once it kicked in, very few could catch him.

Had "adrenaline plus" been Trainer all along? He never tried to describe what it felt like because his father told him never to concentrate on Trainer. Now Trainer was making himself known. As Bill's mind traveled through his childhood years, he found one thing in common. He could take any number of them in a fight, but in a game of competition, he couldn't compete with any of them.

His memory jumped ahead to when he met and won his wife.

He was walking in the park during his free time while in high school. He couldn't remember a girl that didn't catch his eye, but he didn't catch the eyes of the girls as often. This girl was different. He looked at her, and she returned his smile. With that, he approached her to start a conversation. "Hello, my name is Bill. How are you today?"

His eyes locked on her perfect face. Her hair flowed down her back, guided by the wind to the side. "I'm doing well. My name is Saundra."

"Saundra, that's a pretty name. Do you want to go for a walk?"

"Thank you." Getting up from the park bench, she said, "Sure, Bill. Where do you want to go?"

Bill offered his left hand to her as he said, "There is a walking trail just around the corner. The view is breathtaking. It has everything Mother Nature has to offer."

Her hand slid into his. "You can tell me all about it on the trail."

He could see them walking hand in hand not saying anything. The memory faded as they walked into the wooded part of the trail.

For the first time, Bill recalled the happy times with Saundra. This brought a tear to his eye, but he held it back. He wanted the happiness of the moment to overpower the hurt of the loss. For now, he held the hurt back. There would be time for tears later.

He didn't want to remember any more for the time being. He wanted to wake up. The pain would strike him and break him down, but one name struck his mind and wouldn't let go.

Harry was more than a child's playmate. For a while, Harry was his only playmate. Because of that, in his junior and senior high years, he knew how to handle friends without chasing them away.

Bill was at Harry's playing. His eye caught sight of a book lying on the table. "What is that book?" He picked it up to read the title on the cover, *The Holy Bible*. Just reading the words caused him to throw it down on the table like a hot potato.

"When did you start reading and believing that?"

The words Bill heard didn't matter as much as the feeling of fear that ravaged his body.

"This is my first Bible. My grandmother showed me Jesus's love three years ago with this very Bible. I don't know how much you know about Jesus, but Grandma underlined and marked the verses she showed me."

Bill felt the color leave his face. "It's getting late, and I've got to go."

Bill's mind went black, and the memories stopped cold at that point. He could still feel the trembling fear and sweating as he left the house to never return again. Why did he think of Harry at this point in his life? What had happened to Harry through the past years? Did he really want to know?

5 THE DEMONS

Mary and Henry had sat, cried, watched, and prayed. While Bill slept, they sought the Lord for an opportunity to show Bill who Jesus was to them. The last time they saw Bill, they were drinking to the point beyond drunk, just short of death. All Bill knew of them wasn't anything he would consider Christian. How could they share the change in their lives without Bill laughing?

Again, they sat and stared, prayed and cried for the loss of Saundra and whatever was going on with Bill. Hoping that Bill would wake up and would be willing to listen kept them in his room.

They had the chance to hold the baby and prayed for him already. They had laid their hands on Bill, seeking Jesus's touch for him, but there was one more thing for them to do.

They needed to share Jesus with Bill, giving him the choice to accept or reject. How long they pleaded for such an opportunity just like this. They didn't want it to come under these circumstances, but they knew that God was going to turn it for the best in His name. Right now, all they could do was pray and pray some more.

Henry looked at Mary. "Honey, are we too late to get the message of Jesus to him? Did we miss an opportunity that we should have taken earlier?"

Mary looked heartbroken and wounded. "I think only God can answer that question. Personally I haven't stopped praying that we get one more chance to show Jesus to Bill."

"I just feel like we failed, and now we are going to watch Bill die without even a chance to call on Jesus."

"I know Bill refused more than one opportunity to listen to the message. If he dies, he goes to his own chosen eternity. Though I, more than anything, want one more chance."

"You and me both."

———

Light began piercing the darkness behind his eyelashes. Sleep yielded to the conscious mind, and all his senses began to pick up signals, alerting him to the world around him.

White light coming from everywhere seemed to focus on draining into his unadjusted eyes. The sounds of soft beeps and air rushing somewhere beside him, softly at first, filled his ears. The shiver told him the air around him was cooler than he liked. His eyes focused slowly; he could see the room he was in had white walls and ceilings, a dry-erase marker board with writing too fuzzy to be read, and two people staring at him with a look of excited wanting that he could not understand.

Sounds, then words, "Bill, are you awake?"

"Mary?"

"Yes, Bill, it's me."

"Henry?"

"Yes, Bill, I'm here."

The footsteps entering the room interrupted the exchange. Bill looked to the other side of the bed, noticing the doctor and nurse standing there.

"Bill, I'm Dr. Lockwood, this is Sarah. Do you know where you're at?"

"I'm in the hospital."

"Can you tell me what happened to you?"

Bill knew the answer to that question but not how to explain it to the good doctor. "Last I remember, I was bleeding a lot and pain was shooting up my left leg."

"Do you have any idea why you were bleeding or what was causing the pain?"

It would kill me to tell you. Bill didn't want to explain this and needed a good reason to assure the doctor he was fine now even though he knew he wasn't.

"I don't know. I guess it was just a one-time thing."

"This hasn't happened to you before?"

"No, never."

He could see the nurse pushing buttons on machines, checking printouts, and recording her findings for the record. The questions continued from the doctor, "Do you have or has anyone in your family had any type of heart problems, high blood pressure, diabetes, or anything like that?"

This conversation was not going well, and he knew that it was going in the wrong direction. "Yes."

"Can you specify?"

"My father died of a heart attack when I was young."

Bill was nervous from this line of questioning. He could only wonder if he was going to start sweating again. The doctor filled him in on some things, but they weren't registering because he knew the root of all his medical problems was Trainer. He knew he needed to talk to Henry. He would understand the demons inside because he joked about them with him during some of his drinking binges.

"I want to take a look at that leg of yours. I hear it was really bad just a short while ago."

With the sheet removed from his leg, the exposed bruise looked to be about a week old. The faded green coloring was getting lighter and smaller almost at a rate of speed recognizable to the brain as movement.

"Have you ever experienced anything like this before?"

"No, I can't remember anything like this happening."

"I am going to order some blood tests. See if we can figure out what is going on. Are there any other questions I can answer?"

"No."

"Are you comfortable?" the nurse asked as she finished up her work.

"I'm fine."

"Call me if you need anything."

"Okay."

He watched her walk away then rolled his head back. His mouth opened, as if to say something, and closed again, thinking better of it. Too many ears were present, and there was no way to verbalize it clearly yet.

Bill's mind had nowhere else to go. It went to the picnics, dinners out, and hours of watching the sun go down on the porch. Saundra had loved that view, and Bill doubted she could get enough of it. Tears started running into his ears as the loss and shock settled into pain as though someone was cutting his very heart into small pieces.

He blinked the tears out of his eyes and said, "Saundra?"

Mary turned to Bill and said all that needed to be said with her eyes. "Bill? Are you hungry?"

Bill couldn't answer. "Henry?"

Henry looked down on Bill. "Yes."

"What do they know about Saundra's death?" Bill wasn't trying to be strong. He had been hurting, and he knew he had to let it out.

Bill waited as Henry sorted out his thoughts before Henry replied, "They told us there was just too much internal bleeding. They couldn't get it under control."

Bill could see Mary's sob as the pain of loss shook her body.

He sniffed once, blinked twice, and controlling his voice, asked, "How is my son?"

Henry replied, "Better than you right now. The nurses up there are taking good care of him. They say—"

Bill interrupted, "He is getting better every minute. It's shocking how he is responding."

Henry couldn't believe he knew that. "Yes, how—"

Bill held up his hand, staying his question, "Before you ask, I can't answer the question. I can say it sounds so real in my dreams, and I have too much time to dream."

Henry asked, "Are you seeing Saundra in your dreams?"

Bill looked at Mary. "Not everyone in this room would be able to handle the answer to that. Could I speak with Henry privately?"

"Sure," she replied. Then looking to Henry, she asked, "Do you want some coffee?"

"Sure, sounds great."

Mary left for the coffee shop.

Bill waited for the room to clear. "Do you remember the demons we joked about when we got drunk?"

Henry knew immediately what he was talking about. "Of course, I couldn't forget them if I tried one hundred years."

Bill just said, "One of them was talking to me when I slept."

Bill didn't know what to expect as a response from him. The concern written on his face said it all. "I believe you, and

I want to help you." The concern showed on Harry's face like a spring storm cloud.

"I don't know what you would call it, but I might be demon possessed."

"Bill, that is a serious statement. What makes you think that?"

"I can't go into detail without risking more medical problems. This demon is the cause of my medical problems. He never learned to control his stress, and it shows up in all the ways I demonstrated to get me here."

Henry took a minute to absorb what he just said. "That's quite the problem. Bill, I have to tell you something. The last time you saw us, you know, the path of destruction we were on. Mary and I were heavy into partying and openly denying God. The demons taunted me day and night all those years. One day, a church—"

"Church? You went to church?"

"Let me finish before you condemn me as insane and reserve a bed for me in the mental ward."

"Okay."

"One day, a church held a meeting in their front yard. It was that church right across the way from the farmhouse. We had work to do but could hear every word the people sang and the pastor said. Bill, something inside both of us told us that what he said was right. We were going to die, and we needed Jesus to save us from the torment we were headed to."

"Torment. That doesn't make any sense."

"Does talking to demons in your dreams make any sense to you?"

"No, go on with your story."

"We hadn't gotten any work done and knew beyond the shadow of a doubt the truth. We both stopped pretending and playing, fell to our knees. Bill, we took Jesus Christ as our Savior that day in the front yard. I know you're ready to stop listening right now. I implore you to listen on because this is the answer to your demons."

Bill knew Trainer well enough to know the stress was already on the rise. He wondered if the sweat was his imagination or really starting up. "I don't think my demon wants me to hear this."

"I know your demon doesn't want you to hear this. Jesus took away all my demons right there. I haven't had a drink since that day and haven't seen the demons running up the walls from the withdrawals either. Bill, there is only one answer to your demon, and that is Jesus Christ."

A long silence ensued. The silence continued until the nurse came in. "Hello. My name is June. I'm here to take a few blood samples for the lab."

Bill closed his eyes, opened them again, and said, "Where is the army?"

The door opened immediately after the question, and four others walked in and took their positions silently. The one on the left side uncovered the leg so the doctor could watch as she took the blood.

"You acted rather violently when we tried this before. Do you know why?"

"No, I don't." He knew better than to answer that question.

"Okay, we're going to try to take the blood without any harm done. I need three tubes this time."

Bill's arm flopped out, and his eyes closed. "Any time you're ready."

The needle entered the vein. The sweat started to form but didn't worsen. He could hear the nurse, "One tube, the second tube, the last tube, and we are done, with nothing more than a little sweat. See, it wasn't bad at all."

Bill knew Trainer had prepared himself and hid long before any needle entered his body. "You must have been imagining all the problems."

One of the orderlies that came in said, "Then I imagined it too. You fought so violently, it took everything we had to hold you down. That was not my imagination."

Bill looked at the orderly. He was a big man, muscular, and didn't look like he needed help with much. He knew the strength and speed Trainer could fight with and what he was up against. "I'm sorry. I'll try to avoid that in the future."

All of the staff left.

———

"Henry?" The look on Henry's face said it all to Bill.

"What did you see? You look like you saw a dead man get up and walk."

"I think I did," Henry replied. "I could hear down the hall the first time they tried to take blood. The second time, they were more prepared, but you gave them a fight like it was your life itself they was trying to take. This last time, you just let out a little sweat and laid still."

"I told you the demon affected my health. Any time they try to take blood without the demon being aware, he is at risk of being taken from me because he travels my body through the bloodstream. It wasn't me that was fighting. The demon really was fighting for his life."

"Bill, are you serious? It is as simple as taking the demon out of the bloodstream, and you are done with it?"

"Yes, but I'm almost guaranteed a heart attack for attempting such a procedure. As well, getting the needle close enough to pull him out on purpose would take more than a simple act of poke and pull. You saw what happened when it wasn't prepared."

"Good point. What would it take to get rid of the demon?"

"I can't go there—and won't, for my health's sake."

"How much does this demon know?"

"Everything I hear, see, or sense, he knows."

Just then the door opened, and Mary came in with two cups of coffee in her hands. "Is it okay for me to come in now?"

Bill looked at her and said, "Thank you for understanding. I wonder what's on the TV right now."

"Resting well?" Trainer asked, starting up a conversation while Bill was still awake.

"Yes," Bill replied.

"You need to know that if you start talking about me to others, I can inflict a lot of pain, making conversation impossible. I will defend my identity with everything I know."

"I will not test you in that manner. Your identity will not be revealed by me."

Trainer seemed content with that assurance. "Good, we understand each other. I am a secretive person and will not tolerate secrets leaking out to those who don't need to know." Trainer was not going to mince words or actions on this matter.

"I fully understand." Bill made it clear that the conversation could end with that.

Trainer became silent, allowing Bill to rest and heal. Trainer could feel Bill's body relax as he drifted off into the world of unconsciousness once again. Time is what he didn't have much of, but he needed to figure out what to do next.

6 THE LIGHT

John struggled with every word, "Fff-re-re-re-re-ddd… trro-tro-tro-ble."

"John, what kind of trouble is Fred in?"

He saw the uneasiness and fear in Peter's face. His own fear caused trembling in his hands. He knew this was going to make talking even harder to understand. His nerves tightened and twisted through out his body.

"H-h-h-ou-ou-oou-se."

Peter shook his head and asked, "What house? Better yet, slow down and tell me what is wrong in a sentence."

John took a deep breath and prayed, *God, I need Your control to make this understandable. What do you want me to say?*

John looked at Peter and started, "F-fred is g-g-g-oing to buy a house. The house is go-go-ing to try to kill him. The house is po-po-sse-sse-sed."

John felt the fear and shock in the room. He could see it clearly written on Peter's face. There was a trust and belief in his message that would never go away.

"John, it sounds like we need to pray about this."

John just nodded his head in agreement and began to pray to himself.

John felt Peter's hands rest lightly on his shoulder as he took up the prayer, "Heavenly Father, we thank You for the gifts You have given us and the instruction that flows from Your word. We thank You for Fred and the many hours of studying he puts into each one of his lessons.

"We pray, Lord, that You would protect and guide him. Keep him in Your hands of grace. We fear there is great danger in his life right now. We pray that You would surround him with a hedge of angelic protection, not allowing any harm to come to him.

"We know You will protect all Your servants. Lord, give him the strength to overcome his fear and follow Your will with all he does. Give us the strength to follow Your will no matter what it may cost. Bring the prayer squad to a place of obedience at all cost. Make us true bond servants with You as Master and Lord.

"Lord, fill us with Your peace and wisdom, guide us in all Your ways. Show us Your direction, making Your path clear.

"We thank You for answering our prayer and keeping us. Amen and amen."

A wave of peace filled the room that seemed to flow from the two men standing there.

—w—

Harry entered the house and ran quickly to where he knew John would be. The hallway stopped him cold. Something in the hallway more than caught his attention, it paralyzed him.

His mind struggled for the words to describe the sight before him. He closed his eyes, "Please, God. This is just a dream. As soon as I open my eyes, this image I see will be gone."

His eyes slowly opened to confirm the fact and focused on the image standing in the hall. It looked like a man—but was more than a man. Fear coursed throughout his body. A voice came to him from the huge yet indistinct form, "Harry, fear not. You and only you can see me. I am here to keep Peter from further attack. He must recover from this one before he can stand in a second one."

"Am I allowed to enter the room?" The sheer size of the protector was enough to scare him; he didn't want to challenge him unnecessarily.

The protector opened the door. "Go. Pray for him. Fred needs you now."

He entered the room hoping to see no more of them. "The note said you were here, so I let myself in." The room was empty with the exception of Peter and John praying. He walked up and joined in agreement in the prayer of Peter.

He felt God's presence in the room. And saw God's glory on John's and Peter's faces. "You couldn't wait for me to bring God in here?"

Peter shook his head. "When I came in here, there was no peace. John told me that Fred was in trouble. He talked about a house Fred was buying. He said it was possessed and was going to try to kill him."

Harry immediately understood. "But how could that fill the room with peace?"

"That did not. We spent a few minutes praying. That filled the room with peace."

"On my way over here, I was praying and really felt a burden about signing some papers, making a big purchase. He was handed some keys, but the keys held some kind of evil power in them. It took seven seconds for his fingers to grasp the keys tight, but when he did, the evil fled the keys. Something like a red smoke rose from them, and they were as gold. I was hoping Fred could shed some light on this."

John spoke slowly, "The hou-se is the b-bi-big pur-pur-chase. It is po-sses-sed with e-e-e-vil. Some...how Fr-red must bre-eak the e-e-e-e-vil po-wer."

"The evil in those keys was nothing to be toyed at. I don't think we have the whole picture yet. Is there something we missed?" Harry finished the statement started by John.

The silence was deafening. Finally, Harry broke the silence, "God isn't making anything else clear. We need to be ready for something big. This needs more prayer before going on."

All three gathered around and prayed, "Father, we understand the message You have given us. It brings concern for the safety of Fred. We know You have a plan for all this. We know You want nothing but the best for Your servants. We seek You now for the courage to walk through this with Fred. We don't know all that is going to happen, but You do. Guide us through this with Your grace and mercy. Thank You for all You are. Amen."

They all felt better at the end of this prayer, but concern remained, mixed with the peace in the room.

———*m*———

Fred arrived in front of the old country home of Peter. The two-story farmhouse showed the care of generations of woodworking hands. It had bay windows downstairs, large multipane windows on the top story, and one lone attic window that topped off the pyramid of the A-frame house. It sat on four acres of land that held two barns and a woodshop. The long driveway came around to the back door then continued to the back barn.

Winding around the drive toward the door, Fred noticed the big trees lining the drive, temporarily blocking the view of the house. By the door of the house, he could see the open field behind the barn and the long tree line bordering the small field.

He had been to this house for the last month and had yet to get over the sight of it. It looked like an old, long letter A with a door. The roofing shingles went from peak to ground. The front looked like it could have been an old hay barn at some time. The back access was wide enough to accommodate the biggest tractor.

Fred drove up and parked in the driveway. The fear and trembling had not left him completely, and his mind could see the green light fingers reaching out for the car. He shook his head, trying to get the image out of his mind. His nerves failed to recover from the trauma that played out. Every image of the green light in his mind sent shivers throughout his body.

He stumbled through the door, thankful that the furniture arrangement gave him places to hold while proceeding to the office. His mind went to the never-ending faithfulness of God who stood before them week in and week out. He knew he had to get this under control and walk up those steps prepared and ready to learn from the Bible study.

Instead, every time his hand released the wall, he wobbled and fell over, having to catch it to restore himself upright. The control he usually experienced was gone. His legs visibly shook, making it impossible for him to walk.

He had the choice to call for help, knowing the other men would come, but his pride kept his voice silent. He didn't want the others to think of him as weak. He trembled again before forcing his legs and feet into motion.

He pushed himself to the edge where the wall stopped and the open floor started. He was still one hundred feet away from the steps with a secure handrail to keep him up. It seemed like a mile in his mind. *Will my legs carry me that far, or will they once again fail me, keeping me from my friends and prayer partners? God, give me Your strength to make it to the stairs!*

He watched for shaking in his leg. He took his hand off the wall and stood for a second before feeling his leg shake again. He knew that the only chance he had was to run and hope the fall at the end was at the bottom of the steps. The stumbling was slow, making the effort to run even worse. One, two, three, he stumbled and hobbled as fast as he could. Moving upright, he kept going until he stumbled into the wall by the stairs.

Maneuvering the stairs was hard, but he made it one step at a time. Holding on the wall and rail, he stumbled to the office to find the three other men gathered around each other praying. He stood silently watching and waiting. It was obvious who they were praying for, though he didn't see how it was possible they would know anything. Only God, whoever it was at the house, and Fred himself could have known what happened just a few minutes ago.

He felt the rattled confusion shift to nervous confusion as he saw the eyes of the other three men in the room. The mix of understanding and concern spoke volumes to him. "What did I miss?"

Harry said nervously, "I don't know. What happened to you on the way here?"

"I saw this house on Power Lane for sale. It caught my attention, but it seemed to chase me off with fingers coming from within. It doesn't make any sense." The looks on every one's faces changed to fear as goose bumps formed over all their arms.

"Fred?" Harry asked the question before anyone else did. "Something from within the house reached out to get you?"

"I know this seems strange. But I can't come up with another way to explain it."

John looked at him. "Som-some-thing? A de-de-de-mo-mon."

"If the house is possessed, then why is it that God wants me to buy it?" Fred asked.

Harry confirmed the answer, "God doesn't tell the whys. He just answers the whats and expects us to obey. That's the way God works. We may not be able to tell you the whys, but we have confirmed the whats for you clearly."

"I understand what you are saying. Right now there are two reasons why I can't buy any house. The first is I couldn't afford another payment. Second, I wouldn't know what to do with a demon-possessed house anyway."

"Fred," Harry tried to make clear what he saw. "It isn't what you would do with a demon-possessed house, it's what God would do with a demon-possessed house. Did you see any indication that you were to buy the house?"

Fred shivered. "Yes, there was sign in the yard that said, 'Fred, you will own this house one day.'"

Harry shivered and said, "That's the house. God has showed both John and I that you will buy that house. It will try to kill you. There's something evil about that house."

Fred replied in a sarcastic fearful tone, "It is already trying to kill me, and I haven't made a move toward buying the house!"

"Fred," Harry seemed to try to exude peace, "you will be holding this Bible study in that house."

"I thought it was going to try to kill me. Dead men don't hold Bible studies." Fred knew that sounded bad, but he hoped his friends would understand.

"I know what you're saying. You have said yourself that a prophet sees the mountaintops and that the details in between go unknown. I am telling you the mountaintops." Harry knew that was not comforting but had to be said.

Fred sat in a chair, let his head collapse into his chest, and prayed, "What is going on? Father, I don't understand."

The other three men gathered around him, laid their hands on him, and prayed. Fred knew the Spirit's power that flowed from them; something about this time told him God was all over the situation and in control of it all.

Fred conceded to the authority of God, "Do your will with my life. Make it yours."

The prayers continued for a while as the clock ticked off the seconds. After all the prayers had ended, the men looked at one another silently, saying with their eyes, "We're in this together."

"Thanks."

7 THE REFLECTION

Henry sat with his wife watching and waiting again. This time they took each other's hand and prayed over him. He had been in and out of consciousness for two days.

Henry looked to Mary. "Honey, let's slip out for some lunch. We have been in this hospital ever since the accident. I think we both need a break. When I was looking out the window, I noticed a little Italian restaurant across the street. What do you think?"

Henry watched Mary glance over to Bill before saying, "Sure. I think we're both in need of some fresh air and a good meal. We can tell Sarah where we are going in case we are needed."

Henry helped Mary up from the chair she had made her home over the past few days. She looked frail and in need of some rest. Maybe he could convince her later to go home for a soaking bath and a good night's sleep. His heart ached to bring her grieving to an end, but he knew that only time and God could do that.

He watched as she approached Bill and lightly touched his cheek. He held her by the elbow and guided her through the open door.

—∿∿—

Bill awoke again. The room was quiet and looked empty, and a feeling of loneliness filled him. His hand quickly reached down and found the TV control. His parched throat was a bad sign. How long had it been since he drank water? It had been long enough to have an empty glass on his bed tray. He looked at the control panel in his hand. The emblems on the buttons indicating nurse, on/off, TV channel up/down, and bed up/down. He found the button for the nurse and pushed it. He didn't have to wait long.

Sarah walked into the room. "Is there something I can do for you?"

"I need a water refill. What could be done about that?"

"I will be right back with some ice for you."

He looked up to the blank TV screen and began thinking about what had happened.

What will it take to get rid of Trainer from me and my son? Just how much of Trainer is beatable? The first thing that Bill needed to know was can Trainer be blinded or deafened. The second thing was how much of this Jesus is real and how much is make-believe for the weak?

He started with the first morning events. The reason for the blood in the morning was apparent enough. Trainer finally made his presence known when my son was close to being born. Now he is all but demanding that I have two more sons. The DNA-driven multiplication he is using must be based on one or two failures, so at least one must fully cooperate and continue the line no matter what the others do. I know that is the first step of the plan. Trainer is not discussing any more of the plan either. If there are no more children, there is the chance that he is going to be delayed another generation.

Trainer is working on getting to the Power Lane house for instruction. He has to learn. The information I need is also in that house. Who will get more information if I go to the house on Power Lane? Why is he trying so hard to get that information?

Henry talked about Jesus as the only answer to the Trainer problem. Trainer's reaction was initially to hide. After that initial reaction, was there one? Did he say something to me with the silence in that conversation? I might not know now, but there was a memory of Harry. Didn't he talk to me about Jesus? I wonder if I could find Harry now.

The door opened, and Sarah walked in with a cup full of ice. "Here is your ice. Let it melt in your mouth slowly."

"Thank you. Could I ask for one more thing?"

"Sure. What is it?"

"I need a local phone book. I would like to see if an old friend is still in town."

She walked to a drawer, slid it open, and took out the local phone book and handed this to him with this warning, "Long distance charges will be added to your bill. Local calls are free."

"Thank you."

Bill quickly remembered the name to look for. He flipped to the *R*s and started walking his finger down the list. Randell, there's his dad. His finger worked its way farther down. Harry, I believe he stayed close. Let's see if he is the one I am thinking of. His finger rolled straight across the page to the phone number: 555-7915; this was just a local phone call. He wrote it down on a piece of paper Sarah left for him. After closing the phone book and setting it aside, he waited for the first person to come back to help him.

The door was left open, giving him full view of the hall through the door. The commotion and activity was constant. People that were visitors were distinct from those employed by the hospital. Curiosity was starting to get the best of him. He hadn't seen his cell phone since he got in here. With all the wires and hoses hooked up to him, it wouldn't surprise him if he was peeing into a catheter. How long had he been in the bed? He decided not knowing was better than finding out.

Bill turned on the TV just to get some noise in the room. He debated on calling the nurse. He had called her just ten minutes ago. The last thing he wanted was the nurse coming in all the time anyway.

Just as he was pulling his finger away from the nurse call, Sarah walked in to check his blood pressure and miscellaneous checks for the chart. "Bill. How do you feel?"

"Better. Thank you very much. Do you know what happened to my cell phone?"

"Yes, I will get it for you when I get done."

"Thank you."

While she took his blood pressure, she asked, "Are you having any pain?"

"No."

"Are you going to stay awake now?"

"I hope so. I understand I am a new father, and I would like to see my son."

"Yes, you are. The doctor instructed us to let you see your son if you can stay awake long enough. He wants you to stay awake in here first."

"That's what I figured."

The checks done and marked on the chart, she retrieved his cell phone, asking, "Did you find the number you need?"

"Yes, I think I did. Thank you."

"Just don't get excited. It looks like you are through the worst of it."

"I will take care not to."

"I will see you soon. Lunch should be here in fifteen minutes."

"Okay."

He watched her slip out of the room, picked up his cell phone, and dialed the number on the paper. He listened as the ringing came through on his phone.

"Hello."

Could it be? Should he say something or just hang up? It had been years since he had talked to Harry.

"Hello."

"Hello. Is this Harry?"

"Yes."

"Do you remember Bill Collins?"

"Yes, Bill, is that you?"

"Yes, we talked about something back when we played together, and I have a question about it."

"Go ahead, ask away. I'll see if I can remember."

How can I word it? He blurted out, "Can Jesus Christ help me with demons?"

"Yes, Jesus is the only one that can help with your demons. Can you tell me more about what is going on?"

The sweat started to bead on his forehead with a warning thought, *"Get out of this conversation now. I have the ability to make it your last."*

"Not now. I am in a bad place to talk right now. Thank you, I have your number, so I can call you when I can talk. Would that be okay?"

"Sure, any time."

"Good-bye."

He hung up the phone. He doesn't want to talk about Jesus. Interesting. He logged that into his memory banks and continued resting calmly with the TV as his only company.

———◆◆◆———

Harry was sitting reading his Bible in his chair when the phone rang. The call had surprised him, but what shocked him more was who was asking about Jesus. The thought that Bill would think about Jesus was way more than he would ask for, let alone dream would happen. Bill hung up quickly, but to Harry, the conversation just started.

"Father, I thank You for the surprises You provide daily. I can only assume You are working in Bill's life or he would not be asking about You. Continue to seek him out and draw him to You. Bring him to a place where he will take You as his personal Savior and Lord. I pray that You will not leave him alone until he takes Your free gift of salvation. Amen."

He picked up his phone and speed-dialed Fred.

"Hello."

"Fred, remember me talking about Bill that I played with as a kid? We prayed for him a few times not knowing why."

"Yes."

"He just called me asking about Jesus and demons. I think Jesus is trying to reach him. Can we do an emergency prayer conference?"

"On it. We are tied in to the conference line, and the text is out to call it. Tell me more about what he said."

"When the others are on line with us."

Two more beeps quickly came in. "What's going on?"

"Harry, your call."

"Today I received a phone call from an old friend that has always hated even the mention of Jesus. He asked me if Jesus could help him with his demons. He couldn't stay on long, but I think we need to pray together about it."

"Amen, you start, Fred. We will pray with you." Peter knew they did the same thing for him, and that's the reason he's in the squad now.

They each took time to pray for Bill's situation, whatever it was. Bill would remain on everyone's prayer list until God indicated otherwise. Fred thanked them all for being available and disconnected the conference line.

8 THE VISIT

Day 3 came and went. Bill hungrily devoured the food for the first time since being admitted. The refreshment of the cool water trickling down his throat felt more like a granted, undeserved honor. After three days of nourishment coming from an IV tube, even the mediocre-tasting hospital food was a rich blessing to his taste buds. The morning sun shone bright in the window. He could almost feel the warmth of the sun and could see Saundra and him walking in the early light of the morning.

It was already better. Mary and Henry were in the room waiting for him to wake up. Henry was the first to introduce the new day. Mary was visibly more cheerful. Bill knew the day would be good and looked forward to seeing his son, at least he hoped to.

He heard the nurse walk in the room. "Sarah, would it be possible for me to see the baby?"

Sarah smiled and said, "Let me check into that. It looks like you are doing better."

She went to work checking all the monitors and writing information down on the charts. "Bill."

"Yes."

"I need to get your pulse and blood pressure."

Without a word, he flopped his arm her direction. "This looks like a good day to be out in the sun."

"Yes, it does. Everything is well. It looks like your appetite has improved. You keep this up, and you and your son may be doing just that. The doctor has to approve your release, but I know he liked your improvement yesterday. It appears really good."

"Am I going to see the doctor today?"

"He should be in shortly."

He turned his focus back out the window and listened to Sarah walk out the door. He learned to tell most of the people by their footsteps and could greet them by name without even seeing them. He heard approaching footsteps.

He rolled over toward the door. "Hello, Doctor."

"Hello, Bill. I hear you want to see your son."

"Yes. I'd like that very much."

"From what I've seen yesterday and today's continued improvement, I don't see any reason you can't. I spoke with the attending pediatrician and found out that once the paperwork is filled out, your son is ready to go home. I think after lunch, if all goes well, we can get you and your son released to go home."

"Great."

"We're going to have the nurse remove all these monitors and the IV. I think we can get all the paperwork around while you are visiting with your son."

That was the best news that he could've heard. Mary and Henry were ready to take him to the nursery to see the baby. The time came to go to his son. The wheelchair waited in the room, ready to take him to the nursery. With a newfound excitement, he got into the chair, worked himself to a comfortable position, and got ready for the ride.

Henry asked, "Are you ready to go?"

Bill confidently said, "Let's go see my son."

Away they went. The long walk down the hall never seemed to end. Step by step, as he got closer and closer, excitement rose with the thought of holding his son.

———✺———

Bill took in the plain white hallway while moving slowly along the way. Passing the pictures and doors that dotted the hall, he felt excitement and desire grab him, wanting only to see his son for the first time. Pain only entered the picture when the awareness came that Trainer would also get his chance to see Cadet as well. That was something that he would learn how to deal with later; for now, his priority had to be with his son.

Mary asked, "What are you going to name your son?"

Bill hadn't thought about that at all. They had talked about it as a couple many times but never settled on one name. Soon he would be naming his son, going through the paperwork that needed to be done. "What would you name a son?"

Mary wasn't expecting such a question and wasn't sure what to say. "Saundra always liked *Samuel*, but I like *Bill Jr.* Either one would fit nicely."

"Hmmm, Saundra had talked about Samuel. I didn't really want to have a Junior in the family—it goes against the family grain. This would be a way to positively remember Saundra for the love she shared with me no matter what I did to deserve it." Bill rolled down the hall with a tear rolling on his cheek. "You don't know how much I wanted to share the joy of a son with her. I will never forget her."

Bill allowed his mind to stroll back to their wedding day. He was overjoyed on the day they were to be married. He hadn't seen her all day, and the best man told him that he was charged with keeping him from seeing her until she walked down the aisle to him. He knew there was going to be no getting around his best man. He wasn't bigger but was enough of a friend to know how to get the team to work together. When he got by one, there was another one in the way. He tried to make it look like he was not concerned about that, just wanted to take a walk. He wasn't walking alone anywhere. The men standing up with him and Henry acting together were completely effective to every attempt.

His heart ached and longed to see her as the wedding started. He waited with the pastor for the bridesmaids and groomsmen to come down before finally hearing the bridal march. The sight he couldn't believe. He couldn't fathom her beauty. He could never imagine her more beautiful than at that moment. The broad smile on her face led him to want her all the more.

He never wanted to forget that day and could easily recall it on command.

Henry spoke up from behind him, "None of us will ever forget her. She will live within our hearts forever."

"Is there nothing that can relieve the pain and loss?" Bill's heart still felt torn to pieces.

Henry replied, "Yes. Jesus alone can help with the pain. We will never forget her, and her death will always leave a remnant of the pain to deal with. Jesus Christ replaces the pain and loss with His peace."

Bill made no comment about that and wondered when the wheels on this chair were going to start moving again. The long silence wasn't making the trip any easier. Bill was excited, lost, and hurt at the same time. All the emotions came crashing and crumbling in on him.

Henry broke the short silence, "No matter what you believe, you have been given a perfect son to care for. You are ready to teach that son what he needs to know."

As the elevator dinged and opened, Bill said, "How am I going to raise him alone?"

Henry pushed the button to take them to the third floor. "Why do you have to raise him alone? We are a short distance from you, and we did well enough on Saundra that she married you. We can help you all the way."

Bill knew nothing else to say and finished the ride up to the third floor in silence. The elevator opened and gave him a break to change the conversation, "Looks like maternity is right there. What are you suppose to do when you don't know what to feel?"

"Just hold him and smile. Your son will guide you. Don't ask me how, I just know he will." Bill took it in, letting it become a deep thought.

Bill thought the nurses had more paperwork than three big trees could have made. After signing his life away what seemed like a hundred times, they allowed him to see his son.

Bill looked at the boy he just named Samuel and smiled. His mind raced with memories of Saundra. Times of laughter, times of tears, and times of celebration all crowded in his mind. Somehow Bill had an idea that all those memories were going to be mixed with the new ones this boy was sure to bring into the overall picture.

———

Mary missed her daughter deeply and had cried so much she thought there were no more tears left in her eyes to shed. Deep down in her heart, she knew what Bill was thinking about or thought she did. The stories told over the phone repeated in her mind. "Bill, I could not express her love for you with mere words. This baby was going to be her gift to you to show you how much she really cared."

She could see that Bill was suffering from the loss himself. The smile that crept on his face was emptier than were the smiles she was used to. She wondered when those smiles were going to return. She knew that her own was filled with hurt and pain. The difference, she noted, was the joy of Christ that backed and supported hers. She continued to praise God for the stability He continued to give.

She could not imagine going through this loss without God to help her. She could see Bill working through the pain with no help from anyone. Now was the time to let him think through all he heard and make the decision he was going to make on his own time. She knew he had made no final decision and God wasn't done working on him.

—◈—

Bill could remember the first time Saundra spoke to him about Jesus. "How was that church you went to?" He couldn't remember her going to church before that time, though her girlfriend had invited her many times before. As far as he knew, this wasn't church really. She was invited to go to the special game night being held in the gymnasium of the church. He didn't want to go to anything church-related, so he stayed home to work on a special project that he wouldn't have time to do later.

He could distinctly remember the look on her face when she walked through the door. She glowed with something he never saw before. She walked by him with a light striding step as if all her worries were taken away. The one thing that shook him the most was the freedom. It was like she left the house a slave, but something happened that set her free.

"Honey, what happened today? You look different."

Still silence, but at least she turned to acknowledge he existed. "I don't know how to tell you without you getting mad."

"Why would I get mad? Let me in on the secret."

"I found a Friend that loved me before I ever loved Him."

"Who was that?" Though he wasn't sure he could handle the answer.

"I found Jesus Christ when one of the ladies told me what He did for her."

"Jesus Christ is just a crutch for some people who have no other way to cope."

"Jesus is a lot more than anyone can describe. You have to live through Him and abide in Him to understand Him. If what I saw is any indication, I want to abide in Him."

"Sure, you have it your way. There is more to Jesus than I can understand, that I can believe. You're as full of it as the other Christians."

He blanked the thought out. How can anyone abide in Jesus as they say? You can't see Him, but you abide in Him. Yes, Saundra was right. There was more to Jesus than he understood. More than he was ready to understand.

He focused his mind on Samuel and began babbling in baby talk to his boy.

———*∽∽*———

Trainer felt the presence of Cadet in hiding, fearful of everything and everyone. His inability to get to him had already allowed the first of many mistakes he would make. When in hiding, listen, learn, and teach; the order was of utmost importance. He didn't have to call. Cadet would feel him and come running for the safety and the important instruction he would provide.

Trainer didn't have to wait long; along came Cadet. He recognized the security in an older, more experienced Trainer. Cadet came for protection from the unknown. He settled in as close to the felt source as he could. Instinctively he knew not to leave the host body and to look for instruction from an educated source.

Trainer connected to Cadet and said, "I'm here. Come to me and learn." He settled in on this connection.

Cadet settled in to listen and learn. Trainer began the training, "The first thing you need to know was how and where to hide. You can hide in several places in the body. From the experience of all the Trainers, there is a spot between the lungs just under the big bone that you can sit for a long time without being found. You can keep the connection in that hiding place. If you go to it now, I can show you where it is."

Cadet rode the veins around the small body and found a big bone between the lungs and stopped up against the bone on the inside.

"That is the spot. That is where you hide. Now, you can swing quickly into the lungs. Once in the lungs, you can get into the small blood vessels and ride throughout the bloodstream around."

Trainer's instruction continued, "You need to hook into the eyes, ears, and nose. From these points you will see what he sees, hear what he hears, and smell what he smells. As far as talking goes, that must be done through the brain. You have that hook already in place—use it wisely, and he will say anything you want him to say."

Cadet had absorbed everything he had said.

"One more piece of final instruction, when you place the hooks, they will bring a stinging pain to the part you hook on to. Don't hook on to a lot at once, wait for the pain to subside."

Cadet was ready to start learning.

—◈—

Bill had Samuel resting peacefully on his arms; the smile on his face, the love flowing from Bill into him gave a peace and comfort that calmed him into sleep. Bill was in no hurry to put him down or give him up. No nurse or doctor tried to take him away either. Mary had already promised to help Bill understand what the cries meant and how to keep him fed and safe.

The memories of two nights ago haunted Fred. No matter how much he prayed, surrendering to Christ the entire situation, he couldn't forget the fingers reaching out for the car, or the web sign rolling down to reveal its message. He just couldn't shake those memories out of his mind.

At midnight by the clock, he had picked up the phone, paused, dialed Harry's number, and stopped. Why would Harry be up at midnight? He has to be kidding. They had an agreement that they could call each other any time of the night and they would be available.

Deep down, he knew Harry would be available but just could not push the talk button to start the phone connecting to the other party. The fingers groped at his mind, never quite grabbing hold, not making a clear message.

Flipping the phone closed, he said, "Enough is enough. All I have ever done before was start praying, and shortly I am asleep for the night. This night is no different."

Fred dropped his head on the pillow, closed his eyes, and started praying. Expecting sleep to come quickly, he prayed over every need in the church, the prayer group, and the people directly in his life. The only situation he had not prayed about was that house. In fact, he avoided the topic entirely; he made sure he avoided it. The total time he prayed, he saw the glowing green fingers groping, never grabbing, but reaching, just the tips a distance away.

Frustrated, to a point of pleading, he prayed, "God, can you just take this image out of my mind. If you want me to have this house, make the way for me to get it. Please, give me peace from this image of the fingers reaching."

God closed the door to the thoughts, closed his eyes, and he seemed to drift to a half-sleep state but never fell asleep.

Two hours later, his eyes popped open trembling and sweaty. He was breathing so fast that his oxygen level had to be going down. His racing heart desired to stop dead against the impulse signal from the brain. His eyes searched the room for the clock. He found it on the floor, digital readout saying, "2:00."

His phone had disappeared from the stand beside his bed. Immediately his eyes went to the spot on the floor where his clock still lay. The phone had landed eight feet away from the clock open. The digital screen was completely black. Would it work? Was the battery still good?

He didn't know. What he did know was that he had an intense need to talk with Harry. He bent, spun around, and landed on the floor across the shoulder, landing squarely on the back of his head. Dizziness filled his head. If he had not been lying flat on the floor, he would have landed there soon.

He never was the fighting type, and now he seemed to be fighting to get his phone in his hand. The worst thing was that he could not see the enemy he was fighting. He ventured that standing or bending wasn't going to happen anytime soon. Belly crawling was the one way that he could and would use to get to his phone.

———ƒⱱ———

Harry jumped out of bed and crashed to the floor. Looking at the clock, he saw it was 2:00 in the morning. Inside his spirit, he knew instinctively to pray for Fred. He raised himself to his knees and prayed.

———ƒⱱ———

One hand reaching forward, the opposite knee forward to crawl, he pushed with everything he had and got nowhere. Instead it felt like someone was holding his ankle, not letting him go anywhere. Looking back at his ankle, he saw absolutely nothing holding him. Praying, pushing, struggling to one goal: get that phone.

Suddenly, with a forward movement, he took all he could get and finally reached the phone. Touching the buttons, he turned it on. It stayed on for one second then flashed, went dark. The battery went dead, and now he couldn't make a call. His struggle has just begun. Absolutely frustrated and in pain, he dropped the phone back on the floor. "Now what? Where to now?"

The memory shot into his head: "Computer…landline… phone call." With all his energy, he got up on his feet, took one step after another to get to the computer room. Every step was as if he had a small child sitting on each ankle, holding on to his leg. His muscles tensed, pain screaming in his legs, but he had to go—had to call, had to keep moving in spite of the pain.

The hallway seemed to lengthen with every step. His steps seemed to get shorter and the fight was constantly getting harder. "Have to keep moving, must keep moving."

———ↄↄↄ———

Harry continued to pray, but he knew he had to get to Fred now. His phone went directly into voice mail. He got dressed as fast as he could. With all he needed in his hands, he flew to Fred's as fast as he could get his car there. On the way there, he made two phone calls. He had to get the prayer squad praying. John and Peter were called and asked to pray.

The conversations shocked him and blessed him. They were both farther away and on their way to hold him up from whatever was going on. Speed was of the essence and priority 1. The road could not have been longer or more enduring. The prayers never stopped. Whatever was wrong, the prayer squad was already awake and moving.

Harry was into his own world; he saw Fred's house fly by his car at seventy-five miles per hour. "Shoot! Lying hard on the brakes, he brought the car speed down to get it turned around. He turned into the next available drive, stopped, backed out reversing direction, and shot back to Fred's. He fired into the drive and stopped the car beside the Gremlin.

He jumped out of his car and ran to the door, turned the knob, and slammed into the locked door. Bouncing back off the porch, Harry stumbled into the Gremlin, caught it for balance, and stepped up back to the porch. He fished in his pocket for his keys, found the key given to him back when the prayer squad started. Putting it in to the lock, he twisted the lock and spun the doorknob pushing it open. Slamming the door shut, he ran in yelling, "Fred! Fred, where are you?"

———∞———

Fred still struggled to take any more steps at all. Movement that seemed impossible before had come to a complete stop. The weight got heavier and his legs sorer; each step got smaller as he stepped.

He could hear the clicking of the door lock; the door opened then closed; the voice calling him he recognized. Exhaustion setting in, his attempt to scream was more of a squeak. He managed to bang on the wall, making enough noise to be heard.

———∞———

Harry immediately ran without a word toward the noise in the house. He ran to the bottom of the stairs and heard the front door open again.

He heard footsteps running in, leaving the door open. "Fr-Fr-Fr-Fr-Fr-ed!"

He knew by the voice who it was. He replied, "Upstairs, John."

John ran to the stairs just behind Harry; both sprang up the stairs skipping every other step. Harry caught Fred, allowing him to slump into his arms. John started immediately praying out loud. Fred was sweating, pale, and looked as if he had been running for way too long.

John's prayer was smooth and even; the words flowed from his mouth smoothly, and the answer came almost as quickly as it started.

Just as Fred started to get strength, a voice called up to them, saying, "Where is everyone?"

"Come on up to Fred's room, Peter."

Harry had already started to maneuver him into his bedroom. The strength of Harry and John kept Fred up fighting. He wasn't walking with their help; he was being drug by the two men as they prayed. Peter came in and joined in the prayer.

With all three men praying and laying hands on him, a low growl filled the room and echoed from all around Fred. The volume increased; all four men felt fear and terror filling the air around them. This fear hadn't come from them but from a power or person that was unseen but in their presence. The more fear they felt, the harder they prayed.

Harry asked, "Who are you?"

In a voice more like a growl and howl, they heard, "We are Master Trainer. We will not let Fred buy that house!"

"In the name of Jesus, leave this house!" Harry found himself leading verbally in prayer to bring peace back into Fred's place.

The growl left the voice and turned to a long howl that echoed for several moments. "NO!"

All of a sudden, it was gone. The presence that called himself Master Trainer had left in a hurry.

They all four collapsed, praised, and prayed on the floor for a long while letting the peace flood the house.

When they got off the floor and got to where they could talk again, "What was that?" Peter started the conversation up.

Harry replied, "They call that demon oppression. The difference between possession and oppression is possession is living within, while oppression is controlling from the outside."

Peter didn't know what to say. He knew the situation was serious and asked, "What do we do?"

Harry plainly responded, "Fight with the weapons God has given us to fight with. We will have to work together as a team, with Jesus as the leader, to break the power of the demons." It was obvious that this fight was just beginning.

9 POWER LANE

Master Trainer had split into two parts. All but two of Legion had stayed at Power Lane to stand watch; Aiden and Keegan had gone to find their known enemy. They had entered the tattooed portion of the roof. The tattoo looked like two circles, one inside the other, with an x over it. The remaining line cut the circles in half from top to bottom.

From the moment they entered the tattoo, it had began to protrude and take on a three-dimensional shape like a spaceship. After a short time, the shape distanced itself from the roof and, like a vapor, streaked through the air like a lightning bolt.

From inside, it looked like a ship, but it had no steering controls. It floated in the air moving about on its own, shifting from place to place, combing the ground below with all the knowledge of all the Master Trainers from beginning to end. The hunt had started. They knew what the Gremlin looked like; but no matter how much they searched their minds, they could not find anything else that would be a clue.

A feeling, something inside them, swirled around feeling a threat. A threat they knew before; this had to be the enemy. Though they could not see, they felt the Gremlin and knew he was close to it. They seemed to be slowing, lowering, and leveling off. Shifting to the angle of the roof, the vessel landed, leveled, and looked like a tattoo on the roof of the house.

They both sensed the presence of the real enemy here. He would be easy to find and even easier to stop. He has already been haunted by the memories; now to feed on those memories.

They found him in his room resting. They were not expecting someone standing beside the bed. This person was tall, strong build, with wings. The wing closest to Fred shook him and woke him up. The man spoke, "This one is protected. You have no right to him, leave!"

Aiden responded, "We are two, you are one, and what can you do against us both?"

"I stand with the power of the Creator and Lord, I can stand against you."

"I am Aiden-Born of Fire, and this is my friend Keegan-Fiery. Who are you to stand against the power of Hell?"

"I am Randolph-Strong Shield. I can stand against the power of hell because I stand in the name of the Lord, Jesus Christ, the creator of heaven and earth."

"Randolph, we have the power of two. Do you really believe that you alone can beat us?"

"Aiden, I am never alone. You misunderstand who is alone."

"I am tired of this verbal volleying. Let's see what you are really made of." Aiden and Keegan together charged. With one swift move, Randolph sent Keegan stumbling into Aiden, knocking them both to the floor. Aiden shot up to his feet first.

"Quick, I can see you aren't going to be as easy as I thought." Keegan looked dizzy but was on his feet.

Randolph was not moving, still holding the space between Aiden, Keegan, and Fred. Keegan faced Aiden and said, "Plan B."

Keegan slowly approached, bracing for attack; Aiden lingered three steps behind. Randolph, stern and ready, drew out his wings to full spread, protecting the entire bed area of Fred. "Do you really want to play this game?"

No answer from either attacker. Steadily moving, spreading out in a left and right flank, both attackers sprang with full force. Randolph shot both wings striking the attacking force. Keegan flew backward crashing to the floor. Aiden dropped immediately to his feet to flail sideways at the blow given by Randolph's hand. He dropped by the wall, unable to get beyond the wing of protection.

Randolph reiterated with power, "Leave now!"

Aiden stood to his feet, regrouped with Keegan, stared at him, and each poised for a new attack.

Randolph looked at them. "The game continues. I am still ready to play."

Aiden glared back at him. "This is no game. When you go down, so will your friend. His indecision will kill him. We will take great joy in ending his life."

Randolph was not shaken and did not answer, standing firm, ready for whatever they decided to throw at him.

Keegan mocked, "Fear got your tongue?" He took two steps at Randolph.

His wing snapped, striking Keegan to the ground. Aiden backed away and braced. Nothing; there was no more movement from the warrior they faced. The silence in the spirit world was deafening, the currents ripping through to the core of its essence.

Aiden drew out his flaming sword and said, "Are you ready to face the fury of hell's fire?"

Randolph slid out his sword. "Any time you are."

Keegan was just rising to his feet and could feel the strength seeping out of him.

Aiden placed one foot in front of the other, looking for the flash of the wing. None came. Stepping around to the side, Aiden drew Randolph's body to an angle that left each spirit in a line. Randolph stood firm, holding his ground.

A leaping charge from Aiden and Keegan were answered with a blow of the sword. The force of the strike sent Aiden back. At the same time, Keegan leaped for Fred. All he could get was his phone and clock before the strike of the wing sent him sailing forward crashing into the wall.

Aiden struck again, this time just catching the wing of Randolph. He returned the strike with a blow of his own sword. The sword met the shoulder and neck of the spirit, sending him flailing off balance backward with a quick spin to face Keegan; the wing struck Aiden with enough force to drop him. As he spun, his sword reached out and slashed the air above the bed, sending Keegan down with Fred's alarm clock and phone on the nightstand.

Keegan quickly lifted the phone, drew the energy of the battery into himself, and dropped the phone as the mighty wing smashed again into his head. He flailed back to Aiden. His sword lay on the floor on the other side of Randolph and Fred.

Aiden and Keegan gathered together and planned a strategy for a minute. They braced themselves for the attack. Aiden put his sword away, and Keegan lunged forward alone. Randolph quickly countered the one attacking. Aiden stepped twice and jumped over Randolph and landed squarely on Fred's chest.

He fed his mind with enhanced memories and disrupted his sleep.

Keegan locked on to Randolph, containing and occupying his attention. Keegan felt the thud of walls but wasn't letting go. Every flutter of the wings tried to shake him off, but he remained locked.

Aiden kept feeding the mind, weighing Fred down, causing dizziness and inability to think.

Randolph couldn't shake Keegan but began sending in thoughts. "The phone." It was dead and useless. "Computer. Landline. Phone call."

Aiden acted as a weight, causing resistance, making it harder to move. With each step Fred took, he hooked a claw into the floor adding resistance. He laughed and hissed with joy as Fred found it impossible to move.

Just then, Seth, Harry's guardian angel, came up, whipped out his sword and slapped Keegan across the back, knocking him off. The two stood side by side, silent, each knowing what was going on without being told. Almost as quickly, a third angel came. William drew his own sword and held the line between Fred and the opposing demon.

Aiden whipped fire from his sword at them all and lashed forward. He was met with the fury of light from William's ready sword.

Keegan and Aiden showed fear and shock as a light from nowhere filled the house that only the spirits could see. What they saw was an angel twice their size in stature and build: the warrior, Alexander stood behind them, holding a sword twice the size of theirs, and bellowed out in a great voice, "Leave now. In the Name of Jesus Christ, Father of heaven and earth. Leave!"

They both took flight to the ship and fled back to Power Lane.

Alexander looked at the other four and said, "Well done. They are safe for now. Continue on the lookout for the war has just begun."

Looking to the sky, Alexander reverently said, "Yes, my Lord," and left as quickly as he came.

———*∞*———

Aiden and Keegan descended on the house Moloch had claimed as his own. They knew this was not going to be a good report and it was not going to be easy. Trying to recall what went wrong, they replayed the events again in their minds. They had faced "Jesus's servants" before and had easily taken them. What was so different now?

"Aiden, Keegan, report," Moloch commanded with force.

Aiden stepped up. "Master, the man lives."

"What? Why?" Moloch's anger thrashed out at Aiden. "This was a simple murder. Why can't you kill him?"

Aiden had not gotten off the floor in submission. "He was Jesus's servant, and his guardian angel wouldn't let us get to him."

Moloch flashed fire. "Have you not fought and beat guardian angels before?"

"Yes, Moloch, but this one had more power and were joined with friends."

"Aiden, I know what you are capable of. These excuses are unacceptable. What will it take to kill that man?" Moloch's expression was clear.

Aiden answered, "We must sap the strength of the guardian angels. His wings were powerful weapons that could stop the fight immediately."

Moloch had listened attentively. "A warrior, a shield, guardian angels have specific specialties."

Aiden answered, "This one was a warrior. He was joined by three other warriors of the same capabilities. The worst part is…he was joined by a warrior twice his capability."

—◆◆◆—

Moloch steamed, "A colonel!" Memories flashed in and out of his mind. He had been cast out by the colonels before and knew the level of the fighters had to increase. "Who was the colonel?"

Aiden replied, "Alexander, the great protector."

Moloch flamed up, "We have Legion available to fight him. Who was the human?"

Aiden looked to Moloch. "John, the one we almost killed a while back."

Moloch shot fire at Aiden, sending him backward on the floor. "Your failure! Your only failure was the one that can roust the entire plan! Now I need the others to clean up two of your messes."

Aiden had stayed down. "Myself plus the 'power team' can clean up Fred. It will take longer to clean up John."

Moloch shot out, "What do you plan to do to beat this guardian angel?"

Aiden's answer had to be good or face another burst of the fire Moloch was capable of. "Their power is based on prayer. If Fred has no time to pray, his guardian angel loses his strength. We attack when he is the weakest."

Moloch thought about the answer and raised his hand, allowing the fire to swell and grow and fall back. "Don't fail. Failure will cost you everything."

Aiden trembled while saying, "I won't fail."

———

Alexander and Boris watched the entire conversation with Jesus by their side. He looked to Boris, "Who do we send to help Randolph?"

Boris looked to him and said, "You are going to be busy with Legion. I am capable of working with Randolph. I know the plan and who I am taking on. The prayer strength is strong. God will take care of the rest."

Alexander replied, "You have your work cut out for too. Stand strong in Christ and you will not fail."

———

John had not slept since getting home from Fred's. He had struggled with so much. He could not stop thinking of the time where his prayers were not stuttered words, weak and fragile. There are times that he wondered if the words didn't shatter on the roof over his head; though he had been told that doesn't happen. Since he wasn't going to sleep anyway, he gathered his Bible and began reading the Psalms of David. His reading brought peace and assurance that God was truly in control.

Now he was on his knees in prayer, thanking God for the miracles He provided, seeking strength to make it through this day. Struggling to chase away fatigue, he continued to pray. His workday started late and ended with an e-mail to the company he was doing the project for. He liked being available most all the time and served as a prayer warrior on three request lines.

He knew the prayer squad was in trouble and needed the Lord to carry them through. His prayers were extensively concerning the prayer team and someone he didn't know named Bill. He just had a son, and John's prayers always sought God to show him His love, grace, and peace. Obediently he had placed Bill on his prayer list and prayed for him daily; even though he didn't know the man personally, he was sure that his time with God was important to the prayer squad.

—◆—

Had it already been a week since the last Bible study? Fred knew little rest and less heartfelt peace. Already, for a week, his mind raced with the memories of the signs, the late nights, and now his job was on the line. Knowing the importance of the meetings that will be happening, he fell to his knees, seeking counsel and just maybe a shoulder to rest on for a little bit before starting off a new day.

His prayer time in the morning has always been the highlight of his day, and now it was more than just a place of communing with God; it was a necessity to draw strength to get through the next hours ahead. It was now that he was thankful for the grace and strength God continuously provided. At times like these, God drew him close and loved him, covering all of his weaknesses. His thoughts raced in and out, disrupting any focused thought that was there. Though the prayer was scrambled and seemed to be gibberish most of the time, he knew the prayer was clearly understood by God, and that was what really counted.

The time came—go to work, get these meetings over with, and then deal with the results afterward. The prayer squad would be praying now anyway. How could anything go worse this week anyway?

—◦◦◦—

Harry heard the beeping of his alarm clock. The time had come to pray. He got to his knees on the carpeted floor and began thanking God for the blessing and victory the previous week. He sought God for the victories to continue in Fred's life as he goes to the meetings scheduled for the day.

God gave him a special message in his prayer. Get the prayer squad together and tell them to start a week of fasting and seeking the face of God. He had gotten that message before, and John had almost died that week. It was in the power of fasting and prayer that John lived through the battle that ensued. After the last battle for Fred's life, he started then and prayed right on through breakfast. John and himself had both said that angels fought hard last night to protect them; Fred for sure.

He had an idea that Fred and maybe the whole team was in this for the long haul now. He didn't have to have the details; he had seen enough last few nights to have an idea. The day was slow at work, and he wasn't needed in the shop anyway. With a quick call to the manager, he was off to John's in a flash. He wanted John's assistance with praying on this matter more.

———

Peter had already driven to John's place. He wanted to understand more of what had happened two nights ago. John and Peter were as close as Fred and Harry. Peter had accepted Jesus as Savior the day before John's battle that almost took his life. He hadn't really prayed much before that night, but he did in a way he hasn't understood since that night.

Because Fred was unsure of the results of some meetings that was taking place today, the team gathered together an hour early tonight. All anyone knew was Fred's job will be affected in a good or bad way by these meetings.

He took the five steps and got to the place where he prayed. The church kneeling bench had been a sarcastic gift from a friend that since decided not to talk to him. He knelt on the bench and started praying.

—◆—

Jesus, Alexander, and Boris looked on to all four members of the prayer squad. One man was going to meeting after meeting. The other three men gathered together praying.

Alexander said, "The guardian angels are getting stronger now. It doesn't seem possible that they will need more help."

Boris looked at Alexander. "From what you explained to me, this battle is not at this moment."

Jesus looked at them both. "You two need to understand, I am working to make it possible for all the team members to be together tomorrow. Satan is coming to talk to me. The prayer squad is going to be the topic of this discussion. Aiden, Keegan, Legion, and Moloch will be the least of the problems you two will face."

Together Boris and Alexander asked, "What?"

Jesus continued, "Satan wants to send a special army of his to the families of the four."

Boris said, "You're going to stop him, aren't you?"

Jesus looked, and a tear came down his cheek. "I will only allow him those that already belong to him. Your assignment is to defend any of the family that belongs to Me. You have as many angels as you need at your disposal. If Satan himself appears, call Me. I will take on Satan Myself."

Alexander asked in shock, "How many will die?"

"Too many." Jesus knew the cost but would not force any man's hand.

Just as they finished, Satan barged in. "Jesus, we need to have a talk."

Jesus replied, "I know." Alexander and Boris placed their hands on their swords but didn't draw. Jesus looked at them. "He will not attack me in my house. You two know your assignment, prepare your troops and allow us to talk."

10 THE EXIT

Bill relaxed in his room, excited about the news from the doctor. Samuel's doctor and his doctor released them to go home. This excitement was boiling over into Trainer, but he was not concerned about that now. He was ready to go pick up his son and take him home.

The only matter delaying this now was the signing of the paperwork. Now, he had to wait and slow his mind, allowing him to keep calm and settled. No more panic needed to make matters reverse themselves again.

He made himself slow down and relax. The wait made him anxious enough without adding to it. The room was lonely with no one else in it. Henry and Mary left earlier to get his stuff out to the car and get the car ready for the young baby. Now there seemed to be a void in the room, creating uneasiness and tension.

Bill allowed himself to drift into his old thoughts. He saw Saundra putting the wood cross with a crown of thorns on her nightstand by her bed. He never said anything to her about it. That was her thing, and she was allowed to put on her bed stand what she wanted to remember before going to sleep. His was almost empty with the exception of a small wood block that was passed down through the generations. No one knew what it represented for at least three generations, but Trainer would not let it go. They kept it for the sake of peace with the internal spirit that could cause so much pain.

It looked like a wooden doll or something. To make it fit in the room, he put wood-carved works of art around the room. This one, he could find nothing like. It was only a foot tall with a face that looked angry. He could almost see the evil in this piece.

The eyes were carved deeper than he thought would have been necessary. The ears were a shape that he hadn't seen before. They were not a half oval like most he saw; pointed didn't really fit either. Lying against the side of the head, the ears appeared to be just ugly.

A chubby body, but that was normal. The wings on its back and sword on its hip were more than he could understand. The name "Moloch" under the statue was not understood either, but there was a definite fear that was attributed to that doll.

He shook his head, looked to the door, and wasn't sure who he wanted to show up first. It didn't matter anyway. The door was still closed, and no one was coming to open it. An image of the cross nagged at his mind. It was empty, and the reason, according to Henry, was Jesus raised from the dead and lives forever at the right hand of His Father.

Henry told him it is understood with a step of faith, and without it, no one can understand it. There was no one to ask there, but he knew who to ask and how to get a hold of him. Did Harry have the right answers? If not, he was the most trustworthy of all those that he knew. There was so much he didn't understand and didn't know how to word the questions to get the answers. Was this God really there?

He didn't know what to think, but it was better to ask someone than to drown in confusion that can only result in depression. "Jesus, help me understand this stuff."

—◦◦◦—

Jesus heard the prayer and knew who to call. "Aaron, I need you."

"Yes, Lord, how can I serve you?"

"I need you to go to Bill and help him understand what he needs to know so he will accept Me as the gift he needs for his sins."

"Yes, Lord, is there any special instructions with this case?"

"This is your normal situation. No special instructions."

"Yes, Lord." He immediately flew off to Bill to begin his work.

—◦◦◦—

Mary slid into the room quietly. Her eyes met Bill's immediately. "Hello. Is everything ready in here?" She could see that he spent more time thinking than getting himself dressed. He had managed to get his shirt and pants on before she arrived. His face showed nothing of the happiness the situation called for.

"Is Saundra on your mind?"

"No, I can't get this image out of my mind. I thought about Saundra, and the thought reverted back to the image. Every situation seems to come back to this image. I don't know what to do with it. I just don't understand it. When I get home, there is someone I want to call to talk to. I hope he can help."

"Is there something I can do to help?"

"There is that closet that needs checked to make sure it is empty. I am mostly packed up but don't want to leave anything."

"Okay." She knew his thoughts weren't about what might be in that closet, but his answer said that she wouldn't be of any help on the subject.

The closet still had a bag on the floor to be pulled out. She pulled it out and put it with the remaining stuff to go to the car.

While Bill slid into the restroom in silence, she fell to her knees by the chair. "Dear Jesus, You know what is going on in his head. Send him someone that can reach him with Your truth. I have done all I can do."

She wasn't sure she felt better, but at least she could get God's help with the situation.

She didn't see Bill for several minutes. When he came out, he looked ready to go, complete with a smile on his face.

As she stood up, the nurse came in with a wheelchair. "Is anyone ready to go get a little boy?"

A burst of excitement lit the room. "Yes. The chair is for me?"

"Yes, the car seat is waiting to be loaded and taken to the car. There is a little boy who is looking forward to seeing his father again."

"And a father who is looking forward to seeing his little boy again."

Bill's heart was full of joy and bursting with excitement as he rode in the chair to the nursery. He was not going to just visit; he was getting his son and taking him home. This was real happiness. He refused to let any depressing, confusing thought or image appear in his mind. *This is going to be a good day from now on.*

———

Henry was sitting patiently, listening to the radio at the hospital patient pickup when he saw Mary, Bill, and Samuel heading toward the exit. Excitement and anticipation had filled all of them all morning long. Now they were truly on their way.

A smile formed on his face as he knew this too-long stint was over. All of them could relax for a second, work on training and raising Samuel the way they knew how. There was a lot to teach the young boy and not enough time to do the teaching in. There was also the concern for Bill and his personal salvation. That would be a matter of prayer. He never got into whatever he thought the demons were, but did he really have to know all the details?

The smiles he could see on their faces said Bill's concern about the demons was not a priority at this moment. It felt good to see Bill so proud, up and moving again. He saw way too much of the stillness and unconsciousness in the last few days. Besides, just the sight of his wife made him smile from ear to ear. Could there be a more beautiful sight to see? He couldn't think of one.

Henry watched Mary as she listened closely to the instructions given just before they left, marveling at her beauty and her love. He knew she would be the strong one in raising this little boy; the motherly love would pour from her very soul into Samuel.

"Honey…honey…Henry."

The last shout of his name yanked him out of his thoughts. "What…what do you want?"

"Some help here!"

Henry quickly opened the door, got out, and opened the back door of the car. The look on Mary's face showed the frustration and revelation that she knew he was not in this world.

"I'm sorry. I'm getting lost in thought again." He used his eyes to beg without words.

"I know you were. You are forgiven. A lot has gone on in a very short period of time."

"That is the reason I married you. You know all of my weaknesses and still stay with me."

"That is because I still love you."

Bill interrupted the conversation, laughing, "Okay, you lovebirds. Can you take me home before you get a room?"

Henry said with a smile, "Sure, we can continue this conversation in the car."

"Can you install a window between the front and back seat so I can concentrate on Samuel?"

Henry, Mary, and Bill laughed together as they finished loading the car and headed home.

———

Bill watched Samuel's eyes aim from one place to another. They stopped on things of bright color or movement. They never stopped long on any one target before heading off to the next target.

Bill was concentrating on his son and what he had learned about Trainer. He had to find a way to find out what information Trainer gave Cadet. As well, he needed to see if there was a way to blind Trainer as he thought. He had too much to think about and even more to learn. It seemed his world turned upside down a week ago, and just now the doctor felt comfortable releasing him from the hospital. In this last week, his wife died, his son was born, and he learned that he had someone or something living inside him and wanting to use him for its (his) own purpose.

Bill refocused on Samuel trying to connect to the boy without the actual physical contact. He knew it wasn't the best way, and eventually he would have to have the contact required by Trainer to connect. He didn't know exactly what he was going to do about that, but he suspected that would resolve itself over time.

———

Mary had not stopped praying since she found out her daughter and son-in-law were in the hospital. Now she was leaving the hospital, proud to be a grandma and still numb from the loss of her daughter. Her concern for Bill heightened in the wake of his anger and silence that was unaccustomed to his natural behavior. That was the second concern. The first concern was that Bill didn't respond to the message Jesus continued to give him. How long will this have to be the focus of my prayers?

Henry reminded her often about how long it took the message Jesus gave her before she responded. God would have to break through the hard crust protecting him before he would respond to the message. She knew that was of Henry now, that through the loss of Saundra and the new complications of life presented by Samuel, the thick crust would crack and crumble off, allowing him to hear and respond to the message of Jesus Christ.

This trip home would be a joy and a tough time at the same time. They had become accustomed to that. There has been a week of pain and joy all mixed together. Henry and Mary spent most of their time praying or talking to Bill, the remainder spent holding little Samuel.

"Is everyone comfortable and buckled in?" Henry asked.

Bill said, "More than you can imagine." That brought chuckles from everyone in the car as they proceeded out of the hospital parking lot toward home.

11 THE OPEN DOOR

Satan headed out of the conversation with Jesus ready to create havoc in the lives of the prayer squad. His army was ready for the instructions of their master.

"We are limited to inflicting injury on those in the family that still belong to me. If they belong to Jesus, they will be guarded and we will be fought." Satan didn't get all he wanted but would take what he received. The mission didn't change.

"One important detail: when His children pray, He will answer that prayer. He will fight you with the strength of the prayers going up. Our mission to keep His children from praying is still an important mission. Those that are on the attack, stay there. The rest of you take a family member and inflict as much pain as possible. We have permission to kill them if we want to. Don't hesitate. The loss of life is a powerful weapon and stops most from praying."

Moloch asked, "What can we do to the prayer squad?"

"The prayer squad will fight us tooth and nail. We don't have permission to touch them. Getting their schedule full to the brim so they have no time to pray is the best chance we have against them. There are many good things to occupy their time. Use all of them if that's what it takes."

—⁂—

Aiden and Keegan led Legion to John. John had just sat down to eat his evening meal when his mind went wild with thoughts he had not entertained since his salvation.

He couldn't clear his head from the thoughts running around no matter how hard he tried, prayed or praised.

Legion had come for his mind first and threw the thoughts at him one after another in a machine gun fashion. Just then Elliot jumped between John and Legion, catching every thought that was tossed at John and throwing them back to Legion.

John started praying with a clear mind, and the words flowed with freedom, unabated from anyone.

Elliot warned with force, "You have no right to be here. Leave now."

Legion replied, "You think you can stop me. Oh, little one, take me on now." With that, he multiplied and drew swords.

Elliot said nothing while drawing his sword, lit with a brighter light than he himself was used to. Legion stood unafraid, ready when Alexander appeared.

"Legion, what are you doing here?" His sword drawn and lit nearly blinded the horde of demons. Without a word, Legion and his horde attacked, swinging their fiery swords at the two angels. Both angels immediately swung the light in half-moon-shaped blades, cutting and slashing at the demons, sending the demons backward with a flash. The number of attacking demons decreased by the power in the angels' swords.

Elliot and Alexander flared out their wings to fully cover and protect John from the attack. Legion hissed, still strong.

Alexander said, "Elliot, follow my lead. We are stronger than they are."

"Yes, Colonel." Elliot continued to stand strong.

Legion and the horde leaped again, flashing fire all around them. Just as quickly, the sword of the angels sliced the horde; they dissipated them into space or sent them flailing backward looking for a stronghold.

Quickly, Randolph, Seth, and William joined in the fight, swords drawn. As the horde flew at the angels, they slashed and cut away at the horde. The light and fire from the swords was easily deflected from any harm to John.

Legion drew back and regrouped. Silently the demons took positions high and low as if stacked upon each other. Alexander took the high position alone. "You four have the low attack." All five angels took a full wing-spread-defense stance and locked together.

Legion looked at the defensive front. "Do you really think you are able to hold our attack? It will only take one time, and we will have our way with John. As they say, the rest will be history."

Alexander shot back, "You still have to get past us, and you know that at this moment, the five of us are stronger than all thousand of you combined. We are not getting weaker with every strike. Can you say that about yourself?"

"Attack!"

The horde flew in the divided front, swords pointed and focused on killing the angels. The defensive blows to the swords connected hard. The sparks lit the air all around. A quick slash of the angels' swords sent the demons tumbling backward, and red smoke rose from the ranks.

Legion gathered what remained of his power, united into a single form, and said, "I will have my day. You can count on that."

Out of nowhere came a flurry of thoughts that confused John. Something or someone was attacking his mind with a vengeance. Though he sought God with all his heart, the thoughts flowed one after another. He began singing praises to God, but the thoughts still flooded his mind.

Finally, as quickly as the thoughts came, they stopped. He continued to praise God while finishing his evening meal.

He couldn't clearly identify what was happening, but he knew something was very wrong. Whatever it was, it felt as though a war was surrounding him. Just then he recognized it. It was the same thing that woke him up when Fred was under attack. The gut feeling came with instructions to go to Fred's. This time, it came without instructions, which could only mean one thing. He was the one under attack this time.

———∿∿∿———

"John, where are you?" Fred yelled as he, Harry, and Peter burst into the house.

John could feel the added strength from the second they entered the house. It took him a second before he saw the three terror-filled faces storm into the entryway of the dining room. Before they screamed again, he held out his hand and said, "Here, you found me."

The prayer squad laid hands on John and sought God in prayer. The prayers flew heavenward. Their strength empowered the angels in the fight. With that strength, the feeling vanished leaving only peace behind. The remainder of the meal was shared with all four of them.

———∿∿∿———

Alexander looked at the army with him. "You four seem to be together a lot."

Randolph replied, "United we are strong. Together, I don't believe that anyone can beat us."

Alexander warned, "With their prayers strength behind you, you're right. As their prayer strength goes, so will yours. There have been times that I could not stand off against Aiden alone because of the lack of prayer support."

"What can we do to keep the prayer support up?" Seth asked. Alexander looked at them. "There is nothing you can do. Everything depends on them."

Alexander saw the warning was understood. Randolph said, "We can guard them well and hope they stay together and strong. When they are together, they pray."

———✳———

Legion retreated to Moloch's, defeated and beat up. Stumbling into the main room, he bowed before Moloch, saying, "Master."

Moloch looked at Legion. "Tell me John is dead."

Legion knew trouble was coming, "John is not. He gathered together with the other three and his colonel. Their power together is greater than any that we could have ever imagined."

Moloch's anger flashed in flames. "It is time to leave them alone with the exception of outside temptations. I can have Aiden and Keegan start the thoughts leading them into their own sin. They will break the power of God in their lives. Legion, I want you to attack all those in their families that already belong to us. Kill some of them, make them sick. Make them so busy with life that they don't have time to pray."

Legion smiled. "Yes, master, they will not be able to think about praying when we are done."

Moloch cautiously smiled. "Good, make sure it happens."

Legion left Moloch to begin his work.

12 THE FUNERAL

Bill was out of the hospital for two hours when the first arrangements were made for the funeral. Being forced to deal with the death of his wife was almost too much to handle. For the first time, an array of emotions overpowered his inner being. Looking at the body erased all doubt of her death. Bill felt every emotion in a short time. The emotion he felt now—anger.

He could hear Trainer saying, "Once the baby was born, I can no longer control the woman. I do everything I can."

The words echoed in his mind over and over again like a perpetual song. The anger began to boil in his blood. He could feel the sweat forming on his brow as his blood pressure pulsed hard in his veins. He knew what was coming next. "Not now. The time will come that all this can be expressed without fear of any particular retaliation." He closed his eyes and forced himself to express his feelings in tears. The back seat of the car was as private as he was going to get for a while anyway.

He could hear Mary trying to talk to him but shut out the words. His own sobbing made it difficult, if impossible, to answer anyway. He buried his head deep into his hands to muffle the sound. As he thought of the loss of his wife, he allowed confusion to overtake all other emotions and thoughts. All he wanted now was to find out if Jesus could help with this pain.

His shoulder was shook by someone. He raised his head to see Henry. "You're home now. Do you want us to stay with you for a while?"

He thought for a second then said, "No, you can go home. I will call later to check on Samuel. I need some time alone to clean up the house and prepare for his homecoming. I will call you if I need you."

He unbuckled his seatbelt, slid out of the car, and walked to the front door of the house. "Oh great, how long has the front door been open?"

He carefully scanned the room. The house looked like everything was there. He could see where the blood had dropped on the floor and dried. He stepped into the house, knew exactly where the blood trail went, and relaxed a little as he closed the door. "First thing's first, make sure nothing was taken then call Harry." He walked through the house, searching the rooms for items missing or out of place. He was relieved to see that nothing was out of the norm in any of the rooms.

He sifted through his wallet and found the paper with the number on it. His phone in hand, he dialed the number. "What am I going to ask? What is he going to say? Is this really the right thing to do?"

"Hello."

"Hello. Harry?"

"Yes, this is Harry. Bill, is that you?"

"Yes, do you have a minute?"

"Several, how many do you need?"

"I wish I knew. Would you be willing to come to my place to talk?"

The voice of the Lord inside him said, *"Harry, go. Everything is in my care."*

"Yes. Where are you living?"

"I bought the place that was the main house of the dairy farm at the edge of town. Do you remember it?"

"I think. It is on the corner of Washington and West?"

"Yes. The whole neighborhood used to be a dairy farm. This is the oldest and biggest house in here."

"You have the old main house?"

"Yes."

"I can be there in twenty minutes."

"Good, see you then."

"I'm on my way."

—⟳—

As soon as Harry hung up the phone, he felt as though a clock had started ticking away in Bill's life, and he knew he had to act quickly. Two buttons pushed on the phone connected him to Fred.

"Hello."

"Fred, start the prayer squad praying. I am going to Bill's at his request. I don't know any more. I'm gone."

—⟳—

Fred hung up the phone and placed the call to Peter.

"Hello."

"Peter, my place for an emergency prayer meeting."

"I'll call John, and we will be there soon."

—⟳—

Peter ended the phone call with Fred and immediately called John. He heard the phone ringing on the other end.

"Hello."

"John, I'm on my way to pick you up. Emergency prayer meeting."

"K."

Peter learned the code John used over the phone, and it was already made clear what to do.

—⟳—

Fred thought about how long it had been between these situations. It was never too long. These were emergencies and to be dealt with in that manner. His prayer room was where the meeting would take place. It was time to go. The prayer room was surrounded with God's peace even in situations of this nature. His study was vacated in a hurry. The five steps he took to the prayer room went as quick. Just seconds later, he was on his knees, praying for Harry and Bill.

Peter wished he lived closer, but things were as they were. He drove faster than he should have but managed to get to John's in record time. He blasted on the horn as he turned into the drive.

John was out the door, in the car, saying, "Go."

Peter threw the car in reverse, out the drive, and like a cop, threw the car in drive and took off. The car was moving fast when John asked, "What?"

"Don't know, John. Fred doesn't call with that language often, and when he does, there is no time for questions. He will fill us in when we get there."

All Peter could hear was John praying for someone named Bill. He took the role of number 2, agreeing in prayer himself. The rest of the trip was spent in prayer right up to Fred's driveway.

They got out of the car, ran into the house, and headed straight for the prayer room. Fred was already in prayer for

Harry and Bill. Peter gave up understanding how things happened. He was filled with wonder and awe as he noticed that the prayers they were praying on the way to Fred's matched those of Fred's prayer word for word.

———∽∽∾———

"Harry won't be here. Bill called him and wanted to talk to him. He wanted our prayer support. What we are praying for is Harry's supernatural knowledge of Bill's need and him to accept the knowledge he receives. Who wants to start? We keep going till he calls us with results."

Peter and John knelt at the bench. John said, "I'll start."

All three were kneeling on the bench as John started the prayer.

———∽∽∾———

Bill was struggling with how to put into words what he wanted to say. He tried to think it through for the hundredth time when the knocking on the door startled him. "Harry?"

Harry was a little confused but spoke through the door. "Yes."

The door opened. "Harry, come on in."

As Bill stepped to the side to allow Harry to enter, he said, "Please don't mind the mess. I just got home from the hospital and haven't had a chance to clean up yet."

Bill sat in a chair and waited for Harry to take a seat across the way.

"You may not know how I feel, but I want you to be patient with me. Can you do that?"

"Sure I can."

"The pain caused by the death of Saundra is so great that I can't bear it. I've heard that Jesus can help with the pain. Can He?"

Bill was withholding information from Harry at the time because he was unsure of Harry's reaction. "Yes, He can but only if you allow Him to. I am so sorry for your loss."

"Thank you. I will be burying her ashes the day after tomorrow. I got the chance to say good-bye today. Samuel is being cared for by her mother and father. So I can take today to sort out myself."

Bill noticed Harry sat quietly, waiting for him to sort out his thoughts before he continued, "I don't know how to deal with the pain."

"Bill, I myself have never lost a close relative. If it is anything like losing a dog, it makes a hole so deep and so big in your soul that it seems that nothing can fill it. Am I close?"

"When it's your wife of twenty years, it is more like a canyon. Yes, you're right."

"Jesus doesn't take away the pain. He does fill the canyon, giving you someone to call on when the pain is the worst. The only way I know how to describe what He does is to help you replace the pain with something that brings joy to you. I know that even Christians cry at a great loss, but there is a peace that is unknown by any other."

"Why would Jesus want to do that for me?"

"To answer that question, I have to refer to His own words. John 3:16 says, 'For God so loved the world that He gave His only begotten Son, that whosoever believeth in Him shall not perish but have everlasting life.'"

"What kind of love is that?"

"Romans said it this way, 'God demonstrated His love toward us, in that while we were yet sinners, Christ died for us.'"

"Even now God loves me? Does He know what I have said about and to Him?"

"The best part of the verse I just told you is that yes, Jesus knows all your sins. It doesn't matter. He would have gone to the cross for you if you were the only one on this earth to die for."

"Have you experienced anything like you are talking about?"

"Can you remember me talking to you that one time as children about Jesus?"

"Yes."

"I was not always true to Jesus as some might think. I went looking for a substitute for God's grace out of a bottle. That wasn't a substitute; it was a mask that left me worse than when I started. It just got worse the more I drank. I almost drank myself out of a home and a life. God placed Fred in my life about two and a half years ago. Through him I found that the love of Jesus isn't conditional upon me. The only condition He gave was His blood. So I took that love, and Jesus welcomed me back with open arms and helped me with the alcohol. Can you name one other person that would do that?"

"No, I can't." He knew that Trainer would not tolerate much more of this conversation and decided to end it. "Harry, due to time and circumstances, I am going to have to ask you leave. I will call you when I can talk again."

"All right, can I pray for you before I go?"

"You will have to make that a prayer on the road. I will call you when I have more time."

—⁓—

Harry heard the voice of the Lord again, *"You have done well. It is time for me to do more work with him."*

He got up and left for the door while saying, "I look forward to talking to you again."

Each exchanged a wave as he left the house.

Harry got to the car saying a quick prayer. "Lord, I don't understand what You are doing, but I know it is best. Reach Bill with Your word and the testimony of Your saints."

Backing out of the drive, he reached with one free hand for the phone. How was he going to put into words the strange conversation he had with Bill and the abrupt ending? He didn't understand why Bill wouldn't or couldn't allow Harry to pray for him right there. He received Spirit confirmation that he was done with all that he was to do at that time.

He rolled to a stop at the stop sign. A quick look in the rearview mirror told him he was alone on that road. Two buttons pushed, and in a short minute, he would be connected to Fred.

"Hello."

"He listened to me, and God told me that my work was done for now. He didn't accept Christ today."

"John said something while we were praying. He told us that the demon in Bill is similar to the one in the house. Did you feel anything from there?"

"I can believe that. There was a spirit presence there, but it didn't feel like the powerful demon of the house. I don't doubt John though. I don't know what to make of it."

"I'm on my way to give you guys the details."

Bill felt conflict inside. It was like there were two voices inside him. Trainer's voice was angry and confused. The other voice was calm, quiet, new, and reassuring in a positive way. The conflict raced through his mind, trying to toss confusion into the picture. One phrase kept ringing through his mind, "The truth does not need anger and force to make its point."

Had Trainer said anything without using anger, force, or threats to make his point? He tried hard to think of something but couldn't find anything, unless it was just mute conversation. Then he tried to think of anything he heard about Jesus that was said with force or anger; again nothing came to mind.

If truth required no force to make its point, then who best exemplifies truth?

—◈—

"These thoughts will get you in trouble. You know what I am capable of. What do you plan to do when I reinforce my will on you?" Trainer cut into his thoughts with more force than he wanted to use.

"Is that what the other voice means about truth?"

"So you want to know the truth. I own you and will fight to make sure no one takes you."

"Own? That is an interesting choice of words. I can believe that is truth. There is a problem."

"There is no problem." Trainer tried to keep his voice calm and under control.

"Oh, there is. You see, I don't want to be owned. I don't see anything in you showing me love. You are clearly showing me that you only want your gain no matter what it will cost me."

Trainer wanted to enforce severe pain on any part of his body, but Aaron was right there stopping all pain. "You just remember that Trainer is your master and must be obeyed."

"I understand," Bill said.

—◈—

The prayer squad was all together. Harry started the account of what happened. "The biggest thing that happened was that he heard the word and thought on it. The word of God will not return void."

"Amen. It sounds like Bill just needed a gentle push to get on the direct path to Jesus. We can only pray that he stays on it," Fred spoke more visually with his hands than he did verbally.

Harry said to them all, "One more prayer before we break up to our homes?" He reached out his hands to start. The rest of the three took hands, formed a four-man circle, and prayed again.

———◆◇◆———

The day came for Bill to bury his wife. The funeral home was well prepared. The pastor spoke with him, making sure all the arrangements were met and ready. Now he stood in front of a table that contained three of the most important things to Saundra. First was the Bible that sat on the nightstand for the last five years or so of their marriage. Second was a plastic statue that meant so much more than he could understand. He tried to remove it once. He put it back after she searched the whole house for two days. He remembered her not sleeping for more than a few hours before searching once again for it. The third thing was a vase with a silk rose that always stood as a reminder that he was true to only one woman, and that was her. It was given to her at their wedding. The only other thing on the table was the box that contained her ashes. Beside the table stood pictures of Saundra; both sides of the table were filled with flowers and plants that had been delivered from family and friends alike. He smiled as he thought of how happy she would be, being surrounded by the things she loved.

The guests began to arrive, looking at all the beauty around and the memories that flowed from the different pictures of Saundra's life. The most important thing was young Samuel being in Bill's arms. Samuel's eyes focused on a plain box. Bill tried to convey to the young man the love he had for his wife. He didn't know if he actually succeeded, but it was worth the effort.

The feelings piled up inside, and he pulled one hand free from Samuel and dropped a balled fist on the table. "Why did this happen?"

A tear dripped from his eyes and ran down his cheek. *I miss you so much. I want you back so bad.*

A hand from behind on his shoulder startled him. Mary softly spoke in his ear, "It's all right to cry. Let those tears be replaced with joy."

He turned to her, grabbed her, and sobbing tears, said in a broken voice, "How long will it hurt?"

"Bill, I can't answer that. What I can tell you is that we love you and want to help and so does Jesus."

"Thank you, Mary. It's good to get reassured of that especially right now. I think I need to sit down."

They both moved to the front-row seats reserved for the family, sat down to get the tears under control.

The guests started milling in his direction. Through their hugs and words, they showered him with strength and encouragement that he desperately needed. The time came to sit down and start the funeral. As the family stood up and started speaking about Saundra, the tears that flowed from many of the faces would have filled many a jug.

Then Saundra's pastor stood up and began his message. Bill kept hearing a calm voice with no force, and the pastor continued to claim that Jesus made her life complete and that same Jesus wanted to make his life complete. All he knew to pray was "Help me."

Again, all of the talk about Jesus had no forceful tone. "Truth does not need anger and force to make its point."

With that, he decided that Jesus must be true, but was this the time to trust Him? When was the time to trust Him? He decided it may be time to talk to Harry again. He was curious what the Bible had to say about it. Harry would be able to answer his question.

13 THE FAMILIES

After dinner, Fred looked up at the prayer squad. "Anyone up for being blessed?"

The answer came quick and unanimous, "Yes."

Fred started, "I went through five meetings to find out in the sixth meeting I am interviewing for a job opening with the company that would allow me to work from my home. The sixth meeting they confirmed that I had the job. As long as I get the e-mail to them on time, I only have to show up on the job site once a month."

"Hallelujah!"

"Praise the Lord!"

"That's fantastic!"

The prayer squad raised their hands to the Lord and praised for the provision.

Harry looked at them. "Guys, can I make a recommendation?"

They locked their attention on him, "Go ahead."

"It was obvious that something is going on. Fred this morning and John just now—we are under attack. This house has something to do with it, but it seems to be a minor part. I am not sure what it was all about, but this I do know: it is serious. We have all felt the attacks, and they are from the pits of hell. We need to meet daily, pray with each other and for each other. If you two are vulnerable for attack, we are too."

"I agree. We are under a more severe attack than I have seen." Fred continued with understanding, "The house scares me beyond what I can describe in words. The house may have more to do with this than we think. I hope you understand that God is working in the house situation, and it is clear. God has a plan and is seeing it through. Are we all really ready to walk through it with Him?"

—⁓—

Legion found an uncle of Fred's with a weak heart, and it easily stopped at his command. The uncle fell to the floor, grasping at his chest. His wife came running with the phone as she called 911. The ambulance arrived and transported him to the hospital.

Making all the phone calls to the family members, she could hardly say the words. Her mind still hadn't accepted the events of the last few hours. "Fred, this is Aunt Carol."

Hearing from her was a shock to him. "What's going on?"

Aunt Carol's voice began to crack. "Your uncle Bud had a heart attack, and it doesn't look good. He is at the Stepping

Stone Hospital right now. They are doing everything they can for now."

Fred immediately turned to the prayer squad, "It's Uncle Bud, he had a heart attack. I am going to the hospital now."

"You go, we will start the prayers going up now." As he walked out the door, the prayer squad was on their knees, praying.

———✦———

Boris started his flight. The vial in his hand was to be poured out on Uncle Bud. Jesus didn't speak the mission. He handed Boris the vial, and the rest didn't need to be said.

Boris tucked the bottle in his cloak and withdrew his sword. "I have a job to do, and I will do it."

A small part of Legion was over Uncle Bud in the path Boris needed to take. The demons drew their swords. "He is ours, and there is no one that can save him."

The prayers were surging power into Boris. "It is time to deal with the mission and not you."

The demon swished his sword, cutting the air in half. "You will have to deal with me before you will deal with anyone else."

Boris saw Fred enter the hospital room. Behind him Randolph came in. He pointed at Uncle Bud then the demon in the path. The light off Randolph's sword caused the demon to turn for just one second. While the demon was distracted, Boris shot at him, piercing his sword all the way through him.

The demon melted around his sword and dissipated away as smoke. A quick salute of thanks, and Boris was on his way.

Boris landed and anointed Bud with the oil; he waved at Randolph and returned to God's kingdom.

The drive to the hospital was hectic and filled with prayer. He didn't know what else to do. Fred's emotions ran on overdrive. He felt shock at receiving the message of his uncle's condition, which brought with it a haze that kept him from thinking clearly.

He focused on getting to the hospital without further incident. "Once I'm in the hospital, I will have more accurate information to make an evaluation on. Just get to the hospital for now." The verbal talk helped slow down the confusion, allowing him to focus on one thing. He remained focused until he parked the car.

He didn't want to think. He just walked to the entrance doors of the hospital. At the entrance, he felt the strength of the prayers and knew he needed all of it that could be provided. He opened the door and started the walk toward the room where Uncle Bud lay.

The feelings of confusion and doubt tried to rise to the forefront of his mind. "Jesus, give my mind clarity and ease of knowing what to say to accomplish Your will in here today."

His steps didn't get lighter, but he knew that God placed him there for a specific reason. Now was the time to be ready and willing to be used. God already prepared him for that, but was he really ready to go where anyone could take him? He put the question aside and knew the Spirit of God would bring to mind what he needed, when he needed it.

The plain white halls were long and took more time than he thought it would. He used the silent walk to try to remember when he last saw Uncle Bud and Aunt Carol. The last time he could remember was at the family reunion.

This was the one day in the middle of the summer that all of the family gathered together and caught up with the events of the year. Grandma and Grandpa were always there. Several of his aunts and uncles made it year after year, but Uncle Bud hadn't been able to be there for the two previous years. This year, Uncle Bud and Aunt Carol made it to the celebration. They lived in the area again and looked excited about the opportunity to find out what was going on with the family.

Uncle Bud was a well-built man of medium height. He kept himself fit and firm with a steady exercise program. Fred was searching the crowd for some of the cousins who regularly attended, the ones who were always willing to go over to the park and play anything that involved a ball. He might not have been the most talented, but they allowed for his inabilities and had fun anyway.

Fred was thinking back on those days.

Uncle Bud came up behind him. "Fred?"

"Yes."

"It's been a long time. Do you remember me?"

"Yes, a little. I was a teen last time I visited you."

"Yes, you were. What are you up to these days?"

"I am working in an electronics firm, and I just started a Bible study."

"What are you doing there?"

"I am in the quality control and repair division. What do you do?"

"I just moved here two weeks ago. I work in engineering."

"Engineering. It should be easy for you to get work in that field."

"Yes, it is."

"Do you have room here for your aunt and I to sit?"

"Sure."

For the remainder of the day, they sat and talked. Before leaving, they exchanged phone numbers and promised to talk to each other. They had kept in touch, but it had been sporadic.

Now he stood in the room where that same uncle lay unconscious.

"Fred, I'm glad you could make it."

"Hello, Aunt Carol. How is Uncle Bud?"

"No change yet. He has not woke up yet."

"I called you because I've thought about what we talked about at the family reunion."

"What do you think about it?"

"I purchased a Bible and tried to read it but got lost and struggled to understand it."

"That is why I lead a study group for those who struggle with that. I try to make it clearer. God always gives me insight into His word."

"That sounds like it would be good to go to."

"You are welcome to come with me."

Fred didn't know where to go from there, so he turned to Uncle Bud and looked at him. "Do the doctors have a guess as to what they expect from him?"

"Not really, they just keep saying that we'll have to wait and see. I hope he wakes up soon. The sooner the better."

Fred saw sudden movement. Bud's eyes opened, and he started to try to talk.

Bud was lying on the bed unconscious; his mind was drifting through memories from his life. The noises around him drifted into his ears faintly. He couldn't be sure of who was there or how long they were there; time was slipping through his fingers.

Suddenly, a bright light surrounded the images in his mind. The images vanished into small particles, drifting out and away from his mind.

"Bud." A soft low voice filled his head.

He didn't know if he was talking out loud or just in his head, but he responded, "Yes."

"Why do you reject me?"

Bud was confused and intrigued at the same time, "Who are you that I am rejecting you?"

The voice remained quiet, "I am the Savior, come to save you from your sin."

Bud didn't comprehend any of this clearly, "What are you talking about?"

"Let me play it for you in your mind."

His images turned back in time to a plain-dressed man riding on a donkey. The crowds gathered from all directions, their coats, reeds, and anything available to them they laid on the ground before the donkey. The shouting "Hosanna" rang in his mind. The entire crowd worshiped, calling this man king.

A flash as if time sped up and flew on by; then it slowed to normal-run speed. Three men napped on the ground, interrupted by that same man who rode the donkey. He spoke to them, scolding them for something, and disappeared. Two more times this happened. Army troops and one man different walked up to this same place where the others were.

More silent conversation; whatever was going on, the army arrested this man. He was revealed by a kiss. Bound and chained, they pulled Him back to a trial. All the way back they hit Him, spat on Him, and yanked and jerked Him around on the chains. The pain was evident on his face. He refused to speak. He could see the words were mocking, teasing, and hateful.

From one trial to another trial, the man was taken. This one, a one on one, was short, merciful, and the judge could find nothing wrong with him. He was sent to another trial. The beatings kept getting worse. The spitting, the insulting words and hitting continued every time He was taken some place new.

Back at the second trial location, he could almost hear the crowds demanding something. Then the leader takes this man to a post in the center of a courtyard. Two tables on either side of this post contain punishment methods too severe for Bud to understand. He was chained to that post, and two guards picked up a reed pole. They were ordered to whip this innocent man with them. The pain was all the more clear as he dropped to the floor of the courtyard. With the beating done, this man stood shaking and trembling in pain.

The two guards went to the tables and picked up whips of some sort he had never seen. They had nine leather straps coming off the handle with something sharp on the end of each one.

Bud couldn't imagine anyone using those for punishment, and then he had seen the straps come down across his back. The ripping the flesh apart and off made him want to close out the images. Over and over again, the whips landed, tore, and pulled off small portions of flesh off the body of this man.

Bud could hear himself saying, "Wait." The images froze. "This man is innocent. Why was He being beaten like this?"

The quiet, still voice returned, "Because you will need the forgiveness for all of your sins."

"Stop!" Bud could not fathom what he just heard. "He did this for me? Why would He do that?"

"That man was me. My love for you was the reason that I did this. There is so much more to show you."

The voice had Bud confused, but he continued to watch. The replay started back up. The whips continued until there was nothing left to whip on his back. This man was rolled over on his back exposing his front. The blood flowed to the ground already, and now the whips flew again. The front of his body beaten to the point the He was not recognizable as a man.

Still alive, amazingly, He was returned to the second judge. The crowd could not be satisfied; they were angry and demanding that he be punished more. The judge tried something, but it didn't work the way the judge thought it would. With tears in Bud's spirit, he saw them place a cross on this man's back.

Bud could not imagine Him having any strength left, but He picked up that cross and carried it until He was no longer able. A man was chosen from the crowd to help Him carry it the rest of the way, all the way to the top of a big hill. Once there, He was laid on the cross, nailed to it, and hung there. There were two other men, one hung on either side. All three died that night on that cross.

The other two were taken and dumped off the side of the hill, landing on a mountain of bones. The man in the middle was placed in a tomb. Some time later, Bud saw this man standing outside the tomb, telling him, "You have rejected my love. I am showing you what my love has done for you. I am the way, the truth, and the life. No man comes to the Father but through me."

Bud wept as he asked, "How can I find you?"

"Ask Fred. He was waiting with the answer." The voice left, and he woke up.

Bud looked around a hospital room and knew immediately where he was. Fred was first to meet him. "Uncle Bud?"

"Fred, I saw a man that was so badly beaten and crucified on a cross. He said He did it for me. Will you show me what He meant?" Bud could only see the images vaguely, as through a fog, but would never forget them.

Fred started explaining salvation. "God made us to be with Him always. Sin entered the world, separating us from God. Jesus went to the cross, died so we can be made right with God again. You see, through Jesus's blood, God forgives us from our sins and makes us right in God's eyes."

Bud was silent, but teardrops flowed from his eyes.

"Uncle Bud, if you believe you have sinned, Jesus died for those sins, and has risen from the dead. God will forgive you of your sins and save you from them."

Bud looked through the tears. "How?"

Fred asked, "Will you follow me in a simple prayer?"

Bud just nodded his head yes.

Fred and Bud went through a simple prayer, asking Jesus to forgive them and save them. In the background, Fred could hear Aunt Carol saying the words.

Fred looked at them both. "Come to my place. I'll bring you to the Bible study I lead. There you will learn and grow in your new faith by being in His word, the Bible."

With the arrangements made, God had grown his meeting of four to six. Fred prayed, thanking God for all He had done, and left to have the Bible study.

—✲—

Boris returned to Jesus, "Lord, mission complete."

Jesus said, "Well done."

Boris noticed first the angel approaching. "A fighting army is approaching."

As they left for the gate, Jesus said, "Let Satan in to talk to me."

Boris and Randolph knew immediately what to do and where to go. The armies of the Lord gathered at heaven's gate, awaiting the enemies' strike. Randolph told the armies, "Satan only goes through. All the rest must remain outside."

The armies nodded in consent. Randolph drew out his sword. "The armies are coming. Be on your guard and ready."

The Lord's army all drew their swords. The light blinded anyone coming in its path.

The noise of thousands of wings whirred around, the sound was deafening. No orders came, just a firm stance from all in the Lord's army. Satan came in the lead and became visible first. The sky darkened in the shape of a huge triangle. Satan hissed something, and the triangle loosened its shape; the demons drew their swords of fire and moved in fast.

The swords began to strike, and everything became a blur. The sparks flew, and the front line held strong and firm.

Randolph silently escorted Satan to Jesus, then returned to the battle.

Boris and the others had not stopped moving. The fighting continued hard. Just as quickly as it started, a loud hiss overpowered all the other sounds, and the demon horde retreated with Satan in the lead.

Boris and Randolph went back to Jesus. "What was that conversation about?"

Jesus said, "A misunderstanding of what I meant between Mine and his."

Randolph said, "You are still claiming the elect."

"Anyone that will come is mine. I will protect those that will come to me."

"The fight is going on still. Be ready to fight." Jesus looked at them both and reiterated, "Be ready to fight. We are not done."

"Yes, Lord," was all that was heard, and they were gone.

—⁂—

John's dad pushed his old lawnmower around the yard. His health had been as close to perfect as humanly possible, and today he felt better than ever before. His strength had come from years of training—physical and mental. He had no reason to believe anything was going to change today. In his fifth lap around the lawn, he felt a stream of pain that began at his ankle and went up through his leg, then nausea, dizziness, and finally silence. He was declared dead on the scene and taken away.

His wife picked up the phone to make the worst call she had ever made in her life. "John, your father passed away today. He was bitten by a snake and died before anyone had the chance to help him."

John was silent, still. In disbelief, he asked, "Mom, yo-yo-you're tal-tal-tal-king a-a-a-bout my dad? When did it ha-ha-hap-pen?"

"Yes, John." His mother's voice cracked, and tears formed in her eyes. "It happened just a few minutes ago. The paramedics got here, but he was already dead."

John could hear the tears and suffering. He hung up the phone in disbelief. How could this have happened?

John dropped to his knees. "Oh, God, my God, what is going on? Do I not deserve a chance to pray and heal as Fred did?"

John did not hear an answer from God; his friends knelt beside him praying. As he continued praying, "Was there no way to save him too?"

John knew that he had tried to show his dad what the love of God was all about before. He could hear the words his dad had told him repeatedly, "I have left God out of my life, and that is the way I way I want it. Don't ever bring Him up again."

For the last month, he had grown so cold that no matter what John said, he just let it go in one ear and out the other, without a thought. "Jesus, give me the strength to get through this."

——❦——

Randolph and Boris watched the scene play out. Once the attack was evident, Boris held out his hand to take the next vial. Jesus said, "No, Boris, not this time. Satan is taking this one with him."

Boris's hand dropped to his side, his face saddened, and he said, "Yes, Lord."

——❦——

Seeing John's distress and hearing his words, Keegan prompted John to think. "What kind of a God would save one man and kill another? Fred is his favorite. Seek revenge on Fred, and you might be the favorite of God."

The words were largely ignored by John, but a seed of doubt had been planted.

Keegan heard a warning, "Not all at once you will have many chances. Seeds turn to cracks, cracks turn to holes, holes cause the biggest buildings to break and fall down.

——❦——

His mom was still on the phone. "John? John?"

His quiet reply came through the tears, "W-w-wh-when is…the fun-fun-er-er-al?"

"We don't know yet, we are just leaving to go the funeral home now. How soon can you be here?"

"Th-th-th-three hours."

"I love you, see you then." The click signaled the disconnection of the conversation and of his strength at the same time.

—◈◈◈—

Boris looked to Jesus. "They are attacking hard. I am ready to stop this now."

Jesus pulled out a vial and held it out to Boris. "Richard only."

Boris looked with amazement. "Satan wins another one?"

"It's their choice. They chose who won before this day came. It is not a choice that I make, but I will defend their choice because of the price I paid on the cross."

"I understand, Lord."

"Time is getting away, go now."

Boris vanished in a blur toward the car.

—◈◈◈—

The truck driver had driven too long already, but the load had to be on time. He wasn't going to be the driver that lost the account. He pushed the truck fast and hard, without a chance of stopping. Sleep would just have to wait.

—◈◈◈—

Boris approached the car to find two guards, swords drawn. "We have already heard about you and your mission. You will not get past us."

Boris drew his sword. "I want Richard."

"So does Satan. Right now, for you to get him would be punishment for us. You can't have him."

Boris looked down the road to see the truck a few miles away and coming fast. The heckling laughter of the demons burned in his ear, telling him they were aware too.

Boris took aim, pointed his sword to the demon on the left, and flew in attack. The demons held their stance, heckling and mocking, "Come to your defeat."

As the words left his mouth, Boris slashed and dissipated the demon on the left. He rolled to the left, swords clashing against the other demon. Fire and sparks flew, lighting the air. The demon took a hit hard to the side of the head and tumbled away.

Time was of the essence; Boris went directly through the roof of the car, poured the oil on the head of Richard, and went up, prepared to ward off the demon again.

The demon hissed, "You are dead. I will not run," as he kept on course, the sword point headed directly to the heart of Boris.

Boris braced, watched, and when the time was right, crossed his sword, deflecting the demon's sword, and slashed the demon across his neck.

"No!" The demon dissipated and vanished.

The truck driver's head slammed hard on the steering wheel as the demon beside him pushed it down. He grabbed the wheel and yanked it, turning the truck into the opposing lane of traffic. Steward, the driver of the car, tried to swerve to get away but didn't react fast enough.

The metal and plastic folded, crunched, and flew; bodies bounced in the vehicles, and the engine of Steward's car smashed through his midsection. Burning pain shot throughout his whole body, darkness, then nothing.

The phone rang again. All four men looked at it. Fred had just got back from the hospital; he hadn't heard what had happened. John just waved for someone to answer it. Harry picked it up. "John's place, may I help you?"

Harry recognized the voice on the other end, "Harry, Steward was in a head-on collision. He is at the hospital now. They don't believe he is going to live."

Harry's countenance dropped, "I am on my way." The receiver dropped to the holder and rested.

Harry looked at the other three. "We are all going to the hospital. My brother was involved in a head-on collision. Everyone ready?"

"Let's go," everyone said together.

———✺———

At the hospital they stayed together, went to Steward, and watched the indicator lines on the machine go straight. They stayed long enough to see that he had died. Harry promised to be back shortly.

The four walked off to the nurse's station. "Do you have a patient named Richard Boss?"

The nurse typed it in the computer. "Yes, are you family?"

"I am the brother of Steward, the driver." Harry dropped his head. "He just died, and I figured Richard was with him. Can you tell me if he has family here?"

"I am his father," the voice came from behind him.

Harry turned to face the man. He didn't know what to expect, but he saw an average man with worry and fear written on his face. When he looked up, it was with effort. He knew the accident made an impact on that family's life as well. "Would you mind if I talk to him? My name is Harry."

"Come with me." They walked off to the room together in silence, each with deep sorrow on their minds.

"I am going to pray with your family. You can handle talking to Richard," Fred said as he walked back to the room with Harry's family.

"John, go with Fred. I'll go with Harry for prayer support."

Peter and John followed their prospective parties as the team divided to serve where they were needed.

"Harry, this is my wife, Vera." She didn't look up until she was introduced. The anger showed on her face. She was wearing blue jeans with a T-shirt that said "No. 1 Mom."

"This is Richard's sister, Patty." She was dressed like she just finished a sporting event in which she played. The shorts and T-shirt with the team logo, high socks up to her knees and tennis shoes.

"This is his Aunt Molly." She appeared older and slightly heavier than the others.

"Everyone, this is Harry."

They all exchanged hellos. "I am Steward's brother. I hope that Richard is okay."

Richard replied softly, "You are Harry?"

"Yes."

"In the ambulance I saw an image of a cross and a voice told me to talk to Harry about what it meant. Are you that Harry?"

"I believe I am. You saw an image of a wooden cross with three holes in the wood. It was placed on top of a hill, with the words 'I love you' below it."

"Yes," Richard was amazed. "How did you know?"

"I saw the same image. Only I was told to find Richard and show Jesus's power to him."

Richard's mom interrupted, "How could a loving God allow this to happen?"

Harry looked at Vera. "Ma'am, God saved your son. The same God that saved your son took my brother. I believe that

God allowed this to happen so He could save your son from eternal separation from Him."

All were silent, listening to Harry.

"Our sins separate us from God. God knew we needed a way to be restored into His perfection or we would never be able to live with Him in Heaven. God made a way through His Son Jesus Christ. Jesus became the perfect sacrifice for our sins. When He took our sins on Him, He made it possible for us take His perfect righteousness on us. We simply take the free gift God offers by asking Him for His forgiveness and making Him the Lord of our lives."

Harry led all that would pray into prayer. Richard prayed with him, accepting Jesus as his Savior and King. Richard's Father stood up saying, "Thank you. We have tried to show him Jesus for years, but he has refused continually."

Harry sought their faces. "He was ready tonight. God set His plan into action. He was spared death in the accident because of this moment."

They all prayed one more time, thanking God for the gift He gave; then Harry promised to return later.

―✳―

Vera watched as Harry left the room. "You're all crazy. How can you even think that stuff he said is truth?"

"We don't *think* it is true. We *know* it is. I have showed you many times why I know it is. The change in your daughter should be enough to convince any man," Gerald answered with confidence that sent her back to a chair.

"You listened to Harry when it was his brother that put our son in the hospital." The emotion was spilling over into tears.

He said, "I listened to a voice inside me just as did Richard and Patty. We know that you won't respond to the voice until you take the time to get quiet enough to listen to it."

She got up and ran to him, fist formed. "I've tried to listen to the voice you are talking about. It never answers me. I just want to know the voice is truly of God." Her fist slammed into his chest as she said the last word.

"Settle down. You look for the voice in raging fire, tornado winds, and hurricane winds. The voice we listen to doesn't come in those times. We listen to a still, small voice that can only be heard in the quiet moments." He held her hands in his, hoping that she would calm down and listen.

"Let go of me!" She yanked her fist free from his grip. "The voice of such a big god as you talk about should be able to boom over anything."

"I'm sure it could if He so chooses. He chooses to speak with a still, small voice, I think, because it gives us a choice to listen or not. God always gives us the choice to believe or not."

"Do you even understand what you are saying? Does that make sense to you?"

"Honey, God rarely makes sense to me in my limited understanding."

"You say that you cannot understand God. How am I going to understand God?"

"Who asked you to understand? No one understands God. What God asks is that you put your trust in Him without understanding. Do you see the difference?"

"How can you trust what you can't understand?"

"How can you believe in the wind and never see it? You look at the results of it. What are the results of God?"

"Shut up." She turned away and walked to the wall and stopped.

"Dad?" Richard's voice broke through the new silence in the room.

"Yes."

"You know it is hard to come to a point that you would be willing to come to Christ."

"Yes, I do. I also know your mother is angry and doesn't want to listen to Jesus. It is easier to blame Him than trust that He is who He says He is."

The deafening silence in the room couldn't be filled with anything, and Vera doubted anyone had anything better to do than stare at her. "I'm going for a cup of coffee."

"I'll go with you." Patty followed her mother out the door.

—⁂—

Moloch roamed the house from room to room, nervous; yet expectedly, he wasn't told what was going on between God and Satan. He had seen every room of this house a million times, and Trainer had not come to get the logs. This rattled his nerves, but what was worse: he was losing battles for souls and lives to Jesus. Satan was on his way to confront him about this. Legion had nothing but excuses. Keegan and Aiden hadn't been able to break the resistance, and Satan was not going to accept excuses from anyone.

With no answers, his best hope was to have a really good plan to show Satan or lose the house. Is the plan good enough? Will Satan allow me to continue the work?

"Moloch!" Satan's voice rushed into the room with anger. "What is your report?"

Moloch jumped at the sound, landing on his knees and face. "Master, I have good news to report. The plan to keep the prayer squad busy has started and is working. They haven't sat still long."

Thinking deeply, Satan inquired, "How long have they been hopping?"

Moloch knew enough time had elapsed, but the answer had to sound good. "We started before their Bible study started, and that phone has rung off the hook. John is already starting to grow the seed of doubt, Harry will be breaking soon with the death of his brother; and best of all, the plan will divide the prayer squad in half, making it ineffective."

A pleased fire burned in his eyes. "One more question. Why are they still praying?"

Moloch looked at the floor. "I am confident the seeds we plant will take root. The sin will break the power of their prayers, and they will fall."

Satan thought about that, knew the truth of it. "I shouldn't give you any more chances. You have failed me again. I will allow this plan to follow through. If it fails, you will not see this type of power again. Am I clear?"

Moloch feared the fire of hell was already being cast his way. He knew this would not be repeated again; failure was not an option. "It will be done, master."

———◆———

Boris, Alexander, and Jesus sat together again. "I am concerned about the recent attacks. They have not had their needed prayer time." Boris had seen this happen before, and it led to weakness and failure to prevent the harm from being done.

Jesus searched Boris's face. "Boris, we are all concerned about them. What Satan has not seen is that the prayer squad is growing in numbers. That will be important in their future."

Alexander knew what that meant. "So they will not be alone in prayer. Their power will be magnified when they pray as a team."

"Yes," Jesus said, "*when* they pray. Satan wants them not to pray while he plants sin in their lives to break down the strength of the prayer squad."

Boris thought hard about that. "There is nothing we can do to change their decisions until they pray either."

"Yes, the strategy is effective and will very well disrupt the plan. They will make the decision," Jesus spoke the words with tears, hoping they would allow Him to send his angels to help.

—◦—

Vera stormed down the hall. She only got a few feet when she heard Patty call out, "Mom?"

"Your father thinks he has all the answers. How could love create such pain?"

"Love helps us grow. To grow, we have to go through hard times sometimes. Besides, God spared Richard's life. Mom, you still have your son. Think of how the mother of the other young man feels."

"Her son was driving. Do you really want me to pity her when my son is lying in the hospital?"

"Not pity her. I want to you think about what God did to someone else."

She noticed an empty table beside a middle-aged woman and man crying. It wasn't until she sat at the table that she heard them talking.

"At least God used our son to reach one more for His kingdom."

She stopped to continue to hear the conversation.

"Harry was right. God will use this death in a mighty way for His kingdom. We may never see all He does, but we know already God is at work through this death."

"We have much to be thankful for."

She quickly turned to the couple. "What! Thankful? You just lost your son, and you are thankful?"

The couple looked at her. "We are thankful any time God brings another into His kingdom. We will miss our son greatly. We also know that Richard saw Christ through this event. That is a blessing in the storm. God will bring us through the storm."

"You're as weird as the rest of the religious freaks." She stormed off to another table farther away. "Patty, you willingly associate yourself with those freaks?" The anger in her voice shot out like a rocket trying to destroy.

"Yes. That is the love of God. It is a willingness to see one He loves die to save another. No one wants to be here in our or their situation."

"If they raised their son right, this wouldn't have happened."

"Can you see your own selfishness in that sentence? Yet they are thankful for Richard's salvation. Who is in the wrong?"

"Shut up." She turned and faced the wall.

———

Jake drove down the road in silence with his son, Peter. There hadn't been much conversation as of yet, so Peter thought it best to start one. "Dad, I have been praying hard that you would see Jesus for who he really is. Have you thought about it any?"

"I have done more wrong and committed more sins than could be forgiven. I have never seen any man love someone so much that they would die for them like you said Jesus did." The doubt in Jake filled his voice.

Jake saw the countenance of Peter sadden with each word. "I know what you are saying, Dad. I struggled with that too. No one would die for all the people of the world like that."

Jake's head was nodding in agreement.

"Then I found out what it took to die for someone else."

Jake looked at him. "What do you mean?"

"Do you know anyone, including your closest friend, who would give his life to save yours?"

"No." The answer came with deep thought.

"When the opportunity came for you to give your life for someone else, did you?" Jake could see Peter was trying to make a point.

"No." The answer was dry.

"I wouldn't have either. That's what changed my mind about Jesus. He walked to His own death willingly so I could live with Him for eternity. Dad, if you were the only man on this earth, He would have done the very same thing just for you."

Jake's expression changed from dry to disbelief. "How can you say that?"

Peter replied, "You know me, you know what I was like as a teenager. When I graduated from high school, would you have said, 'This guy is going to be a preacher one day'?"

"No, I had you pegged for being an inmate in state prison. In fact, I had already given up on you, waiting to visit you in prison."

"What else, besides Jesus, could make such a change that drastic in my life?" Jake's wheels were spinning inside his head.

The attitude changed from disbelief to why. "Tell me one thing. Why would He....why did He do that?"

Peter simply said, "Love, true love."

The tears rolled down his cheeks; for the first time in his life, he prayed, "Jesus, if what he said is true, save me. You know I have sinned a lot. Forgive me of those sins and make me Yours."

———∽∽∽———

William stood firm around Peter, knowing he was alone, without help. The enemy coming against him was not one but many. The sneering laughter of the demons made him aware of his standing alone.

He braced for an attack from all sides. His wings spread out as far as they could, sword drawn, holding position. The demon leader stopped the horde. "What are you going to do alone?"

William looked at them. "Whatever I possibly can."

Legion knew that failure would bring harsh punishment from Moloch and came prepared to kill Peter and his father. Killing one of the prayer squad right now would make a real impression on Moloch, especially since his last meeting with Satan.

William knew what he was thinking and also knew that with every attempt, he would need full power and concentration. He felt something from above; he recognized it as a supernatural strength coming directly from God.

"William, no one else can see me, but I am here helping you."

"Boris?"

"Yes, William, it's me."

With his confidence supported, he stood strong. "You have no right to Peter, and I will not allow you to take him."

The demon horde drew their swords, lighting the sky with the fire. The leader prepared his horde, "Are you ready to fight?"

William stood firm, holding his defensive position. "You should know that Jesus is in control of this situation. You cannot take what Jesus has not given you to take."

"We shall see about that." William was ready for what was coming next.

"Attack!" The demon horde heckled and flew toward William. The sound of their wings filled the air. William's strike was quick and consistent. His sword and wings moved quickly, deflecting the horde. They were held on the first wave of the flash of his sword, striking and cutting.

The leader's sword came high over the blocks, and the strike was aimed directly at the shoulder of the warrior. Just inches from striking its target, the sword deflected up over his shoulder and head. The light from this new sword was greater than of William's. Boris stood visible beside William. "I don't think you heard William. You have no right to Peter. We will not let you take him."

From the heavens flew a flash of light. "Boris, I am Bevan. I am here to fight."

Boris looked at this young warrior. "Who are you assigned to?"

"Peter's father, Jake has accepted Christ as Savior."

Boris nodded his head. "Then what are you waiting for?"

"Your word, captain." The sword of light flashed out with surprising speed.

The horde leader said, "Horde, they are three. We are many. Attack!"

"Make that four." Alexander flew into the line beside Bevan.

"Boris, you lead the team. Protect these two with all the power of heaven."

"It is done." Boris commanded again, "Keep the line solid."

The other three angels together said, "Yes, sir."

The horde flew, swords pointed straight at the four targets. The wall formed by the angels was stiff and had curved around the car. The slap of the first demon on the wall sent immediate flashes of light from all four swords. The demon horde bounced and rolled as they were slashed, and many dissipated on the second wave. The third wave came seconds after.

The fury of the continuous attack left a red haze floating in the air. William had pain coming from somewhere, and Bevan showed his youth. With every flap of Bevan's youthful wings, William and Alexander followed to keep the wall firm.

Rolling back, the horde gathered and collected for another wave of attacks. Bevan's wings fluttered, anxious for more fight. Boris commanded, "Bevan, hold your position. We are to defend only."

Bevan says, "Yes, sir."

The horde waited. "Boris, we have no retreat. To give in now would be worse than anything you can dish out."

Boris calmly said, "Make your choice, pain from me or Moloch? We are not giving up."

———✵———

Jake drove in prayer the rest of the way to Fred's house. "Good, they're all here. I want to introduce you to the prayer squad."

By the time the car had stopped in the drive, Fred was waiting at the door. "Welcome, come in," Fred directed the statement to Jake.

Jake, unsure of what was going on, said, "Thank you. My name is Jake, Peter's father."

With a hearty pat on Jake's back, he said, "We have coffee and beverages on the table in there."

"Thanks." Jake headed inside to the coffee.

Peter lagged behind, tapped his heart, telling Fred his father had accepted Christ as his Savior. "How about something to drink?"

Fred gave a thumbs-up and went in behind his guest. "Peter, do you want to introduce your father to everyone?"

"Dad, this is Fred, John, and Harry. Everyone, this is Jake, my father."

They all shook hands, and when Jake took his son's hand, Peter said, "Welcome to the family of God."

"Amen," the unanimous cry of all four of the prayer squad came.

———

Just as quickly as they entered the house, Randolph, Seth, and Elliot came up through the roof, swords drawn. "Need some help? We have been waiting for a good fight."

The horde leader yelled, "Attack!"

The horde flew into action, swords swishing from side to side, cutting the air with fire. Boris got behind the other angels as they formed the wall. The slashing of their swords cut into the front line, dissipating all but one. The second line drew back with amazement of their new-found strength.

Unanimously, the entire angelic team said, "Leave now!"

The horde fled back to Moloch with fear.

The prayer meeting at Fred's lasted two hours. Boris stayed behind on the roof while the others went through the roof, standing firmly behind their assigned believer while they prayed.

14 THE DATE

After the funeral, Bill decided to take a walk around the town. Half of the block was owned by the funeral home. Right behind the funeral home was a neat row of houses on small lots. As he entered the residential area, the dogs started barking and jumping along the fence line bordering the backyards. Nice, three-bedroom homes, most single stories with a few exceptions—up one side and down the other of the street. Nothing seemed different about this neighborhood. As he walked on down, he came to a blue house that stopped him cold.

It was one of a few two-story houses on the block. It had the same blue paint job that it had when he was taken from it after his father's death. The yard was kept cut, and the For Sale sign in the yard was fading. The realtor's number was faded beyond reading. He walked up to the front door. The brown door brought back memories he couldn't imagine he remembered.

He was two years old, and the sun was out shinning bright. He was so interested in that sun that he walked out to the door and looked at the sky. The look of awe left his face. The blue of the sky was there, but there was no bright-orange ball in the sky anymore. "Where did the ball go, Dad?"

"What ball, son?"

"The big one in the sky."

His dad took his hand and walked him off the porch. "That orange ball is the sun. That is what gives us light during the day."

"Sun."

"Yes, sun. It shines light on us."

"Sun lights us."

"Yes, it does."

He ran off in the yard, jumping high to catch the sun but missing.

He looked back on the porch. His dad was standing there with a friend just watching, talking and laughing.

Bill let the memory fade away with a smile. Just for grins, he tried the door, thinking it will be locked tight. The door opened with ease, and a voice from somewhere inside said, "Welcome back."

"Hello." His pulse quickened a bit at the unknown surrounding this entire place.

Silence from inside. He walked slowly in the house, scanning for the location of the origin of the voice. The place looked like someone was cleaning it daily. The furniture looked like it never aged. His father placed a full-length mirror in the entrance hall. He had to look in the mirror and answer the question, "Do you want people to see you that way?"

Now he looked in that mirror and saw something much different than was expected. He didn't see a full-grown man but a child around twelve years old. Tears were streaming down his face; his lips moved, trying to say, "Dad." His own memories could recall seeing that the police pulled him out of the house to place him in foster care.

Could this house be stuck in that year? How long had it been for sale and never sold? Why was the house unlocked? Who held the keys to the house now? He didn't know, but one thing was for sure: he could feel the comfort of his father, mixed with terror from inside that rattled Bill in a way he was unfamiliar with.

Trainer said to him, "This is the wrong house. This will not help me. You need to get to Power Lane, end of story. This house will not bring me the information I need to get the job done."

"What job is that, Trainer? It will take time to get stuff done right. I will get to the house when the funeral dinner and the other stuff is done."

"More boys! The job is getting two more boys. Remember what I told you at the hospital? Shall we walk around and see if there are any single females willing to breed for the cause?"

"I don't think that looking for females for breeding only is a good idea. How about looking for a wife first then let the children thing slip out?"

"Okay. The sooner we get working on that, the better off we are."

"We?"

"Yes, I can still inflict major pain on you. Don't be fooled."

Rather than push this conversation further, it was time to get going to the dinner anyway. He made arrangements to pick up the funeral stuff the next morning. Saundra could wait until the morning.

As Bill walked out the door, he saw a middle-aged woman with her daughter about ten years old down the road. "Is she single? She looks pretty and medically able to bear children."

Quietly thinking to himself, "Cool down on the children. Talk first." His mind could not let go of Saundra just yet, so his desire was to deal with her first.

He walked to his car and started off to the hall for the dinner.

At the dinner, he sat at a table with a plate containing a sandwich, some potato salad, and a little cheese on the side. Though there was much more food to eat, he sat not eating anything. The emotions ran rampant in his mind along the words of the pastor at the funeral. "Saundra has not died, but has gone from us to live eternally with Jesus. We can see her again if we also follow Jesus and take him as our personal Lord and Savior."

He spent more time picking at his food then eating. Trainer continued to prod with every sighting of a female, but they were ignored easily enough. While he continued to pick at his food, nibbling small amounts at a time, he heard from beside him, "Are you going to play with your food or eat it?"

Startled by the voice, he looked at the young woman who sat beside him. She had blond hair, long and flowing down her back. Her hair accented her blue eyes. She was wearing a dark-colored dress that made her natural beauty come out.

"I don't really feel hungry right now."

"I understand, you should at least eat a sandwich. You will get hungry soon." There was a sparkle in her eye that prompted him to eat the sandwich anyway.

While he chewed on a bite of sandwich, she continued the conversation. "Bill, I knew Saundra well. She would have wanted you to take care of yourself and continue to strive forward. I was the fried that she called when she needed a compassionate ear. I'm Rebeca."

"Rebeca, how much do you know about me?"

"I feel like I know you better than my best friend."

Bill thought, she hasn't heard a thing about Trainer. What would she say about all that? "I hope Saundra was kind about me."

"Nothing but. I never heard a bad word the total time we talked."

He could hear her careful choice of words and understood why. He opened his mouth to say something but stopped. Finally he did speak, "No, I can't be too forward." He said it softly, trying not to be heard.

"I am the one being forward. You can say whatever you want to say."

"I have to leave for an appointment soon. If you don't think it is too forward or soon, we could meet for lunch. I need someone to talk to that knows Saundra already anyway."

"Sure, where do you want to eat?"

"Do you know the sandwich shop on the main drag?"

"Yes, I eat there most every week."

"I'll be there about twelve. I'll be bringing Samuel."

"I'll be there with something for the boy. I'm looking forward to seeing you."

She looked at the plate of food and knew that he ate very little. "God, you've got to help me with him. You are working in him in more ways than I know. Give me wisdom to deal with him and the situation he is in."

15 THE HORDE

The time had come for Bill to go see this house on Power Lane. Bill could feel the pull from the house the closer Trainer got. The sign lit up, like someone wanted him to be sure he knew where to go. "Trainer, I am going where you want me to go. I got all the directions, and I have a GPS system in the truck to get me there. Don't blind me with the signs."

"It's about time. You've delayed my time schedule." Trainer had been insistent ever since leaving the hospital.

"You can blame that on Samuel. He doesn't seem to be on any schedule," Bill chided back.

"Just get there. No more games." Bill could feel Trainer's frustrations building.

Bill looked for 5757 as the car rolled down Power Lane. What he saw was a disaster. The yard was knee-high with weeds and grass. The house was unpainted, rotting wood, no windows had glass in them, the doors hung swinging in the wind. The truck rolled into the driveway by itself. A green glow came through the opening in the doorway. Bill opened the door of the truck and floated out of the truck.

Without his feet ever hitting the ground, each step moved him closer to the door. The spiderweb hung from the entryway stopped him dead in his tracks. He read "Welcome, Bill." He tried to step back to the truck but found he could not. Even when he willed himself to move, it was toward the house.

Bill no longer wanted to know anything that was in this house and now fully understood why his father didn't want him to see it. Forget the logs; they lost any value to him at all. This place looked worse than any he had seen in a horror movie.

He felt a sick, eerie feeling, and his stomach churned inside. With each forced step, he got closer and closer to the house. The smell of the mold and decay began to fill his nose, causing his stomach to roll all the more. Now just inches from the spiderweb, he could see the light beams reaching out like fingers pulling him in the open door.

Still floating, he saw the inside, and it looked like it had been used by every wild animal in the area for shelter. Piles of dry poop and stains littered the floor where animals had urinated and left. They combined with dead carcasses lying around the house that made for an odor that could not be tolerated.

He swallowed hard to keep himself from throwing up. His heart raced. His eyes as wide as a saucer, a sign or spiderweb or something hung from the ceiling. In front, it read "Welcome Bill." Just a few feet behind, it read, "Fred, leave now."

His mind was racing faster than his heart. Who is Fred, and what does he have to do with anything? Will the logs bring up Fred?

Trainer came from inside, "Fred is the leader of the prayer squad. He hasn't made contact yet, but we believe he wants to buy the house. We can't tell what would happen to the property after he buys it."

Bill knew immediately what to ask, "That does not fit into your plans, does it?"

"No, we have worked a long time to keep this in our possession. We are not giving up now. You are headed toward the basement now. Stay focused, I will guide you."

Bill was already too nervous not to focus. "Stay with the game today, learn tomorrow."

The basement door looked brand-new and opened all by itself. The musty smell associated with basements wasn't there. It was carpeted, beautifully walled, and set for living like a king in every way. The pool table, minibar fully stocked, TV area with the absolute latest in television technology, and the complete lack of spiderwebs left him uneasy and unnerved.

"Bill." The sound of the voice behind him made him jump. Startled, he turned to face the voice. His eyes saw a wood and metal mix exterior with a green glow radiating around it. A squeal escaped his lips, and the trembling of his whole body revealed his fear to the voice, whatever it was.

"Bill, I am Moloch. I am the head of all Trainers. This is a warning: no one but you is to view these logs. We will know if you let someone else view the logs, and you will pay a price that you will wish you never had to pay. Am I making myself clear?"

Bill trembled and couldn't get his voice to work. He opened his mouth to speak but stayed silent. He shook his head in agreement.

In the corner of the basement, a green light lit up. "Bill," Moloch called for his attention, "the logs are behind that wall. You will need to crawl to get in. The information in those logs will be absolutely necessary for both of you to learn and grow. Continue with the plan."

Bill just nodded his head as his feet settled on the floor.

—◦◦◦—

Moloch was upstairs trying to understand the reason the horde leader had failed again. "You not only failed at killing the people, but you also allowed the one that belonged to us to turn to Jesus." His voice escalating as he enunciated the last phrase.

No one dared look up at Moloch, and only one had any right to speak, "We did all we could."

"What!" Moloch threw a slash of fire from his sword, sending the leader back still lying facedown, not willing to look up. "Is there anyone in here that can lead a mission to kill someone?"

The silence from the horde was deafening and angered him even more. "Who! Speak up now!"

The horde was beginning to regret not letting the angelic host kill them with the others. They all trembled.

Satan stood on the left side listening to the report. He heard all he needed to. "Moloch!"

Moloch faced to the left side, bowed to one knee, and said, "Master."

"Moloch, apparently I am not making myself clear. Failure is not an option. Again, you fail me. What do you think I should do with you?"

Moloch was not looking up now. "I am correcting the situation now. I assure you it will not happen again."

Satan glared at the back of his head. "Where have I heard that before? Could that have been at our last meeting?"

"Yes, master." Moloch waited for the blast from Satan's sword that would shred him into pieces.

"Why have you failed me again?"

Moloch continued to stare at the floor. "I have not gotten to that yet from the leader." Then he cowered, waiting to be shattered.

"Who is the horde leader?" Satan demanded.

The leader, now lying in the back of the horde, said, "I am, master."

"Come forth."

He flew low and landed in front of Satan, never looking up from the floor.

"What happened?"

"We thought it was one angel. William was nervous, so we knew he was beaten already. Boris joi—"

"Boris?" Satan's anger flashed. "You are telling me that an entire horde can't take out Boris and one angel?"

"We only had one chance to weaken them. Then they were joined by Bevan and Alexander." The horde leader hoped this was going to free him but knew that was going to look like another excuse.

"Bevan." Fire flashed from Satan on this. "Young warrior. You let an amateur, a guard, and two colonels beat a horde of how many?"

The horde leader looked at Moloch. Moloch pointed a bony finger back at him with relief that some of this fire was going to someone else. "It was a horde of…one…hundred."

"Since when is there an excuse for one hundred demons in a horde to be beaten by four of the heavenly host?" Satan's fire was not flying at anyone but was flaring around every square inch of him.

The horde leader trembled and said, "Four angels didn't beat us. They got to the prayer squad, and their three guardians joined in."

"There are only four members of the prayer squad. How could you have seven angels?"

Satan wasn't buying anything now and wasn't going to like this answer. "Peter's father, Jake, accepted Christ. Bevan was his guardian angel."

"Not only did you fail to kill Peter but also allowed someone to accept Christ?" Satan's hand was now pointed at the horde leader, shooting fire just inches away from his head.

"We did all we could to get to him, we were not allowed."

The fire rolled from Satan's hand, blowing the horde leader off his feet to the back of the room. "Is there anyone that can kill the prayer squad?"

The silence again was deafening. As Satan's eyes drifted from demon to demon, he found no one willing to say the prayer squad could be killed.

He hissed fire from his mouth, "Moloch."

"Yes, master." Moloch didn't want Satan's wrath back, but he had it.

"You have no more chances. I will select one of my soldiers to lead this group. They have to die." Satan vanished while all the demons still looked on the floor.

—⁂—

Jesus looked at Boris and Randolph. "The prayer squad is into more than they understand. Their prayer shield is strong now. The prayer meetings are helping. Satan's strikes are going to get harder."

"The guardian angels are holding their own, and paired up, they are incredibly strong." Randolph was doing more verbal observation than anything else.

Jesus's eyes went to the prayer squad. "You are doing well. The work has just started though. The guardian angels are doing everything they can and holding off many demons. Keep your eyes out for a new horde. This battle is getting ugly."

Randolph and Boris together said, "Yes, Lord," and left to do what needed to be done.

—⁂—

They all arrived together at Peter's house, praying and thanking God for the protection given at the house on Power Lane. All of their hearts were starting to slow down, and the extreme tension they felt subsided into a livable calm.

Peter asked, "What was all that about?"

John answered, "The e-e-e-n-n-n-e-my a-a-a-ta…at-ta-cked."

Harry provided further detail. "Out of six family members we have prayed for, two did not accept Christ as Savior. This means God has used us three times to bring victory in the lives of our family members. Plus, Richard has also joined the prayer squad and Bible study. God has shown me, and I believe John as well, that the attack was on Jake. Because of Peter, he was not allowed to follow through with the kill. Now Jake is a believer too, hence the attack has turned to us."

John shook his head. "Sca-sca-sca-sca-sca-ry-ry."

Jake asked, "Am I the reason for all that trouble?"

Harry looked at Jake. "You are the result of God's blessing and answer to prayer. That is the reason for the attack."

Fred continued, "We were attacked before you. Now the victories and the continued prayer will drive the attacks. God is protecting and keeping us. This is a good example of what happens when God works in your life."

Unanimously the whole group said, "Amen!"

Fred looked down to the floor, took the deepest breath as he could, and continued, "What we saw today was the easiest we are going to have for a while. We have started incorporating daily prayer nights voluntarily. What this should show us is that we need to get together every night to seek God and pray."

Harry dropped his eyes. "We need to be working in pairs as well. Richard is really struggling right now. I didn't feel the power that I felt when we prayed together unified. Satan will try to attack us alone. God tells us, 'Where two or more are gathered together in my name, there I will be also.'"

Peter asked, "I noticed that when we pray together, John doesn't stutter, and God moves in a way that I can't comprehend. It's like we are protected more or something."

Harry said, "I feel it too. I know that is because the unseen spirit world is getting reinforced and the enemy has to flee. This is exactly why Fred said we had to pray in pairs."

Fred sought God for the words to say. "The only thing I can think of is God wants to continue the work in us and through us. The enemy will be coming harder and more often. The strongest weapon we have against them is prayer. It is time for us to work in pairs, using the strongest weapon available to us."

"Amen!" The whole group agreed and set aside the time to pray together with each other every day.

—⁓—

Satan was back in his office. The fire burned on everything but consumed no air or particles from above. "My horde, come forth!"

Immediately, the larger, most skilled of all the demons came from all directions and bowed in front of Satan. "Master."

Satan looked at the thousands that appeared. Their power individually was more than one hundred of the demons currently at work on Power Lane. Their size was twice as big. The toothy grin on their face caused a smug smile to form across his face. "Nassor, I have a special job for you."

Nassor, bowed right up front, faster and stronger than the rest, looked up to Satan. "Yes, my master, my service to your will."

"There is a group of believers called the prayer squad, kill them all! You have the group already there plus one hundred demons behind you. Do whatever you have to do."

"Yes, master." Nassor looked up and glowed red. He drew his sword and slashed the air; then raising the sword over his head, he said, "It will be done."

Nassor swiftly turned to the demons and began calling names.

—⁓—

Randolph, Boris, and Jesus watched without surprise at what was being said. Randolph looked to the other two. "Are you going to assign an archangel to match Nassor?"

Jesus said, "I already have. Meet Ailith."

Ailith walked out, a big angel, the look of power and strength written all over his face. If Randolph and Boris hadn't known he was on their side, they would have withdrawn in fear themselves. Ailith said, "Nassor is mine. I have selected my hundred archangels to go with me, Lord."

Jesus said, "You and your men are to wait here. You will know when to go into action."

Ailith took his place on the other side of Jesus, waiting for the command to go. "Yes, Lord."

Jesus looked to his angels. "The fight will be harder than ever. Satan is going full force for the prayer squad. Be ready."

All three said together, "Yes, Lord."

—◦◦◦—

Bill saw the brick that was glowing and was partially out, and he pulled at the brick; it slid easily out revealing a switch. His hands were jittery and shaking as he groped for it initially but never switched it. His mind reeled; he was confused and scared, and wanted to leave, but knew trying now would be a mistake.

He steadied his hands, slowly reached for the switch, and flipped it to the opposite position. A section of the wall slid up exposing a doorway half the height of a regular door. The room behind it was lit with the green glow that came from everywhere and nowhere. Just being near this room was too much; he would not enter.

"Trainer, I am not going in there."

Moloch answered with a flash from his sword over his head. "Go now."

Bill crawled in the doorway, into the glow, and scanned the room for the logs.

He quickly found them and reached out to take the top log off the first pile. The cover read, "Trainer Log, Thoughts of Joseph." This one he knew was for him. On the next pile, the cover read, "Trainer Log, Thoughts of Trainer, Written through Joseph."

His heart had not slowed down, his desire to get out of that house even stronger than before. Bill, you've got to get this done and get out of here.

He slid the logs through the door, crawling out behind them. Grasping the logs and getting legs under him, he stood up on shaking legs, stared into what he thought were the eyes of Moloch, and said, "No one but me sees them. I will learn what needs to be learned. I am going home with them. Is that permitted?"

Moloch nodded his head in agreement.

Bill nodded while he walked up the stairs to leave the house. Moloch watched carefully as he left, looking for nothing specific. Just as Bill got out of the house, Nassor entered.

—∽∾∼—

Moloch went to the main office of the house. The green glow radiated all over the room. It was without any furniture and immaculate in appearance. This time Nassor was waiting for him.

Moloch looked at Nassor, asking, "How may I help you?"

Nassor said, "You can leave my office until I call for you."

Moloch was irritated and demanded, "I don't know who you are, but this is my office, and I've had it for over one hundred years. You may leave now."

Nassor said, "This is now my office. You will wait until I am ready and follow my orders. Leave."

Moloch stood firm. "Who are you?" The anger in his voice rang out.

"Nassor, I've been assigned to complete the task that you could not complete. I will call you in shortly for a debriefing."

Moloch drew his sword. "Nassor, I am not giving up my office just on a word."

Moloch watched Nassor draw his own sword, twice as hot and twice the size of his own. "Anytime you are ready. I will never lose to you." Nassor was firm in his words.

Moloch didn't back down, "I have beaten the best that have come against me. I am ready to take you too." With a flash, he flew and slashed his sword.

Moloch was surprised at the quickness in which Nassor moved away from the attack. Nassor replied, "You really are not a challenge to me. If you give up now and yield to me, it will be easier on you."

Moloch launched again, slashing at the air where Nassor was. Moloch felt Nassor's sword pierce him with a movement as quick as lightning.

Moloch whirled around; the pain stung every part of his body. The sword of Nassor flew, slashing again. This time Moloch fell to the floor one wing bent up and tore.

Nassor said, "Have you had enough? I will call you back when I am ready to talk to you. In the meantime, go tell your minions Nassor is in charge."

Wounded and hurt, Moloch backed out of the office. "Yes."

—◦◦◦—

Moloch met his minions in the main living area. His second-in-command came to him and began work immediately on his wing. "What happened up there?"

Moloch, still hurting, said, "Later, in private." Moloch faced the horde. "The master has appointed a new leader over the house. I will still give your orders to you, and you will still answer to me. It is just that we have a higher-ranking demon in the house temporarily."

The horde hissed and placed their hands on their swords.

Moloch held up his hand. "This is a good thing. We have help to get rid of some of the things that have plagued us. Power Lane will be stronger for this."

Though Moloch wanted to see the support he saw, he knew fighting now would not help the situation. *Why not use them until I get what I want, then the horde can oust these intruders, and I will be in charge again.*

Moloch made one last statement, "Remember who we have to fight. The prayer squad must go down. Let's work together as a team to get this done."

The horde hissed and jeered the prayer squad, committing them to their deaths.

―◦◦◦―

Nassor had been watching with his second-in-command. "He will work with me for a short time. He'll try to rebel when he thinks the time is right. Your warriors will have to fight to keep the peace. Don't back down."

"Yes, master."

―◦◦◦―

Boris, Randolph, and Ailith watched the scene on Power Lane with interest. Ailith looked to the others and said, "Satan is trying to negotiate with Jesus now. What he will give, I don't know. This I do know, our job has just gotten harder. Are you ready?"

Boris and Randolph gripped their swords. "We are always ready."

Ailith said, "I've got one hundred archangels in my command. We will fight with everything we have and win."

—◦◦◦—

"Moloch," Nassor called out.

Moloch entered the office that was his and said, "Yes."

Nassor commanded, "I am to be called master by you too. I don't need to force this issue, do I?"

"No, master," Moloch said.

"What do you know about the prayer squad?"

Moloch knew he was only going to reveal the minimum to him. "There are eight of them now. We have faced Randolph, Seth, William, Elliot, Alexander, Boris, and the new one, Bevan. They become stronger as their numbers increase."

Nassor thought, *Randolph and Boris, two colonels?* He looked to his second-in-command, "Familiar with any of the others?"

"Yes, master. Seth, William, Elliot, and Alexander are good but need a lot of prayer support. I have never met Bevan."

Moloch interrupted, "Pardon, master, I have a crew working on keeping them busy so that they don't have time to pray."

Nassor looked up, nodding his head. "Working on weakening them. Good. Something is being done right."

Moloch looked with anger but held it inside.

Nassor asked, "Is there anything that you can tell me about Bevan?"

Moloch said, "We have never seen him until the last battle. He doesn't have much experience. The other angels made up for his errors though."

The second-in-command nodded his head, knowing all he needed to know. "Is there anything else I need to know?"

"We are attacking the families now. We are killing those around them, trying to break their spirits."

"Good move." Nassor thought about the struggle they were already in. "How many have died?"

Moloch didn't want to answer that. "Two."

Nassor's silence made Moloch uncomfortable. "We will need to work on that. How often are they getting together to pray?"

Moloch was even less interested in that question. "Once a week is the latest report I have."

Nassor looked at Moloch. "Send out a spy, he is not to attack but to find out how well your plan is working so far. We will attack soon on all fronts. Go get the spies in the sky."

"Yes, master." Moloch hated having to say that, but he was not given any choice in the matter unless he could beat him in a fight.

16 THE BLESSING

Richard was home from the hospital, and Vera was relieved to have him back in their home. She watched closely as Richard slept on the couch. She wasn't listening to the warnings that she was overprotecting him. She wasn't letting him out of her sight for another night at the least.

"Vera," Gerald's voice broke the silence of the moment, "he will be just fine there even if you don't stare at him."

"I know. I am still so scared that something will happen, and I want to be on the phone getting help immediately if it does."

"It's okay. You can come help me with supper. We will be able to hear anything that goes on in the living room."

"Okay." Vera joined him in the kitchen. Vera looked at what Gerald was preparing and realized he didn't need any help with it. "You don't need help with supper. What am I doing in here?"

"You're in here so you don't worry about Richard by standing over him, staring all day and night."

Vera shot Gerald a look of disgust. "You worry about him too. I'm not alone in that."

"I have to admit that I was concerned ab—"

"Concerned? I think *worry* best describes it." Vera's interruption came with frustration and anger.

"Vera, I want you to relax. You're going to worry yourself into the hospital with an ulcer."

"I know. I'm sorry. I just love him so and don't want to lose him."

"So do I. That is why Richard is here sleeping so we can be here for him if we are needed. Right now we need to be more concerned about getting some food ready for him to eat. He should be waking soon."

"All right, I can help with that. I guess I can try to relax a little bit too."

"Thank you."

Vera was looking into Gerald's eyes when she jumped, startled by the arms that were wrapping around her from behind. "I love you, Mom."

Vera nestled in her son's arms. "I love you too. Are you hungry?"

"Do you have a horse ready to eat?"

"Just half a horse with bread will do. The doctor said to hold you back. You might get fat." She wanted to keep him close longer. She knew that eventually he would once again leave the house to live on his own. However, his words of assurance and the hug filled her heart with hope.

Vera watched her son walk away with a sandwich and chips. "I am so glad I have both of my boys. I can't imagine life without any of them." Vera wrapped her arms around Gerald and didn't let go.

"Your boys could not imagine life without you either." Vera heard his reply as he wrapped his arms around her, pulled her tight, and kissed the top of her head.

—◦◦—

"Hey, sis, what ya got on the agenda for today?"

"Not letting you get in trouble. What do you have in mind?"

"Sis, would I do something to get in trouble?"

"You've been out of the hospital for less than one day. You really have to ask?"

"All right, I give. I was thinking about going to the prayer meeting tonight. I got the address. Since Mom isn't about to let me drive anywhere, I need a ride."

"How far is it to the prayer meeting?"

"About ten minutes at the big a house. Harry will be there with friends."

"I'm not sure Mom is ready for more of Harry right now. I will take you and pray with you. You have to promise not to play matchmaker for me."

"Spoil all the fun. I'll concede and call it a deal."

"When are you planning on leaving?"

"It starts in about an hour. That should give you forty minutes to doll up."

With a look that only a sibling could understand, she said, "I'll ignore that comment and get ready."

"Thanks, sis, I knew I could count on you."

Vera heard the conversation and called out, "You will be held responsible if he is hurt. Is that clear?"

"Yes, Mother. I will make sure he behaves, even if I have to tie him to a chair."

"You better."

Richard chided, "Can't get anything past her."

"Me either. You will behave if I have to force your hand."

"Be nice, sis."

"I will only do what is necessary to keep you in line." She took off to get ready.

———⟋⟍⟍———

Patty put on a pair of jeans and a plain sky-blue button-down shirt. She combed her shoulder-length hair and put on a little makeup. "Doll up. I am going to look presentable." She looked in the mirror and decided that was enough for the occasion. She headed down and asked, "In your opinion, am I dolled up enough?"

Richard smiled at her. "Smashing, the ball gown can wait for the first date."

"Ha-ha, are you ready to go?"

"We can go. I promise to be nice."

"I promise to get you back in the car."

They heard Vera call from another room, "Take it easy on each other. I want you both back here in one piece. Understood?"

"Yes, Mother. We better get going before she decides to get us both. She could take you easier than me."

"I'll answer that on the way."

They both headed out the door to the car. A loud "I love you both" trailed them.

Just a minute later, they were on their way. Richard asked, "Are you trying to impress anyone in particular?"

"Can't a girl look presentable without trying to impress a guy?"

"I don't know. I haven't seen you dress up for any other reason."

"Unlike you, I don't just think about the opposite sex twenty-four hours a day, seven days a week." She finished the statement with a smart-aleck twist of her head.

"Oh-ho! I see how it is. Well, sis, we'll see about that when we get there."

"You bet we will." With a big smile on her face, she drove on to the prayer meeting.

—⁓—

She saw the door to the house was open. She walked in with her brother to a big room. On one wall was a long table with food, plates, and flatware on it. In the middle of the room was a small section of chairs gathered in a circle. She heard that group consisted of four men. Now she saw eight others, besides herself, gathered around chatting and eating. She saw only one other woman in the room, and she was older than most of the men.

She scanned the room again, this time trying to recognize anyone else besides her brother. Her eyes stopped on the young man that was with Harry in the hospital room. There was something about him that made her want to know more. Don't make this obvious or you will never hear the end of it from Richard.

This young man was a few inches taller than she was, clean shaved, dark eyes, and hair combed neatly to one side. He was wearing blue jeans and a pullover golf shirt with a logo on the left chest. The shirt hung semi loosely on his strong frame. She could see him talking to another young man, not as interesting to her, but apparently close to him.

Richard broke her train of thought. "Sis, are you looking at John or Peter?"

"No one in particular; I thought I recognized one of them. Don't you go thinking anything."

"Sure deal. Let's go get something to eat."

Patty walked directly to where John and Peter were talking. "Excuse me."

Peter looked at her and smiled. "Hello, may I help you?"

She tried to keep the stars from shining in her eyes. "Where is your restroom?"

"It's the men's room down the hall. There hasn't been a woman in this house since I was eighteen. It's the first door on the right."

"Thank you." She proceeded down the hall, noticing the plain wall was covered with a lightwood shade paneling. She walked into a small bathroom with a toilet and a sink. It obviously lacked a woman's touch. Plain medium colored paneling with no pictures and only one mirror a little bigger than her. She continued to look for something indicating that this room was used for more but couldn't even find a toothbrush. The image of Peter remained firmly planted in her mind as she relieved herself and cleaned up. Taking extra care to make sure nothing was out of place, she washed her hands and walked out to get a snack. *Maybe I should ask him to help me with my food and drink.*

She got to the table, and Peter was there placing another dish of food on the table. He pulled a plate from the stack and offered it to her. "Better get your plate now. Fred will call the meeting to order soon."

"Where are the salads and vegetables?"

"This has always been men. When men provide the food, those things don't typically make it to the table. Don't be bashful about bringing those though. We will eat almost anything put in front of us."

"I can see that." She put some of the cheese and crackers and some slices of meat on her plate. "Could you carry my drink for me?"

He took her drink. "Where are you sitting?"

"Anywhere you are." *You didn't just say that. Where is Richard? He didn't hear that, did he?*

"Follow me. My name is Peter."

"Hi, Peter. I'm Patty." She followed him to the circle of chairs.

"You can sit here. I will be back with more chairs."

"Thank you."

She watched as he brought the chairs, expanding the circle without concern if her face showed her feelings or not. She could see others saying things to him, but it didn't seem to get to him at all.

In a few minutes, he was seated beside her, with John on the other side of him. She saw Richard on the opposite side of the circle looking at her with that "what did I tell you" look clearly written in his smile. She just looked at him, snubbed her nose up, and said to Peter, "Are there normally this many people at the prayer meeting?"

"No," Peter returned, "four is normally the maximum. There have been other things happening that led to the group growing to over twice its size."

"What happened to Richard happened to others too?"

"More than you can imagine. Two of our direct family members have died. We ourselves have been under attack in other ways. It is certainly keeping us hopping."

"Why is this going on?"

"Well, we suspect it has something to do with a house. You'll understand more as the prayer time goes on."

"That doesn't make any sense."

"Whenever God is going to use us in a mighty way for him, we come under some kind of attack to prevent it from happening. This is the biggest attack we have ever been under. We can't imagine what he wants us to do to cause this type of attack."

Fred called, "It's time, guys. Let's get started." The voice came from around the corner.

She saw Fred walk out, looking like someone hit him with a Mack truck. The three others there knew that look well. Power Lane was on the move. They sat him down on the chair in the center of the circle and formed the triangle around him. Harry looked up and told the others there, "You came here to pray. There is no more of an urgent time than now. We won't go into details with you now, but you can see the need with your eyes. We are going to ask you to gather in a smaller circle and pray. God bless you all."

The prayer squad knelt and prayed over Fred while the others gathered in a larger circle around the triangle, locked hands, and prayed.

—◈—

"The way your love has caused you to hurt when your son was hurt is the same way I feel when you walk away from Me without a second look. You are My daughter. I have placed you where you are protected and guided you in the way to the light. Your choices cause Me the same pain you felt for the last few days. Come to Me and remember the love that brought you here."

The words rang through Vera's mind, repeating them as a broken record until she looked to Gerald and said, "I keep hearing some words in my mind. Would you help me understand them better?"

"Of course, tell me what they are, and I will do what I can to help you understand them." He couldn't imagine what the words may be, but immediately Acts 9 came to mind.

She repeated the words and saw Gerald sit beside her with a Bible in his hand. "The words you are hearing are from Jesus. Jesus spoke to one other in person. It is recorded in Acts. I'm just going to read it to you. Is that all right?"

"Sure, I may need you to help me understand it. Are you willing to answer any questions that I may have?"

"Of course," he answered. "Here it is—written in Acts, chapter 9, verses 1 to 18. Are you ready to hear?"

"Yes, I believe I am." Vera looked at Gerald with anticipation.

> But Paul, threatening with every breath and eager to destroy every Christian, went to the High Priest in Jerusalem.
>
> He requested a letter addressed to synagogues in Damascus, requiring their cooperation in the persecution of any believers he found there, both men and women, so that he could bring them in chains to Jerusalem.

As he was nearing Damascus on this mission, suddenly a brilliant light from heaven spotted down upon him!

He fell to the ground and heard a voice saying to him, "Paul! Paul! Why are you persecuting me?"

"Who is speaking, sir?" Paul asked. And the voice replied, "I am Jesus, the one you are persecuting!

"Now get up and go into the city and await my further instructions."

The men with Paul stood speechless with surprise, for they heard the sound of someone's voice but saw no one!

As Paul picked himself up off the ground, he found that he was blind. He had to be led into Damascus and was there three days, blind, going without food and water all that time.

Now there was in Damascus a believer named Ananias. The Lord spoke to him in a vision, calling, "Ananias!"

"Yes, Lord!" he replied.

And the Lord said, "Go over to Straight Street and find the house of a man named Judas and ask there for Paul of Tarsus. He is praying to me right now, for I have shown him a vision of a man named Ananias coming in and laying his hands on him so that he can see again!"

"But, Lord," exclaimed Ananias, "I have heard about the terrible things this man has done to the believers in Jerusalem! And we hear that he has arrest warrants with him from the chief priests, authorizing him to arrest every believer in Damascus!"

But the Lord said, "Go and do what I say. For Paul is my chosen instrument to take my message to the nations and before kings, as well as to the people of Israel. And I will show him how much he must suffer for me."

So Ananias went over and found Paul and laid his hands on him and said, "Brother Paul, the Lord Jesus, who appeared to you on the road, has sent me so that you may be filled with the Holy Spirit and get your sight back."

Instantly (it was as though scales fell from his eyes), Paul could see, and was immediately baptized.

Then he ate and was strengthened. He stayed with the believers in Damascus for a few days.

Tears welled up in Vera's eyes as Gerald read the words from the Bible. Her head fell in her hands. "Save me from myself. Forgive me for the pain I have caused you." The rest was sobs and tears. Immediately she could hear the same voice in her head. *"You are forgiven, My daughter. Remember Me."*

—◦◦◦—

Gerald watched her head fall into her hands and knew she had no questions. He raised his head to the wood plaque he made from the woodshop behind the garage. He read the passage of scripture held there to himself and to God for the thousandth time.

Again and again the rods slashed down across their bared backs; and afterward they were thrown into prison. The jailer was threatened with death if they escaped, so he took no chances, but put them into the inner dungeon and clamped their feet into the stocks.

Around midnight, as Paul and Silas were praying and singing hymns to the Lord—and the other prisoners were listening—suddenly there was a great earthquake; the prison was shaken to its foundations, all the doors flew open—and the chains of every prisoner fell off!

The jailer wakened to see the prison doors wide open, and assuming the prisoners had escaped, he drew his sword to kill himself. But Paul yelled to him, "Don't do it! We are all here!"

Trembling with fear, the jailer called for lights and ran to the dungeon and fell down before Paul and Silas. He brought them out and begged them, "Sirs, what must I do to be saved?"

They replied, "Believe on the Lord Jesus and you will be saved, and your entire household."

Then they told him and all his household the Good News from the Lord. That same hour he washed their stripes and he and all his family were baptized. (Acts 16:23–33)

Gerald softly cried, "Thank you, Jesus. You are so faithful to follow through with Your word. Thank You so much. This is the hour that You have chosen to reach the last member of my family. Thank You again."

He looked at Vera and saw the tears coming down her cheeks. They got up, walked to each other, hugged each other in a loving embrace, and wept tears of joy together.

———

Richard and Patty drove home in silence. Richard was shocked about the events at the prayer meeting. His head was still swimming from what had happened. As he entered the house, he didn't notice anything different. He gently took Patty by the elbow as they walked into the kitchen. The sight that greeted them was as normal as every other day. However, the air was filled with a sense of peace that he had not felt in a long time. His parents' faces seemed to glow.

He heard Gerald ask, "How was the prayer meeting?"

Richard's face blanked out as he tried to put together words to explain what happened. He spoke first, "There was an unplanned situation that arose. It was a time of praying for special needs."

"Oh, anything you want to tell us about?"

Patty replied, "I don't think we know the whole story."

Richard added, "I don't think anyone knows the whole story. Whatever happened was bad, real bad."

Richard looked into his parents' faces, his distress evident in his eyes.

Before anyone could say anything, Patty said, "Peter said it was no more than an attack from Satan. He looked more concerned than he let on to me."

Gerald said, "I'm sure he is. He's closer to the situation. We can remember them in our prayers as well. We have some news of our own."

Richard looked at Patty and then at his parents. "It is something good?"

The laughter from his parents surprised him but sounded like music to his ears. He watched as Vera walked over to the plaque and rubbed her finger on the outside of the glass that held the printout of the passage of scripture. She read the last line, "That same hour, he washed their stripes, and he and all his family were baptized."

"Your mother accepted Christ while you were away."

Richard felt shock, joy, and love embrace his very soul. "Let's go give Mom and Dad a big hug and celebrate with them."

"Please," Patty whispered, "I feel like a wreck."

"This will do us all some good. Don't go leaving the last image of the night being Fred as he walked out to start the prayer meeting."

"Shall I remember his face when it ended instead—since it was so much better?"

"No, we both need some celebrating to get us past tonight. You are going to turn around, get the pitcher of tea, and we're all going to celebrate God's victory tonight."

"I don't feel like it."

"Patty, I'm not moving until you get going to the table. You are not winning this time."

She turned away from Richard, her body still shaking with fear in every step she took. When she got to the table, she dropped into her chair and took the glass of tea her mom had prepared. When all four were seated around the table, Gerald asked, "What happened tonight?"

Richard started, "Fred is the leader of the prayer squad. That is what they are calling themselves. It took the other three of the original squad to get Fred seated, and all we did was pray."

"Dad, it looked like something tried to kill him or got so close it could be mistaken as death." Patty could feel her body shaking as she spoke.

"Patty, is it really that bad?"

"Worse, Dad. I might not know much about it, but those three had fear written on their faces at the sight of him walking out. I would say something tried to kill him and just missed. Whatever it was, it left behind the battle scars for all to see."

Patty watched as her dad stood and said, "This sounds like an emergency. We can all come together and pray again. It sounds like there can't be enough prayer about this."

Patty's heart was heavy and light as they stood to pray. She held tight to her mom's and dad's hands as her father led them in prayer, thanking God for the victories of the day and the burdens overshadowing their friends.

Father, help me to be strong in You during this time. I need You to help me forget the look on Fred's face and the fear on the faces of those closest to him. Father, thank You for bringing my mom to You, making our family complete in You.

The prayer ended with Gerald thanking God for saving and uniting his family. In unison, they all closed with, "Amen."

17 THE LUNCH

"Go away!" Trainer shouted for the thousandth time at whoever it was staying persistently outside Bill's body. Trainer ventured to the outermost part of the body once to try to attack the spirit outside. That left a memory that he didn't want to remember but was foolish to forget.

He saw the spirit, staying and watching. He didn't mind that as much because the spirit was allowing him to do what he wanted to and to go where he wanted to go without a fight. Until he started hearing the name *Jesus Christ*, then the spirit outside was stopping him from making Bill not listen. When he applied pain, the spirit stopped it. When he attacked the understanding of the words, the spirit made them clear and comprehensible. When he tried to put out a call for help, it went unanswered by anyone.

The frustration reached a boiling point, and he wanted to attack at close contact to that spirit. He mustered all the strength he could and slammed into Bill's outer arm. Just as expected, the spirit lightly touched Bill's body to stop the pain. The light from the touch pierced into the darkness of the attack. Lighting the space he was in at the time, Trainer was forced to run trembling from the outer attack point back to the darkness of the safe house he made long ago.

Trainer could still see what was going on and the mess of an environment Samuel was left in. It's not that the house wasn't clean. It was well cared for and clean just as before. Everything seemed to come back around to Jesus in one way or another. All of the contact with Cadet was spent defusing Jesus in the life of Samuel. He wasn't defusing Jesus in the life of Bill. He was all alone, left to figure out this mess without any help from anyone.

No matter where he ventured, he was closely watched. That was not the concern right now. Bill had a lunch date with an available girl that did not mention Jesus. Any encouraging sign at this point would be taken. Now it was time to prepare. He checked the communication between the two of them. "Bill?"

"Trainer, you can talk to me when I'm awake."

"Yes, only when I need to. I want to make sure you can understand what I want while you are talking to this young lady."

"Now I am expected to take advice from you on how to get a girl. You want me to rape her on the first date?"

"Be careful. I am not going to make light of this. I need the contact with the child after he is born. Take this seriously."

"I am. If I find another woman to marry, I want her to be a respectable woman. I don't want to get involved with every floozy that walks in my path just to make you happy."

Trainer was rapidly getting angry. "Listen to me. You don't understand what has to happen. Don't insult my intelligence like that again."

"Okay. What needs to happen here?"

"You need to start getting her interest. Let's call this a get-acquainted date. I need to know certain things from her—her desire to have children, her ability to have children, her willingness to start having children."

"All right. That will take time to get all that info. I don't know how much of that she will be willing to answer today. I'll start with trying to get over Saundra. I don't want it to look like I am thinking of only what I can get from her."

"I will lead you in the plan. Just make sure you keep moving on course as it is laid out."

"Okay." Bill went to get ready for the lunch now with the knowledge of Trainer's intentions for this date.

—∿∿—

"Where are you, stupid spirit?"

"I am always close," the spirit answered.

"You speak?"

"Of course. I only speak to you when it is needed."

"I am going to tell you what I need from you."

"You can. Realize that your boss is not mine. I will follow the orders given me by the one over me."

"You are going to leave me to do my work with Bill through this date."

"I can't follow your instructions when they contradict my Lord's."

"Who is your Lord?"

"Jesus Christ."

"No. You will leave Bill now. No more talking. Just go."

"My Lord sent me here to do a particular job. I am not leaving until it's done."

"You have started the fight of your life. I will kill Bill before surrendering him to you."

"That is your choice. The fight will be started by you. I am here for defense only."

"Just leave him alone. He is mine, and you have no right to him."

No more comments from the spirit. He looked around and saw him floating around, staying close just like he was doing before. Trainer's fury reached a boiling point. Bill began sweating for no apparent reason.

"Trainer?"

"What?" Trainer was filled with anger.

"Why am I sweating? Are you trying to kill me while I am cooperating with your plan?"

Trainer calmed himself. "No, I am having another problem and forgot that I have to disconnect from you to deal with this problem. You are still going on the date?"

"If I can get ready without bleeding to death from the sweat."

"You get ready. I will disconnect and deal with this other problem. Don't ask what it is. I don't have time to argue about it."

———〰———

Bill continued dressing for his date with Rebeca, but she was not the one he was thinking of. His thoughts turned to the first lunch date he had with Saundra. He knew he had enough time to sit and cry if he needed to. This was the time to let those memories flood his mind no matter what the emotions were going to do.

He was wearing his only clean pair of jeans and a plain pullover shirt. He spent most of the time washing and cleaning the inside of his car. His hair was neatly combed. He decided he was ready to go pick up Saundra. Just then his foster father stepped into the bathroom. "Squirt a little of this on. Your foster mother likes this a lot."

"Thanks." He quickly put a little on and asked, "What do you think?"

"Go get her, be nice to her. Remember to be polite and courteous, and you'll be just fine."

He pulled the car up to the curb in front of the house. To help calm his overactive nerves, he checked everything one more time. It all seemed to be fine. All the way to the door, he had mixed feelings of excitement and fear. By the time he got to the door, he could almost feel the sweat on his forehead.

The door sounded all wrong when he knocked on it. It opened almost immediately. Standing there was Saundra's father. Bill's mind couldn't get his mouth to work.

"Hello, son."

"Hi. Is Saundra here?" he tentatively asked, not knowing what to expect.

"Yes, she is. Come on in, and we can wait in the living room."

He hesitantly walked in the living room. His nerves still on end and couldn't think.

"You can sit down there on the couch."

Bill slowly sat on the couch across from Henry.

"My name is Henry. What is yours?"

"Bill."

"Bill, I just want to know that you are going to take care of my daughter."

"Yes, sir, I will."

Saundra's voice interrupted any further questions, "I'm ready to go. Let's go to lunch."

He was up, opening the door for her in a second. "I will take care of her."

Both of them were out of house, and the door closed in a jiffy.

"My dad is not mean. He just cares."

"I'm not taking any chances right now." Her door opened, he let her in then closed it behind her. He slid in himself. "I found this little sandwich shop that has good food, or do you have any preferences?"

Bill saw her smile. "The sandwich shop sounds good to me."

He drove off toward the shop, talking as he finally started to relax.

———◆◆◆———

He could feel the same jitters coming now as he was making the final preparations to meet Rebeca. At least he was meeting her at the shop, a place he was familiar with.

Samuel was still sleeping in his car seat, ready to go. He quickly threw all the necessary stuff in the diaper bag, making sure to include warm water in the bottle and extra diapers. He wasn't out of the hospital long when he learned that checking to make sure there was another appropriate change of clothes in the bag was an absolute must. Everything was ready to go to the best of his knowledge.

He loaded up Samuel and the diaper bag into the car, making sure Samuel's car seat was fastened in tightly. As he walked to the other side to slide in, he wondered what was occupying Trainer and if it would be enough to keep him distracted during lunch.

He knew he would be there a little early, but maybe he could calm his nerves a little before she arrived. The drive to the restaurant was quick and easy. He parked the car in his usual spot. His normal table was empty and clean, so if he hurried, he could get it and a drink.

The sign on the front of the building slowed him up a little. "Did I back up in time? When did they go back to the old name?"

The table arrangement was as it was when he first took Saundra to the place. He stepped into the restaurant, sat at a table, and closed his eyes for fear he was going to see Saundra coming in behind him.

He didn't know if he wanted to open his eyes but decided it was the better option. The modern arrangement of the tables, the newer sign "Home of the Triple Decker Burger" made him feel at ease until he heard, "Are you all right?"

"Samuel," he shouted as he was startled back. Immediately grabbing for the car seat, he saw that Samuel was still sleeping peacefully. He looked up more in the direction of the sound.

"Rebeca, you're early."

"So are you, Bill. How about starting early?"

"Sure," he said with a smile.

—⁓—

Trainer was busy dealing with his other problem when he heard, "Rebeca." Trainer turned his focus to the conversation, knowing that the spirit was still there watching.

Trainer told Bill, "Get up, pull out the seat for her. Be a gentleman about it!"

As Bill pulled the chair out, Trainer was curious about the tears that welled up in Bill's and Rebeca's eyes almost simultaneously.

Bill said, "You're sitting in Saundra's chair. She said that it was more comfortable sitting there. I didn't care so I sat over here."

"I was thinking the same thing when you pulled the chair out. We always sat at this table, with Saundra sitting in your chair."

The waitress broke in the conversation. "Bill, Rebeca. I'm sorry to hear about Saundra."

"Thank you." They both said.

"Are you ready to order?"

Bill looked to Rebeca. "You know what you want?"

"Yes, I will just have my usual."

The waitress wrote down her order from memory and turned to Bill. "You too?"

"Sure."

"I'll be right back with your order, and congratulations on the baby." She walked off to the kitchen.

Bill reached down and carefully cradled Samuel in his arms against his chest. "Do you want to hold him?"

"I would love to. I'll take this big guy from his mean father. Yes, I will," she cooed as she reached out and carefully took Samuel, cradling him to her chest. Samuel just looked at Rebeca with broad eyes. "You can see a lot of you in this guy."

"So they say."

There was a silence for a while as they both stared at Samuel. Bill spoke first, "Saundra would sit here when you met here?"

"Yes, she said it was her favorite spot."

He was thinking. "Every time we came here, I sat in this spot at her insistence."

"That makes sense. She used to tell me that she could feel you in a place even after you left it. She didn't want to be away from places where you had been recently. We always met here twenty minutes after your lunch was over. She didn't want to disturb your lunch but wanted to be where she could still feel your presence."

"I never knew that."

"And you wouldn't today if she was still alive. She would never speak to me again."

"Aren't you worried she is going to haunt you for telling me now?"

"Before she was close to delivering, she left me specific instructions in a notebook. I am to tell you all of her love secrets so you never forget how much she loved you."

"I don't think my heart will ever forget her anyway." He stopped there, not wanting to let his emotions run wild in front of Rebeca.

"I know what you're saying. I have a place in my heart reserved for her where all her memories are being stored."

"I try to let the good memories stay in the forefront while throwing out the video of the events before the hospital trip and thereafter. They keep trying to overshadow all the good times."

"Bill, I know there is nothing different that you could have done. I know more about Trainer than you realize."

———◈———

She could see in Bill's eyes what he couldn't say. In reply to his look, she said, "What you don't know is that Trainer can't control women like he can men. When Saundra was pregnant, she could hear and talk to Cadet. He revealed a lot of information to her about what was going to happen. She didn't want you to be alone. She knew what you and your son would need." She wondered if saying more would be necessary.

A tear started down her cheek. "Do I have to say more?" She didn't know that it was said out loud.

———◈———

Trainer searched to find where the spirit was. A new happiness entered when he could not find the spirit around anywhere. "It's time to go to work unabated."

Listening for further conversation, he decided it was time to connect back up and influence the conversation. "I need to find out how much she knows about me and how she found out."

Trainer could feel Bill's thought, *Does she know something that will help me deal with Trainer?*

—◦∿◦—

"I'm surprised that Trainer hasn't come up yet. He likes to take control quickly. This is what I know Trainer wants. He wants me to be able to bear children, be willing to bear children, lastly and most importantly, he wants to have control over the training and experiences of the child. Did I miss anything?"

"No, you didn't. How did you know that?"

"Saundra dealt with the young one for eight months. Though the baby couldn't do anything, Cadet made a home within her through the child. She kept me in the loop and well informed."

Trainer heard that, knew the weaknesses of her knowledge would affect his plan and now was going to be facing all this again.

The waitress came back with the drinks and placed them on the table. "Your food will be out shortly. Do either of you know what each other's usual are?"

They looked at each other and shook their heads no. The waitress chuckled under her breath and walks off.

Bill said, "I think she knows something about us we don't. I'm not sure that is good."

"I get the feeling her knowledge of us apart is what is giving her the advantage in this situation."

Bill began to steer the conversation back to Trainer. "What did she do to deal with Cadet when he got annoying?"

Rebeca knew this was a dangerous question but had to answer. "Cadet was so much like you that she dealt with you both the same way."

"That doesn't help me deal with him."

"Bill, there is one way for you to deal with Trainer. You already know the answer. You have to decide whether or not you believe it."

"To be honest, I haven't thought much about believing it for fear of the reaction I would get."

"I don't know what you can expect either."

The waitress showed up at the table. "Two house specials. Is there anything else?"

They both had Philly steak and cheese sandwich with onion rings instead of fries. They both chuckled at what they saw and said, "No, thank you."

"Great minds think alike." Bill laughed a little louder.

"Would you allow me to pray and thank God for this day and food?"

Bill waited for Trainer's reaction. With nothing coming to him, he said, "It would be fine with me."

This conversation was going the wrong way. Trainer tried to punch a long pain in his side but was stopped short by the spirit. "Go away! Bill belongs to me, and you don't have the right to stop me from doing as I please with him."

"I have the right and authorization from the one who gives your boss the authority to do what he does. My authority is from Jesus Christ," Aaron answered.

"I possess Bill. He belongs to me."

"Then give Bill the choice to continue to follow you or Jesus."

Trainer heard the request, and with all the force he could muster, he said, "Let go. This cannot happen. I have to stop it now."

The spirit kept Trainer from creating any pain or discipline of his on Bill. "My Lord wants Bill to hear and understand this. I will let you go free when His mission is accomplished."

———

She reached out her hands, and Bill instinctively took them. The soft tingle of her hands ran through his arms to his heart and started melting at the fear and pain that burrowed in deep for safekeeping. His eyes were closed, and yet he could see something waiting and ready, but it was not clear. Through the whole prayer, he focused on whatever it was but never seemed to move closer to clear the image up. When his eyes opened, he could almost see a love in her eyes that wasn't there before.

"Let's eat." Saundra picked up half the sandwich and took a bite.

He took a bite of his own sandwich and savored the memory of when Saundra would sit across from him, not saying a word but sharing more love than words could express.

Looking into her eyes, he could still see that love but this time in Rebeca. "What are you thinking?"

"Nothing much, just how lucky I am to be having lunch with such a great guy and special boy."

Bill could feel the blush beginning to color his cheeks. "Now you're sounding like Saundra."

"It's easy to. She was telling the truth. I just got the chance to see why she felt like she did."

Had he started to relax around her? This isn't right. It's too soon. He still should be crying. He forced himself to back off a little and not let too much out yet. The rest of dinner was fun but limited.

—◦◦—

Rebeca drove home thinking about what happened at lunch. She knew he was relaxing, giving in until they had begun to eat, and then it became comfortable but limited. She could feel the struggle to keep himself from feeling too fast. She was comfortable with him and easily saw what Saundra saw in him.

She wondered if she was falling too fast herself. Is this what Saundra wanted? Something about the firm grip he gave her when she prayed just melted her inside. She knew she had to let him deal with Saundra being gone, and really she had time to let him relax slowly. She drove the rest of the way in prayer, looking to God to bring His will about.

Bill drove home with Samuel. "What do you think about her? Would she be a good mother for you?"

He offered nothing but a big stare at multiple places in the car and outside.

"That's okay. You're not old enough to understand this yet. Your mean daddy is just trying to understand how to feel. Is it my imagination, or is there an attraction both ways with us?"

The stare became slow and steady, motionless. "You're right. I don't have to make a decision today. Sleeping on it sounds like a good idea."

The waitress spoke to a coworker, "We'll see them more often. They truly are a perfect couple."

"Keep out of customer's love lives no matter how much you know about them."

"I won't have to get involved. They already are." The waitress walked off to clean the table.

18 THE EXPERIMENTS

Bill thought about trying to blind and deafen Trainer. Something was going on already. He had lunch with a Christian that prayed and still didn't have to face the consequences. He wasn't interrupted by Trainer during the conversation, and he couldn't understand why Trainer was not fighting harder.

Rebeca said something that made him think. "Trainer is just like you. Saundra always dealt with him like she dealt with you."

If I am like Trainer, then why can't I look inside, find Trainer and see what it would take to shut him out? Isn't that what my dad did? It is certainly worth a try. If I can, then I can learn to be in control of what Samuel learns. Isn't that what all parents want anyway?

Trainer came in, "You do realize the full price of what you are thinking about doing? Think hard because I will get the upper hand on this situation. Your father died because he refused to follow the instructions. Are you ready for the fate of your dad?"

Bill thought about that and focused on his inner self. He found himself roaming around and finding the home of Trainer. He saw Trainer float back and forth, getting closer and then farther away. This kept up for a few minutes, then he collapsed back to the outside world.

Wait on that. It's time to hold and show my son some more love. He bent down over the bed and gently picked up Samuel. He cradled his son against his chest, rocked ever so gently to keep him asleep, and lay on the recliner to nap a little himself.

Samuel lay across Bill's lap sleeping peacefully. Bill closed his eyes, seeing the area of Trainer, not speaking, just watching. He watched as Trainer connected to Cadet, communicating with him freely. He could hear what was being said and prepared to work against Trainer's teachings in Samuel.

Trainer grew stiff and silent, turned away from Cadet, shot a glaring look at Bill, and said, "This is my time with Cadet. When I am ready for you, I will let you know."

Bill never withdrew but waited silently for the opportunity to speak with him. Trainer turned his attention back to Cadet and carefully thought through his words and continued the training. He could not train the young one as desired for fear Bill would counter the training.

Trainer glanced back at him, frustrated, getting angry about his consistent spying. As well, Trainer's eyes were closed and his ears were shut again.

Bill opened his eyes. He could still see the inside of Trainer's compartment and realized he had effectively blinded and deafened Trainer. The compartment grew longer; the sounds of the outside world low in volume began to fill the room. Trainer's ears were working again. He was still blind, but sounds were back.

Trainer turned to Bill; he was receding closer to the back of the room. Bill's ears, for what Trainer was saying, were growing silent and incomprehensible. Bill dropped out of the room, took the lesson, yawned deep, and allowed sleep to take him to dreamland.

Bill woke up with a start when the scream from Samuel filled his ears. Samuel still secured on his lap, he picked him up to his shoulder, prepared the bottle, and sat back down to feed him. Bill opened the log of Joseph and begins to read.

My log day 1

Today was such an unusual day. I couldn't turn on the faucet without blowing my top. Blood on my head came off easily but there was no scar to account for it nor was there a cut. For the first time since I can remember, I ran late on getting to work. I started to hear voices in my head but was unable to identify the voice.

This day was absolutely different from any other day that I have had in my life.

Bill skipped several pages of the log to find the last recorded log by his father.

My log day 468

Trainer has punished me severely. It is not clear if I am going to make it. It is time to put these back into the house on Power Lane. Bill, when you read this, be confident that you will not be able to completely fool Trainer. He will make sure the price to pay is higher than you want to pay. I refused to bear another son for him. Because of that, he is trying to kill me. Bill, think through your actions and beat Trainer at his own game.

I will have my last doctor's appointment tomorrow. You will be well cared for.

At that doctor's appointment, he had a heart attack and died; Bill saw the connection and realized what happened to him.

"Bill, pay attention, have the baby burp." Bill snapped out of it and, with care, placed Samuel over his shoulder and patted his back to help him burp.

—◦◦◦—

With an extra hour of sleep, Bill drifted back into Trainer's quarters. Trainer immediately shot around and glared hard at Bill. "I know when you are here. Go out there and open the door for me to hear and see what you do."

Bill remained silent and stayed where he was.

"Fine, you will drift back out soon enough. When you do, I will hear and see everything again."

Silence from Bill began to frustrate Trainer. He couldn't tell what was going on around him, and connecting to Cadet would reveal exactly what he didn't want to reveal to Bill.

He began to appear to pace with impatience, and a different fury began to swell from inside. This one had no effect on Bill at all, but allowed him to openly punish Bill on a whim.

—◦◦◦—

Bill realized this and withdrew to the far back of the room without leaving the room or allowing him to see or hear. Trainer seemed satisfied with that for the time being.

Staying there while going about his day's task, he also found that Trainer wouldn't connect to Cadet and speak freely while he watched.

He had kept him restricted for two hours in the back of the room. He could come forward or move back at will the more time he spent in that room. When he laid Samuel down to finish another nap, he pulled completely out of the room.

—◦◦◦—

Trainer could see Samuel sleeping, without being able to connect to Cadet. Trainer's anger rose up in himself, but he knew this was not the time to argue the point. He would do that at a later time.

—◦◦◦—

Moloch instructed each of the four spies to observe one member of the prayer squad and find out what could be done to weaken them even further.

The first spy found Fred at home praying and praising God in song while he worked getting stuff together for a gathering of some sort.

The second spy found Harry driving his car praying and praising God in song.

The third spy found Peter driving by Power Lane.

The fourth spy found John already at Fred's house. They had been together for a while, talking about what had been happening to the four of them.

—◦◦◦—

"I had been so jealous that your uncle lived and my father died before I had a chance to pray for him. God showed me that he had all the opportunity to accept and he had refused, but your uncle was going to accept Him, and He does not give up on people. I am thankful for that, and God has blessed me with so much since I learned that."

Fred understood where he came from. "I wanted so bad for all of our family members to accept Christ. I wanted your dad to live too. God saw fit to take your dad. I am so sorry for that. What will never change is God's love and guidance."

John and Fred continued to share God's blessings in their lives to each other. The two spies looked at each other. "What happened to the seed of sin that was going to root up in his life?"

"I'm sure the seed was uprooted before it could weaken the angels."

"Moloch will not like this."

The two spies were quickly joined by the third spy. "Is this their night for Bible study?"

The other two looked at the third. "We had better find out and report it to Moloch."

———

The cry of Samuel woke up Bill. He picked him up to quiet him down, knowing that the bottle was the only acceptable answer. Samuel cried the few minutes as he prepared the bottle. Once the nipple hit his mouth, the crying stopped. Bill had intentionally let Trainer get connected to Cadet.

Bill had learned how to feel the connection. Once he felt the connection, he slipped into the back of the room and let the walls ring out what was being said.

Cadet never spoke; instead, he listened and absorbed everything being said. Finally, work the plan. Now it was Bill's turn to learn from Trainer.

"You will have to learn how not to kill the mother of your host children. We need three boys from each host for the next three generations to get the number of boys possessed up enough to get the ball rolling.

"Once it is rolling, then we can work to infiltrate them for the military purpose and the longer-term goal. I have prepared Bill to teach Samuel all he needs to know. As well, I will guide his general direction to keep the course going."

"Military purpose?" Bill didn't know he had said that out loud.

How long has he been here? What does he now know? Bill understood Trainer's thoughts and saw the surprised look.

"Bill," Trainer retorted, "how long…What did you… How?"

Bill didn't hang around to hear any more or answer any questions.

Bill looked at Samuel, taking the milk out of the bottle with greed. This gave Trainer time to gather his thoughts. "What are you doing, Bill? You have to answer me."

Bill felt Trainer traveling down his leg. "I'll have to show you who is the boss. That is just fine. Are you really ready for this lesson?"

Trainer demanded, "What are you doing?" Bill felt Trainer strike; his leg instantly swelling, throbbing in pain as the blood began to drip down his calf.

Determined not to let Trainer get the best of him, he gritted his teeth and tensed up tight from the pain. "Being a cooperative host. I just want to know the direction you want me to go."

He felt Trainer relax; the pain began to subside. "Now you know what happens when you mess around with me. I need you to cooperate with me. Remember, two more male children. I know you and I can make this happen."

Bill left, he had to do some things anyway with Samuel.

———〰———

"Look at how Samuel has grown," Mary said with excitement as she walked in the door.

Mary felt Bill's gaze on her face before looking back down at Samuel. "Yes, he has gotten bigger every day."

"We told you that you would be a great dad," Mary said, reassuring him.

"Yes, you did. You have helped a lot lately. I don't know what I would have done without your help."

Mary looked knowingly at Bill. "You still would have done great. I came over so you could get some work done. Let me take Samuel and get to the task of the job at hand."

Mary reached out and took Samuel from Bill. "Go to work. The company was nice enough to allow you to work from home, show them how much better you are from your home than at the office."

"Thank you," Bill said as Mary watched him reluctantly leave for work.

—ɷɷ—

The desk was empty except for the logs of Trainer.

I hate to lie to her like that. Luckily Saundra insisted on the emergency fund. She hated the attitude that my boss had and feared me being fired. Well, on that, she was right. I don't need to concentrate on this now. How do I defeat Trainer? It's time to get to work.

The cover of the top log read "Trainer's Log, Thoughts of Joseph." With full knowledge that Trainer could see what he was doing, he slid the top log off the bottom. "Trainer's Log, Thoughts of Trainer" glared off the page, and he could almost see Trainer smile inside. A decision he didn't want to make but had to. The cover flipped over with the persuasion of his fingers. The pages were empty. He flipped through the pages and found not a single word written in them.

—ɷɷ—

Trainer looked through Bill's eyes with joy and anticipation. Unable to hold his pleasure back, he watched the cover flip open. "What? Nothing?" Where are the instructions for him from his father?"

—ɷɷ—

Bill smiled and flipped it closed. Pulling the log of Joseph in front of him, he said, "Teach me, Father, what you knew. Where do I go next? What do I need to watch for?"

With pride, he flipped it open. It flipped to page 4 and read:

Trainer's log day 4

I found a way to look into Trainer's quarters. When I did I blinded and deafened him. This didn't seem to bother him at first. It was as if he was going to wait me out and I would go away. It took a little bit but I faded out of the room, unable to hold that position.

The doctors have found a strange tattoo on my right shoulder, one smaller circle in a larger circle with three lines forming a cut-in-half x. He asked me how I got it. I have never gotten a tattoo in my life. The strange thing about the tattoo is that any medical instrument getting near it caused severe heart tremors that lasted only as long as the instrument was near it.

Trainer's log day 5

I learned to look and focus into Trainer's quarters for a long duration of time. Trainer got frustrated and angry. He eventually punished me, more as a warning than anything else. I don't know how far this can go but I will work at it and see what I can do.

The doctor is waiting to hear from me as to when I can change things around that tattoo. I don't think he believed a word I said to explain it but that is beside the point.

Trainer's Log Day 6

When I closed my eyes to focus into Trainer's quarters, I found I could open my eyes and lock my focus both ways. It still blinded Trainer and angered him all the more. It also allowed me to feed you without Trainer being able to teach Cadet inside you anything important.

With this skill at hand, I think I can trick Trainer into not seeing what is going on until it is too late and get him separated with a needle. I know it is risky and will have to talk to the doctor about what he thinks he will need on hand. Trainer may try to kill me.

Bill was already aware of what that would get him. The thought that his father figured out some of this and just didn't live long enough to teach him gave hope to Bill.

"Don't get your hopes up too far, Bill. Your father died trying to fight me with the medical field. I can wait another generation to move on too." The sound of Trainer's voice was angry and forthright.

"Rest assured, I want no more experiences like I had in the hospital this last time. I am not even looking to the doctors. Is that okay with you?" Bill's tone was smart-aleck, but he meant every word of it.

Trainer seemed satisfied.

Bill closed his eyes and focused inside Trainer's resting place, blinding and deafening him. With effort, Bill opened his eyes, still focused inside Trainer's place and kept him blinded for almost fifteen minutes before he was snapped back into his world.

Bill felt Trainer's anger flare. "Don't start that. I can punish you just like your father."

Bill relaxed and laughed. "I know you can. I was just thinking."

19 THE BATTLEGROUND

Moloch's spies were reporting back, but only one showed up to report. "Master, your humble servant reporting."

Moloch asked, "What is your report?"

"The prayer squad is now meeting nightly, praying, and the number has grown."

"How many has the number grown to?" Moloch's frustration with the failures was showing.

"At least five. We will know more tomorrow night. They were saying that the complete team will be meeting tomorrow night."

"There are more than five members, and they are meeting nightly now?" Moloch's anger flashed.

"Moloch." Nassor had heard something and wasn't going to be patient for the report.

"Go back and get more information." Moloch commanded as he went to Nassor.

"Yes, master."

—⁂—

Nassor didn't like the delay, but that wasn't the current issue. "What did the spies report?"

"They are now meeting nightly, and their number has grown. Their total number will not be known until tomorrow night."

Nassor remained steady and asked, "Is this growth due to your failure of killing the family members of the prayer squad?"

Moloch knew that had something to do with it. The silence allowed him to formulate his words. "We can't be sure. But we succeeded in killing two."

Nassor knew an excuse when he heard it. "Your failure has resulted in their growth. This is the problem resulting in why I am here."

Moloch stayed silent and let the comment go until he could better respond.

"What am I going to have to do to break this failure streak?"

Moloch refused to answer.

"Is there any more from the spies?"

"No, master. The spy has returned to gather more information." Moloch felt smug about getting the spy out of the house so he didn't have to answer to Nassor.

Nassor looked intently at him. "We have to start the strike now. They cannot continue meeting nightly to pray."

Moloch knew what he was thinking already. "Keep them apart. Let them work alone."

Nassor agreed wholeheartedly. "How am I going to do that?"

Moloch looked as if he was going to say something but bit his tongue. "They get around by driving cars. If they don't work—"

Nassor got the point real quick. "No cars, no prayer meetings."

"You got it." Moloch thoughts rolled around as a big grin formed on his ugly face. "What if they are all stolen?"

Nassor thought about it and decided he liked it. "Who could we get to pull it off?"

"I have some people that are hungry, tired, and need a place to rest. We know there are at least five of them. I think, with the right influence, they will all have to meet over the phone tonight."

Nassor smiled at that. "Make sure it happens. No mishaps on this, clear?"

"Yes, master." With a flurry of his wings, he was gone getting the wheels in motion.

Two walking teenagers went past the Gremlin. One looked to the other and said, "I bet that car will burn great. Feel like tryin'?"

"Yeah, nothin' better to do."

They walked quietly to the car, tried the driver's door, and it opened quickly enough. The smaller one had the car started in seconds. "Get in, this isn't a fast getaway car."

Both in the car, they puttered off to find a good place to burn the car.

By the time Fred realized what was going on outside, his car was already down the road.

—⚬⚬—

Looking quickly for a muscle car, the young man scanned the parking lot quickly. The shiny Mustang stood out. He checked it for an alarm and found none. Two seconds later, the tires squealed off, and the car was gone.

Harry walked out to the car with the car alarm in the bag. Scanning the parking lot, he could not find the Mustang.

—⚬⚬—

John waited for the computer to spit out the receipt while receiving the final words from the mechanic. "Tha-ank you. I wi-wi-wi-will be ba-ba-ack next we-wee-wee-ek to ha-av-av-ve the ot-ot-ot-her re-re-re-re-pairs made." John was speaking as a young teen ran across the street, jumped in the driver's seat, and disappeared out of the parking lot with the Ranger.

Everyone's eyes gaped open with shock. "My Ran-an-an-an-ger just got sto-ol-ol-ol-len!"

John was thankful that the manager called the police, helping him with the paperwork.

"I hope they find the truck for you soon." The manager meant what he said and drove back to the shop after dropping John off at home.

———∞———

The two men had decided to practice quick and fluid repossession. "There is one, far enough out of the way and quiet."

The truck backed up, raised the front two wheels off the ground, and pulled the car down the road several hundred feet around a corner. Stopping only long enough to secure it to the tow truck, they drove off.

Peter headed out to get some grocery shopping done before the prayer meeting. "What is going on? Where is my car?" Peter was astonished to find that someone would go out this far to steal a car.

———∞———

Jake had put a lot of money into his Malibu. The outer appearance was as sharp as it was on the inside. He decided though to take the minivan up to Carol and Bud from the hospital and arranged to get them to that night's prayer meeting. They would be more comfortable in it.

As they drove past Jake's house to the prayer meeting, all in the van looked shocked at the sight before their eyes. The Malibu had no tires, no doors, no radio; and everything that could be sold had been stripped off the car in the driveway.

"Let's pray right now. We all know Jesus Christ. Let's ask him for help," Jake didn't have any better options anyway.

They were new to this, but prayer seemed to be the answer used by the leaders in the prayer squad. They stopped the van, gathered together, and prayed. The last amen was said, and Jake looked to the group. "Let's get to the prayer meeting. I get the feeling this is going to be a long night."

Jake's phone began to ring. Grabbing the phone in his hand, he flipped it open and said, "Hello."

"Dad, my car was stolen. I can't go get groceries for tonight."

"I've got Carol and Bud from the hospital. We can get something to eat tonight. When would you like us to be there?"

"The usual time is fine. If I give you addresses, could you get Fred, Harry, and John? Their cars were all stolen too."

"Give me those addresses. I might be new at this Jesus thing, but this sounds like the attacks you have gone through before." Jake already had the van backing back out of the drive, away from the stripped Malibu.

Bud asked, "What happened?"

Jake simply answered, "The same thing that happened to me happened to the rest of the guys you are going to meet. They will be better at praying than I am. We are headed to pick up the other three guys then head to Peter's. It is definitely time to pray."

―――✿―――

The van pulled into the driveway at Peter's and stopped. As the doors opened, everyone jumped out of the van. Heading quickly to the door of the house, Jake in the lead, he opened the door and called, "Son, we're here with food."

Peter returned, "Okay," as he proceeded quickly toward the group.

After a long silence, Fred spoke up, "What did stealing all our cars do?"

"Makes it difficult for us to get together. What Satan fears now is us getting together to pray. If we have no transportation, we can't get together and pray." Harry understood where the battle was being taken.

John nodded in agreement, and Harry saw him shiver at the thought. Richard looked shocked. "We haven't been in this group long, but why would someone want to stop you from praying?"

—◦◦◦—

"This group started with two," Fred began explaining. "Our prayers touched the heart of God. God started blessing us. The two of us became three. The three became four. The four of us prayed for two years. God is ready to make a move with this group, which can't easily be explained. Before the move can be fulfilled, God is allowing us to be tried and tested. When we pray, God gets the glory. The enemy of God doesn't want God to get any glory and certainly doesn't want to see souls converted to His kingdom."

Richard finished the thought with a question, "So when we took Christ as our Savior, we put you guys in danger?"

"Danger," Fred recognized the fear, "we were already in danger. You accepting Christ just made the battle level go up. We would have been in danger if you accepted or rejected Christ. Rest assured, you were not responsible for the danger we are in. We entered the fight when we accepted Christ ourselves."

"I think I understand. How are we to fight if we don't know how to fight?" Fred could see Richard was preparing for battle although he was unaware of the full measure of danger.

Fred said, "By prayer and Bible study, that is our greatest weapon to fight with."

"When we prayed in the van, that was doing battle?"

"Yes, that was specifically doing battle. That is the best example of battle you will have in a long time." Fred knew he realized where the battle was to be fought. "Let's pray like that again. Join in if you want to. When the room gets quiet, then I will close in prayer. Sound like a good idea?"

The group gathered around, praying and doing battle in the spiritual world.

—⁓—

Moloch approached the main office with anger. "I will have this place back when the time is right." He entered slowly bowing and saying, "Master, I have a report."

"What is your report?" Nassor was ready for some good news.

"The cars of the known prayer squad members were all stolen." Finally something had gone as planned.

"Good. So they could not meet together?" Nassor looked at him for reassurance.

This is the part Moloch dreaded. "They still have the van. They gathered together with that as transportation."

"What do we have to do to keep them from meeting together?"

The anger of Nassor was obvious and beginning to flare up.

"We keep stealing their cars and we send out demons to bring doubt to the claims on the insurance companies so they will investigate it further before they pay it off. The sooner they pay it off, the sooner we have to start all over."

Nassor quickly realized the truth of that. "How many more vehicles need to be stolen?"

"There are eleven total in the team, three can move around in cars. Those three cars will have to be stolen, plus the van for mass transport must be taken out as well." Moloch was now thinking out loud but knew saying that would keep Nassor secure about his position in the house. Nassor's comfort was important. Moloch knew if he was comfortable, he would relinquish all his defensive help, which would enable Moloch to attack one hundred to one; his best chance to win.

"So tomorrow the car thefts continue and the prayer team becomes less apt to meet tomorrow night?" Nassor started to feel more satisfied with the success of the day already.

Moloch was getting smug. "Master, we will need to send out one of your soldiers to the insurance companies to make sure they don't pay those claims at all if possible. My army seems to struggle with jobs like that."

Nassor listened well. "I think you are right. I have some men that are perfect for the job."

"The spies had reported eight members now. Attacking them caused a growth to the team that doubled their size. I plan to steal from them and keep them from getting together as long as I can." Moloch was reviewing the general plan, knowing that giving details would be unwise. He had kept secrets from Nassor already, but he needed to make sure he still fed him enough information to make Nassor feel like he was loyal to him.

"How much longer will you be going on with the car thefts?" Nassor was now going after as many details as he could get.

"As long as it takes. I will not stop until they are separated and in the most pain I can possibly get them in." Moloch was confident and assured in his words.

Nassor simply assured Moloch of the intention of the real boss. "You know that pain is not the final result desired by Satan. He wants the prayer team dead. By the way, he really means dead, as in eternity."

Moloch objected, "We do not have authority to kill the prayer squad. Jesus will not allow us to kill them blindly. You can count on the fact that He will fight that. We are not sure of exactly how strong their forces are. You came with one hundred soldiers, how many has he come with?"

Nassor listened. "Here is the problem." His frustration was getting evident, "Your army is weak. Combined with my forces, they will take the guardian angels and then kill the prayer squad. That way we get what we want and we try to keep Satan content and off our backs."

Moloch knew better; even separated, they will be difficult to fight and win against. "Master, you are remembering that everything we have done has cost us because they have been able to get together. I am ready to be patient and only attack when they are one on one."

Nassor nodded and agreed, "Patience is good in this situation. We will be better off attacking after they have been lulled to sleep."

Moloch agreed and tapped on the countertop a message that only he and Nassor would understand. "Good, let's call this a plan and keep it in action."

"Agreed."

"I'm getting it in action, master," Moloch said, still playing games Nassor was unaware of.

———•———

Alexander, Boris, and Ailith listened closely to what was going on at the house. Ailith led the discussion, "You can see how they plan to get their hands into our team. We are going to protect the squad but not the property."

"Yes. You are going to allow those demons to give them that hard a time?" Boris was ready to break their plan into pieces.

"Boris, how can they be blessed more if they weren't allowed to lose everything? God's plan is more important than their comfort. The four know this already and will teach the new ones what they need to know." Ailith knew no one would rebel against God's word, so the question was simply a matter of clearing up His firm hold on the circumstances they would be involved in.

Ailith and Alexander knew exactly what their jobs were and had been through this before. "Boris," Alexander said, "you can rest assured that every time something bad happens to them, Jesus already has something better in the plan for them. It will look bad I am sure, but fear not."

Boris said nothing more, waiting patiently for the fight to begin again.

—*∞*—

They watched closely as Nassor, and his second-in-command flew through the roof of the house and toured the surrounding area. The angel of the heavenly host standing on the street beside the For Sale sign unnerved them to no end, but it was not the time to challenge the situation.

The barn in back held secrets that only a past Trainer could know. Nassor knew Moloch was not going to share those secrets with any other spirit that was not privy to them. They would be fought and not allowed to know them without a fight. What was the main secret that would keep out any spirit from that barn? He had not tried to enter himself, and there were more important details to look into at the moment. "Let's go look into the prayer squad right now. Maybe we can come up with a strategy to cut the strength of the squad ourselves."

—⟨∿⟩—

Ailith immediately called his second-in-command, "Let's follow. At the first sign of trouble, we move in."

No words came from his second-in-command, but the nod of his head said more than words could have. Ailith looked at Boris and Alexander. "Watch your post. Be ready to move, these guys can't be trusted."

—⟨∿⟩—

Boris and Alexander nodded, confirming their understanding, and held their hands locked on the handle of their swords.

Ailith and his companion were out and on pursuit, remaining invisible but ever watching and alert for trouble. They followed behind a safe distance and observed with caution, not to make any sounds.

Coming into view was Randolph. As quickly as he saw the newcomers flying overhead, his sword was drawn into battle stance, his eyes locked onto the demons. They were coming high; they looked bigger than him, but he would not surrender. The demon's hands gripped their swords but made no move to unsheathe them.

—⟨∿⟩—

They observed Fred in prayer, drawing on the only source of strength he knew he had. He felt alone and distanced. This was to be a night of group prayer until all the car thefts took place. Now the division left him feeling unsettled, nervous, and afraid. He still remembered the attack in the night not so long ago.

Praying brought relief and courage, but it still had not changed the facts. The insurance company was already refusing to pay anything on the claim. On top of that, they put him under criminal investigation for insurance fraud.

———◦∞◦———

"Moloch is doing his job well. He is going to break them with circumstances, then kill them while they are weak." Nassor knew not to let his eye drift far from the guardian angel. "His angel looks quick and ready. Good, solid prayer strength at the moment. Let's move on to the next person."

Nassor and company moved on over the house followed by Ailith and company keeping watch. Just a few minutes of flight, and Elliot came into view. The two demons were spotted, and Elliot's sword flew out lighting an arc in the sky. His stance was the same as Randolph's. Nassor noted the speed of the sword. "I can see how these angels together can be difficult to deal with."

"Shall I test them one on one?"

"No, we don't want to rouse a fight now. Just learn what we are against." Nassor watched as the end of the phone conversation played out.

———◦∞◦———

"What claim history are you talking about? I have never had to place a claim before." Anger was rousing in Harry with each accusation of the agent.

"Our computer records indicate that you have attempted to fraud the last insurance company you had. Your story will be checked out. If it clears, we will pay as the policy states we are to pay," the agent stated coldly without feeling.

"How long will that take?"

"That is unknown. It depends on how fast we get a hold of the people making the previous claim."

"Can you tell me who made the previous claim?"

"No, I am not allowed to tell you that information." The agent was not helping in any way, shape, or form.

The demon was whispering in the agent's ear to keep the vague answers coming to every question Harry asked.

"What am I going to do about getting around? Can I at least get a rental car?"

"You don't have that clause on your policy. I'm sorry, but without that, you will pay for your own rental car."

"What, I pay extra premium for the rental car service! Why is it not in the computer?"

"I can't tell you that. It is not in the computer, and I am not authorizing a rental car. Is there any other question?"

The slam of the receiver told the agent all he wanted to know. As he finished typing in the notes of the conversation on the computer, he said to no one in particular, "I don't know who he thinks he is, but I am the insurance company. He will abide the rules."

Nassor laughed at the sound of victory and his company broadened a big smile on his face. "This is going to get easier all the time. It is time to move on."

A slide down a hill, a turn to the right, and a flight took them to Seth. Without a thought, Seth drew his sword and rose slightly off the roof of the house. Nassor and companion readied their swords for the attack that never came. From behind them, they heard the swish of swords being drawn. Nassor spun quickly to see Ailith's and one guard's swords drawn, ready to engage. The look on their faces stated their seriousness and presence without any questions asked.

"Sheath your sword, they will not attack, and you know it. I will protect and defend the believer and his angel without a doubt." Ailith was stern and unmoving.

The angels and demons sheathed their swords together. "How long have you been watching?"

"Every move you make, I watch. You can count on that." Ailith made the point clear enough. They held their distance and proceeded with what they were doing.

They saw John fumbling for words, stuttering, his emotions overflowing to God in prayer. His hurt, anger, and stinging pain coursed through him into the air. Nassor's anger flared at what he saw. Ailith looked at his second-in-command and said to him, "God truly does provide. The peace he needs now is already on its way."

—◦◦◦—

The dove descended from the heavens uninhibited toward John, through the roof of the house. It settled on him, smoothing out his words and taking away the anger and frustration that had enveloped him. He had poured himself out to God, "Why are they trying to press charges for insurance fraud? What do they have on me that would make them think such a thing? There couldn't possibly be an honest clue leading to that charge."

Alexander whispered to John, "It is not truth that is accusing you. It is the power of lies and the deceit of Satan's forces causing this. This is happening to the entire prayer squad, and they need to hear from you telling them to continue to Jesus's answer to this problem. The miracle is already in heaven and can only be prayed down to them."

John knew that they wouldn't be meeting together tonight because of this trouble with all the cars. The new members were the exception to this, but that was even starting to change as it became apparent that they had associated themselves with the group.

—⁘—

In the heavens above, the angels and demons witnessed all the actions and stillness but heard none of it. Nassor was content to move on. Looking out to the east, he saw two angels standing side by side. They had already seen them and were gripping the handles of their swords. Nassor's second-in-command said, "Warner and Ojore, I thought we were trying to keep them apart."

"We are," Nassor assured him. "It is time to find out what is going on."

As they approached closer, they knew immediately why they were together. They saw Carol and Bud sitting at the table in their home. Carol was trying to explain to Bud that the insurance company wasn't called yet, but the police just left ten minutes before he got home because the Montego was stolen out of the driveway.

—∾∾—

"I no more than got inside with all the groceries when I heard it start up. I couldn't get out fast enough to stop anyone but could see it driving off down the road. What are we going to do?" Bud could see Carol was close to tears as he pulled her into his arms, resting her head on his shoulder.

"You did all you could. The police will find the car, we will be all right." Bud tried to reassure himself as well but failed. He knew that car was a lifesaver, that it made it possible for him to make the money he did.

"Will you call the insurance company to see about getting a replacement?"

"Sure will."

—∾∾—

Bud grasped his phone and the insurance information and made the call to the claims department. Once on with the claims department, he heard, "I'm sorry, sir, but we have not received premium payments for the last two months. We have not insured your vehicle for the last twelve days."

Bud took a deep breath and relaxed for a second. "I paid my premium a week early over the phone. You must have the wrong policy number."

She repeated the policy number, the vehicle on the policy, and the owner on the policy to him. Bud shook his head, slid his free hand on his forehead, as if to suppress a coming headache. "Sir, is this information correct?"

"Yes," Bud replied, "it is. Can you check again for phone payments made to that policy?"

"Sir, I have looked everywhere I can. The account shows canceled for lack of payment. I am sorry, but I can help you no more." The click of the phone said all he needed to hear.

"No insurance with us, and I don't want to waste time talking about it."

"Honey, we have to prove that the premiums were paid before they will replace the car." Bud had already taken her into his arms and braced himself for the next round of tears.

"What are we going to do now?" Carol sobbed.

Bud thought about the whole situation, and then said, "We're going to prove that our payments are up to date and get the car replaced. I can't do anything today, but tomorrow is a new day." His next thought was silent and said to his and her Lord in prayer.

Nassor could see the hand of the demon horde working already. His face was covered with an evil grin as they continued on with their investigation.

Without moving any at all, they could see Dima flying over Richard coming at them. Nassor became visibly upset and gripped his hand hard on his sword. Ailith and company matched their grips and waited.

Richard knocked on Bud and Carol's door. Bud helped Carol sit down and went to open the door. "Hello, Richard, how are you today?"

"Not good. Two guys drove up in a Mercury Montego. One jumped out, broke the window out of my truck, started it, and followed the Montego on down the road. You only live a block away, and I needed someone to pray with. Do you have a minute?" Richard waited for an answer.

"That Montego, what color was it?"

"It was a sky blue. What difference does that make?" He couldn't figure out why Bud was asking about the car and not about his truck.

"If it had a Mint drink logo on the rear window, it was most likely ours. Someone took it just a little while ago. Come on in. We need to pray." Bud was ready to continue but knew the police needed the information as well.

They both sat down at the table where Carol sat, distraught and confused. Richard looked at her and said, "I think we should pray before we contact anyone else. Whatever is going on is very real and is beyond just one person. Who else could be affected?"

"I believe last night that the five of the prayer squad had their cars stolen. The whole prayer squad is affected. Carol watched the Montego drive off and then heard the insurance company say they weren't going to pay any claim on the grounds that we had not paid the premium. We have had our share of shock. I might not be the most knowledgeable person on prayer, but I can at least try." The look on Bud's face contained multiple emotions hidden below the surface. Richard knew that he was holding together to keep his wife up.

"I'll start, then you can finish." The nod of Bud's head started the prayer.

———∿∿∿———

Nassor was getting angrier by the minute. They were now living close enough to each other that they were walking distance and still getting together and praying. The three guardian angels were on the roof, swords drawn, boring holes into the demons but never raising a millimeter off the roof. Nassor turned around and saw Ailith and his second-in-command, hands wrapped around their swords, ready to draw. Nassor's second-in-command said, "We might not want to get to hasty. We are two against five with strong prayer support. Patience will be better for us. We can gather more information later. We know what we have to talk about. Let's get back to the office."

"Okay." Nassor knew the wisdom in that strategy and flew back around toward the house on Power Lane.

———∿∿∿———

Ailith noticed they were abandoning the mission but never took his eye off them until they entered the roof over the office. "Let's get back. It's time to check on those he avoided." They flew and returned to Jesus's side.

———∿∿∿———

Nassor and his second-in-command sat in the office. "I don't think that just getting the cars is working well enough. What do we have to do to keep them apart?"

"Do we have to keep all of them apart? Even that group of new people will fall apart when those that we're really after fall. Keep the original four apart and kill them. The new ones will fall to anger and emotional struggles with the strength of any imp in hell's arsenal."

That made Nassor think, "Fred is driving distance from them all. Let's find out just how much power the heavenly host really has. It's time to test Ailith and his comrade."

"Moloch," Nassor commanded from the office.

"Yes, master." Moloch was listening.

"Get a horde together and attack Fred now."

"Yes, master." Moloch went to the horde, chose out fifty men, told them of the mission, and went out for Fred.

———✠———

Alexander, Ailith, and forty-five of his chosen flew out of heaven at the same time and headed for a collision course with the horde. The flashing swords lit the way, flying with all the speed they had. Randolph saw the horde and the heavenly team coming and drew his sword, bracing for the collision coming his way.

The dark horde drew their swords and pointed them straight for Randolph. "Kill him first. Then Fred dies with ease."

Ailith led the heavenly charge and reached Fred's roof at the same time the horde did. The swords clashed, lit up the night with sparks, and carried all but one of the horde away from the house. Randolph slashed the one to pieces and continued slicing in the red smoke as the remaining demon dissipated into the air.

The rest of the fighting carried on a few feet away with the smoke of dissipating demons so that no one but Jesus himself could see who was dead and who was alive. Ailith and the team surrounded the house as Moloch returned to Power Lane alone and defeated.

———✠———

Moloch returned to the office, fell to the floor, and just breathed. Nassor looked at Moloch and asked, "How powerful are they?"

Moloch was still, just breathing. Finally able to get sounds out, "The horde dissipated in seconds to the power of the heavenly host."

Nassor looked at his second-in-command. "I think you should take fifty of our demons and see what they are made of then."

"Yes, master." Down to the meeting room he went, picked out fifty of the best, and said, "Follow me."

He flew, and the handpicked fifty followed. The swords were out, flaring red and smoking. "Fred dies tonight. We will not fail." The horde hissed, and laughter rang to the heavenly horde as Boris flew from heaven with the news.

Fred had not gone to sleep and felt a strong need to pray. While seeking the Lord in prayer, he didn't find peace like he had so many times before. He found instead a lonely struggle that he could not comprehend. The phones had quit working, and now he not only felt alone, but also without any help from his friends and support groups. So he prayed for whatever help he could get from God.

The heavenly host had not left the roof of his house and was now on the yard and scattered all around. As the attacking horde flew surrounding the house, the heavenly host took guard positions and braced. The call came, "Attack!" The horde flew hard at the defense.

The clashing of the swords doubled but never fazed the heavenly host defending. The swords continued to clash and light the night sky through the long battle. The red smoke of dissipating demons could be seen on occasion, but not enough for the heavenly host. Finally a retreat call came, and the demons vanished back to where they came from. The second-in-command reported to Nassor, "The heavenly host is strong. They could keep us confused and fighting in ways where we can't see who is coming from where. We lost six demons to the heavenly host. Many are weakened and struggling."

Nassor dropped his arms to his side. "All right, we now know they will match a force of fifty or more. This will be a struggle to first weaken the heavenly host then attack the prayer squad."

"All of our attacks have increased their prayers, increasing their prayer support," the conclusion came as no surprise to Nassor.

The spy entered and bowed to the floor. "Master."

"What do you have to report?" Nassor looked at the bowing spy, unemotional and trying to bore the information out of him.

"Fred has been weakened. He feels alone and rejected by his God. He is still praying, but it is weak. With the new weakness comes weak leadership. Continued attacks on him can break him, and then the whole squad will crumble after him." The spy smiled but kept his head down.

"Though spiritually the angels are beating us, we are beating at the tenacity of the man in charge." This statement made Nassor grin, and he hideously laughed, sounding more like a hiss of terror.

The spy waited for further instructions. After the laughter stopped, he said, "Keep me informed on him, his emotional and spiritual state."

The spy flew back and resumed his position watching Fred.

—⁓—

Jesus watched as the angels returned from the fight for Fred. As they landed in front of Jesus, Ailith said, "Lord, we defended Fred. He is unharmed."

The solemn look on Jesus's face said there was more to the story. "His physical body is unharmed. His spirit is broken and alone. It was your statement to me that said as long as they are together…"

Alexander asked, "Why does he have a feeling of aloneness and isolation? Randolph is already struggling to hold up and getting weaker."

Jesus looked at all three of them. "This attack was for two reasons. First and foremost, find out just how strong we are, secondly to start to crush his spirit. Kill the leader, and the team falls. The demons take out Randolph, and Fred goes down fast."

The silence in heaven spoke volumes. The four searched each other for an answer, and only Jesus could provide, "The answer will come when the time is right. You have done your job well."

Boris broke the three angels' silence, "Just how bad is it going to get?"

"Watch and fight. Your instructions are clear. The rest is for Me."

The eyes of the angels turned back to earth and watched life on earth continue to roll by second by second.

———◈———

Fred could feel the aloneness like an iron bar strapped on his shoulder. Added to that was the pain from bending and praying seemingly without recognition. His restful peace had left him stranded, alone in a wilderness, with no way out. The heckling and laughter started barely audible, "Now what, not even your God could help you."

Randolph had slid through the roof and was positioned in the corner of the room, tired and weak. The power of his sword had diminished so greatly he feared it would be cut in half with any demon's sword strike. None of that is what mattered anyway; he was there to protect Fred with the best of his ability, and that is what he would do.

A little louder each time the hissing laughter came, "You could make all this easier on yourself. End this miserable life. Wouldn't you be in a better place anyway?"

Fred could not explain where all these thoughts came from. He had heard them all before and had been given a verse to combat the thoughts. He drifted back into time to the explanation he heard.

"Hebrews 12:1–2 says, 'Therefore, since we are surrounded by such a great cloud of witnesses to the life of faith, let us strip off every weight that slows us down, especially the sin that so easily trips us up. And let us run with endurance the race that God has set before us. We do this keeping our eyes on Jesus, the champion who initiates and perfects our faith. Because of the joy awaiting Him, He endured the cross, disregarding the shame. Now He is seated in the place of honor beside God's throne.'

"The first part says that no matter who you are or what you will go through in the future, someone has gone through it in the past. They are watching, wanting you to go through it better than they did. Best of all, verse two says that Jesus went through it and worse. He hung on a Roman cross even though the earthly humiliation was more than any man wanted to take. He did it for you. If there was no one else ever born on this planet, He would have done this for you. You are thinking of all the things that are making your life miserable and may even want to end your life now. Jesus did not want to end His life but, for your sake, took on humiliation equal and greater to any humiliation you have ever or will ever face so you don't have to."

That had him asking all kinds of questions and struggling with more weight than at the start of the conversation. The conversation rolled on in his mind and came down to a close, *Do you want to give all this heartache to Jesus, or do you really think you can handle it alone?*

The memory faded away and left but the question replayed in his mind over and over again. In between the question came a little louder, "Jesus could care less. He left you here alone. Now killing yourself is really the only way out of all this."

Randolph tried to fly at the imp talking to Fred to no avail. His strength had been tapped; over and over again he was sent back to the corner, wounded a little more, to watch the battle play out. The laughter aimed continuously at Randolph as he became useless, too weak to even protect a fly.

"I will never leave you nor forsake you. Claim Me and I will be your strong tower of protection."

"Jesus?" Fred was badly weakened and struggled for even one word.

"Yes, My son. Claim Me as Father, for your victory is in Me."

"Father, give me Your victory," Fred said with all the voice that he could muster, but it was enough. Randolph felt strength come into him. He opened his wings, flew at the imp, and struck; but he was still spun into the opposing corner. The imp's sword had taken the hit with some damage. Randolph knew more was coming.

"Father Jesus, You are my Savior and my strength." Stronger with each word, they began to feed his own strength as well. Randolph took flight against the imp. Both Randolph and the imp rolled on the floor, away from Fred.

"You are my strong tower. You are my victory." The volume of his words had begun to increase, and the sound resonated around the room. Randolph's sword flared arcs of light, slashing the air. The imp flew away in retreat through the roof. Randolph stood strong, wings out and sword glowing bright, and said, "No more attacks."

"Thank You, Jesus." Fred was now in victorious prayer. The peace came down and severed the iron bar on his shoulder into pieces. With that, Randolph stood on the roof of the house strong and ready for whatever the demons could throw at him.

Alexander raised his sword giving a victory shout. Ailith turned to Jesus, praising and glorifying his victory. Boris said, "You truly are Lord of Lords and King of Kings."

Jesus looked at them all and said, "No victory can be won in their strength. In my strength, one hundred demons flee with fear."

The angels praised and worshiped Jesus together in unison.

The imp was bowing before Nassor. "Why is he still alive? I can feel him. We broke him, isolated him, made his guardian angel equal to a rag doll, yet you could not get to him and kill him."

The imp could not raise his head. "I not only got to him, but he was just about to commit suicide."

"Why didn't he?"

"He started claiming Jesus. Once that happened, his guardian angel grew in strength and so did he."

"You let Jesus get into the fight. You cannot allow Jesus in the fight with anyone. Take your sword and slash into him, kill him with more than words. Use all the power of hell to shake him until he dies. I don't care how, just kill the prayer squad." His anger burst out in streams of fire. "We cannot lose again."

Nassor raised his sword, and the fire flashed. He brought the sword down hard, cutting the imp in half, dissipating the failure from his presence.

20 THE SEED

Jesus called Adley to him. Immediately he appeared. "Lord, I am ready to serve."

Adley was a small, undistinguished angel sent on special missions. Their skills and gifts made them perfect for the jobs given them. They had no swords of their own, but when their hands were thrust out, the sword of the Lord worked through their small hands.

"It is time for you to assist Aaron. He is assigned to Bill, who is possessed by Trainer. Your mission is to show the light of my word to Bill while blinding Trainer from seeing until he can take me as Savior and Lord."

"Your will be done," Adley said.

"Adley, your mission specifically is to blind Trainer. Go."

Adley flew directly beside Bill and stayed at his side.

Mary sat holding Samuel. She patiently shared her love with the contact. She slowly rocked back and forth while looking at Bill. She noticed the distant look on his face. It seemed he allowed himself to go somewhere that no one else could go.

—◦◦◦—

Bill drifted deep inside into Trainer's chamber. He watched Trainer pace nervously within his secure place. He heard Trainer talking to himself with the appearance of trying to talk through a problem. "The spirit that is giving me so many problems is joined by another. Can this get any worse?"

Bill stopped, silently watching, surprised that he wasn't noticed by Trainer as he entered. He realized quickly the focused concentration on this problem.

He rechecked the screen indicating the two spirits outside the body. Trainer's fist slammed on the screen. "What will it take to get rid of you?"

Bill asked, "Get rid of who?"

"You! This is not your problem. Get out!"

Bill backed off to the back of the room. He listened to the clicking of keys. Experience taught him well. He knew from the looks he was getting that he was interrupting something important.

"You will have to leave. No more spying."

Bill challenged Trainer by staying in the same place. The keys clicked and sharply withdrew as the pain stung then immediately calmed. He was out of the chamber but accomplished his task.

He knew Trainer was still trying to punish him for his actions. He could feel the sweat starting but not getting worse.

—⁓—

"Bill, are you okay?" Mary had noticed the sweating and the inaudible sounds coming from him. "You are bothered by something. What is bothering you?"

She watched as Bill looked to the floor. "You wouldn't understand or believe me if I told you."

Mary started telling her story, "I think you need to hear this now. For four weeks, I heard strange voices in my head telling me all kinds of things. Mostly, just pain, tears, and depression, but I eventually bought into the lies told me by the voice. As a result, I spent three hours debating as to when, where, and how I was going to die. All four weeks I felt like there was a second voice trying to tell me there was another way as well. I kept hearing it, but not fully believing it. There must have been something in that second voice because for those four weeks, I never even attempted to kill myself."

Mary paused in silence and sniffed. "My story gets harder to tell, and I still struggle with it daily. You need to know though, I will do my best to tell you. Please be patient with me.

"The next day, some ladies came to the door with some good news. I felt I needed some at that moment and let them in. Bud had gone on a two-day business trip, so it was better than being alone anyway, I thought. They had no more than walked in when the voice in my head trying to kill me went haywire, continuously trying to warn me they were lying. Somehow through all this, the words the ladies were speaking were heard and started to sink into my thoughts. I didn't follow through with what the ladies said that night and would never be able to forget the love they described. The words that echoed in my head from that time on were, 'Jesus loved you so much that he freely gave his life for you and would have if you were the only person on earth for eternity.'

"Even after that, the voices worked hard to convince me I needed to die and now was as good a time as any. Immediately after I heard that, I would hear, 'Jesus can show you the love that will turn the worst you can offer into the best.'

"I had to know more about this. Was it true? Who was this Jesus? I decided to visit this church the ladies went to. Maybe a clue would be there to the answers to my questions. I got there at nine in the morning, looking for some hints before many people showed up. The propaganda brochure that I read said one thing, but I knew to look to the people to find out the real truth. Soon enough, they started showing up, and some walked by me without a word. Others stopped and talked to me. I asked each one simple question. 'Who is Jesus to you?'

"The answers varied, but the ones that began to stick with me after I left was 'Savior,' 'Lord,' 'King,' and one lady said 'Everything.'

"I listened closely to the songs and the message of the pastor. It was during that time the voice wanting me dead got quiet and the second voice became louder."

"Even then, I didn't respond, but I knew that somehow I had a real and true description of Jesus. It was puzzling how one man could be all that to everyone at the same time, but it was true, and I knew it."

———

Bill wasn't sure what to say but had to say something. Trainer had been battling through him this whole time and made it difficult to understand, but somehow the words were still getting through.

Bill interrupted, "You were a drinker, smoker, and would party for no better reason than that. You had rejected ever wanting any information about Jesus before. You're telling me that this is the same Jesus you were then considering and since have believed in for everything?"

"Bill, you are no different than I was. You are now the one who needs to have the simple phrase ring in your head, 'Jesus loves you so much that he died for you and would have if you were the only man on this planet.'"

Bill lowered his head and trembled as he said, "Not even the voice in my head loves me. How can you say that Jesus loves me?"

He felt Mary's hand on his shoulder as she said, "I can say that because He showed it to me by forgiving me and loving me when I hated Him."

"Thank you for watching Samuel, I have somewhere to go." Bill left before any more could be said; it sounded like a distraction to him.

—————

Trainer and Cadet had been communicating, and through his doubt, he had been trying to teach Cadet all he knew. At this time, that knowledge was minimal, but he had a feeling he would be at Master Trainer's soon.

Bill had not blinded Trainer as he listened intently to Mary's story. Again, this name Jesus came up, and Trainer's ears perked up to hear all that was being said. A strange and new desire came over him to make the conversation end. Instead he held back, as he just listened and watched the two angels outside Bill.

Everywhere he now walked, he could see their smiles and feel their joy. The frustration tried hard to overpower him and make him hurt Bill, or react in some way, but the two angels outside had stopped all that from happening, and he was now left just able to use words against Bill's mind. If things did not change soon, he would be forced to verbally create depression and sow a seed for Bill to take his own life. Cadet had already started to ask questions about this Jesus, and Trainer didn't know how to answer those questions yet.

The closer he got to the house, the more he felt the house upset, rattled, feeling pain, and war. He had already begun to travel throughout the bloodstream trying with everything he had to find a safe place. All his hiding places were shaking and scary beyond what he could comprehend. Frantically, rushing, flowing, swimming, he moved from place to place searching. There was no safe place to hide and no way to fight all this commotion.

His eyes quickly told him why. Though Bill could never see the spirits unless they desired to be seen, Trainer could easily see them all. Outside at the edge of the property was a line of angels forming a blockade that Nassor and the demons could not see through. They could feel Fred riding down the street, but their view had been blocked. The panic had been created and was spreading. The swords were drawn in the house; Nassor and Moloch together were holding control only by brute force and severe punishment, while next-in-commands were on watch for a time to attack.

The cyclist riding by was clearly the reason for the panic. Trainer had become the link, and the commanders were calling, ready to attack with full force. As Bill's car pulled up to the edge of the street, he continued to wait for the cyclist. The cyclist stopped beside his truck and asked, "Are you the owner of the property?"

The word rang out throughout the whole house, "Attack, now."

The demons all spread their wings and flew at the line of the angels, trying to get to Fred. The light spheres from the angels' swords only slowed them the smallest second and were easily engaged with the fire arcs from their own swords.

The collision on the front line was loud and understandably heated. The fight glowed, sparked, and the hissing and swords flying could be seen for miles. Suddenly, at the same time, all the angels thrust their wings forward, rolling back the horde of demons, allowing room for the archangels that flew in from both sides.

Bill looked shocked. "Yes, as I just found out recently, I am the owner."

"Are you going to sell the house?"

"No," Bill said before any thought. "Wait, I might be willing to talk about it." He expected a thrashing of pain, but it never came.

Don't even think about it. Tell him you are not interested in selling, now! Bill could hear Trainer's anger in his mind.

"Do you want to meet somewhere and talk terms?" Bill asked Fred as he pulled out his wallet and flipped through the business cards. He found the card he looked for. *Stop now!* Trainer was so loud in his head he thought for sure Fred could hear it too.

The background picture of the sign had the words "Coleman, Schmitt, and Brand, Attorney at Law."

Bill blinded and deafened Trainer speaking as if in a trance. "Meet me at this attorney's office at eleven a.m. tomorrow."

"Is your number 555-3587?"

The shocked look on Bill's face said it all. "Yes, it is."

Fred said, "I'll call you if I can't make it. I plan on seeing you there."

"Okay." Bill watched Fred huff and puff as he rode off.

—◦◦◦—

The archangels had filled in the space, and the demons collapsed against the new line with a fury, slashing at anything and everything. The swords glared with the fury, and the battle raged on. Nassor and Moloch could hear the conversation but could do nothing to get to them. Every time they flew up to get over the line, so did one or more angels holding the line. The barrier stood fast, and suddenly the link on the other side of the barrier was just as blind. Just moments later, Nassor felt Fred ride off and Bill pulled his truck into the driveway.

"Retreat!" Nassor was furious but was left with no other choice.

The entire demon horde flew into the house, and with Fred safely out of range, the angels flew back to heaven.

—◦◦◦—

Ailith addressed Jesus first, "Lord, the seed has been planted, and Fred has the appointment to buy the house, but he does not yet have the check."

Jesus looked at him and said, "I will provide all the needs."

Alexander said, "The war for the house will be fought on your terms, Lord, and You will control it."

All the angels agreed and praised God for it.

—◆—

Nassor and Moloch met in the office. Nassor began the conversation, "We don't know what exactly is going on. We do know that it is important and someone is taking Trainer out of the picture. Trainer still holds his body position but I fear not the control he needs to win the war."

Moloch said, "I can try to get what is going on and what was said in that conversation. We will need to know to be able to create a plan of attack that will be effective and strong enough to prevent anything that may need prevented."

"That is what I had in mind. Whatever that conversation was about, it involves this house. We will have to defend it with all we have. Trainer will not have the support and control of Bill to do the prevention on his own."

Moloch wanted to know what was going on for his own personal battle but understood the enemy they were dealing with was more than he had handled alone. "I will see what I can find out about Bill."

"Bring me back a report. I need to know what we are dealing with here." Nassor was still thinking more about what was causing their failure to get to the men during the conversation. The angels alone should not have been enough to stop them or blind them.

Moloch left to get into Trainer's brain. The flight there was no problem, and finding him was easy. It was as simple as looking on a GPS screen at a blip, identifying the exact location. The tattoo glowed green, but it could only seen by the connecting spirits. None of those shocked him at all; the two angels on either side of him did. They did not look like guardian angels. They were smaller and not equipped with swords. These angels were consistently nagging at Trainer. Moloch was unsure of exactly what they were doing, but he knew what he needed to do.

His sword flashed red as it unsheathed and locked on Aaron. He accelerated his flight speed and kept Aaron on target. The whistle of the wings caused both Aaron and Adley to look that direction. Their eyes caught the sword tip hot and coming fast. With lightning speed, Aaron jumped off his side to see a red flash cut between Bill and himself.

Just as called on cue, Randolph shot down, sword drawn, and targeting Moloch with a fury. Moloch whirled around in time to deflect the direct attack of Randolph. Moloch looked hard at him, and the fire burned in his eyes. The hatred and desire to kill masked the fear well, but something in his eyes showed glaringly to Randolph.

Complete stillness from both the guardian angel and the demon allowed Aaron to take his place beside Bill continuing to do his work. Randolph focused on Moloch. "Jesus created Bill and bought him with the highest price that could be paid."

Moloch hissed and raised his sword to the air. "Satan is the victor, taking what and who he chooses to take. There is nothing that you or any other angel of God can do about it."

Randolph kept his sword in a defensive position. "The choice as to who Satan takes from Jesus belongs to the people. Who Bill chooses to serve, he will serve. We are only acting on the request of the believers and are limited to Bill's choices. If Bill chooses you, we have to release him to you."

Moloch knew the angel was telling the truth and fired back with a fury, "Let him go now. He belongs to me, and I will not surrender him to you or anyone else."

Randolph still held his position and kept Moloch's full attention, "Again, I tell you, that choice belongs to Bill. You and your entire horde will let him make that choice."

Moloch's anger flashed hot. "This conversation is over." Moloch flew in attack with speed like a streaming comet, the tip of his sword pointed directly at Randolph. He stood unflinching for just a second, then swiftly turned to one side and sliced cleanly into Moloch's back. His sword lit the sky with the arc of the swing; Moloch dropped back, and for the first time saw that he had been led back to the house on Power Lane.

With a screech and hiss, the demons flew from the house, swords drawn and fire filling the sky. Randolph knew his job was done and flew hard in retreat to the protection of the waiting archangels. The horde coming after him saw the angels and stopped short, watching Randolph cross the line of protection.

21 THE BATTLE RAGES

T he next day, Fred met one of the very few of the prayer squad that still had a car. Bud pulled up in the driveway; leaving the car running, he jumped out and knocked on the door. Fred opened the door. "Hey, Uncle Bud, I'm glad you could come. I have the directions on how to get to the office."

Bud said, "Are you seriously considering buying that house?"

"Uncle Bud, I opened the mailbox today, and among all the junk mail and bills in the box was a letter. I opened it to find out who wrote it, and the contents shocked me. There was a check in there for over one hundred sixty thousand dollars. This is when I read the letter. It said that the writer felt led to cut the check to Bill Collins but send it to me. He didn't know why, but that is what he did. Can you really doubt that this is a message from God Himself to buy the house?"

Fred saw the shock pass over his uncle's face. "Does Bill Collins own the house you are talking about?"

Fred had never heard the man's last name and simply didn't know for sure. Over and over again, Fred had received or read a sign that indicated the same fact. "I can only assume that God is in control of the situation and knows what He is doing."

Fred climbed into the passenger seat, and once the car was on the road, Bud started the conversation up once again. "I'm new to how God works, but that would be a far stretch for anyone to get a figure like that and the name on the check just right. God is in control of the situation, but that would be astronomical odds that all those pieces of data would be correct."

"What are the odds that Jesus would come to earth, fulfill every prophecy ever given about who the Messiah is and what the Messiah will do?" Fred was hoping that Uncle Bud would stop and think about what God had actually done for him.

Fred sat silent for a time and then said, "With all that is going on right now—the cars being stolen, the battles with depression, and the insurance companies going as far as to try to get criminal charges on some of us for fraud. You have reason to believe that God is not aware of what is going and how to get His work accomplished in the midst of the storm?"

—∿∿—

Bud had been thinking, heard every word, and it had started to sink in that the image of God he had was way too small, and he was not aware of how big it really should be. He did not want to talk, but he knew he had to ask a question that would get him talking for a while. "I guess I don't have a big enough image of who God is. How big is God?"

Bud drove on, following the written instructions on how to get to the lawyer's office, while he listened to the answer. Fred answered all of Bud's questions regarding God and His abilities. "That is a good question. Uncle Bud, I can only answer that in one way. Put a picture in your mind with four sides like a square. Put in that square everything you know and have ever known. How big is God that He would have taken control all of that inside the square?"

Bud had been following along and was completely honest with him, "That God would not really exist. I just have a hard time picturing anyone in that much control of my life including myself."

Bud glanced to Fred as he nodded his head. "Now you have to put every human and animal on this planet in that square, with everything they know and have ever known. If it is already a big God for just your life then how big is the God that can control the whole world at the same time?"

Bud could not see any borders to the image of Jesus in his head now. Fred looked straight at Bud. "God is so much bigger than what you just imagined that the square would not hold His little toe."

"God is all about faith and trust. God does as much as your faith and trust in Him allows him to do. That is why so many people don't get what God wants to give them. I personally put myself in that category. I have so much growing to do in my faith and trust." Bud could tell that Fred was opening up to him now in a way he wouldn't have done in the past. It was all so that Bud could get an understanding of what God is to each of them, the faith of a mustard seed in something they cannot see, yet they know exists.

"All I have ever seen in you is faith and trust, you can have more?"

Bud heard Fred snicker before he answered, "No human, no matter how close to God they are, can truly say they cannot grow any closer to God. That would be admitting to being equal with God. No man will ever be equal with God."

"You know, Fred, I never looked at it that way. I guess I have a lot to learn, eh?"

"Uncle Bud, we all have a lot to learn and will never accomplish learning it all."

———

Bill knew the way to the law office, and the time had come to get going that way. He understood one more key fact: Trainer will not stand by and let him sell the house and was already nervous, fidgety, trying relentlessly to find out what is going on, what to do about it, and how to go about it. He had showered and changed three times due to the excessive sweating and bleeding. He learned how to feel when his body was working overtime compensating for Trainer, and this was that time.

Adley and Aaron were both working overtime making sure Trainer would not attack Bill with painful strikes, keeping the thoughts Jesus desired flowing through Bill's head and keeping the focus in the direction Jesus needed to do the work only he could do.

Trainer was attacking at points in the legs, arms, and back trying to cripple him, hurt him somehow, but all to no avail. Adley had been standing in the way of his vision and hearing for a full day now, and no matter how Trainer attacked or threatened to clear the way, Adley remained; he was blinded and deafened by this insistent refusal to give in to his authority.

Bill was visibly shaking with light pink sweat beading on his forehead. He couldn't think and didn't dare reveal anything to Trainer for fear of more physical problems. He had refused to think of anything except "go to the office." As far as Bill knew, that was the only thing Trainer could hear, and that was how he wanted it.

For the first time in a long time, he walked freely to the Benz, opened the door, and started it. Just keep the car between the lines and you will be just fine. The Benz rolled easily out of the drive into the road ready to go.

As Bill started on his way, it seemed that an army stood inside his skull as prisoners. They all had jackhammers, pounding at the inside of his head, trying to get out. Pain shooting through the roof, he just wanted to stop and go back, but he could not make himself do that. Instead, he forced himself to go on and drive, keeping his eyes open and focusing on the road over the army in his head.

———∞———

Jesus had called Alexander and Boris to him. They were standing there awaiting instructions. "Bill is on his way to the lawyer's. Make sure his car stays on the road and gets there."

Together in unison they said, "Yes, Lord."

———∞———

Alexander and Boris saw the Benz driving down the road, weaving and jerking from one side to the other. Alexander pointed to Boris and then to the passenger side. Boris nodded in agreement and headed that way. Alexander and Boris, in position, bounced the car from one side to the other side of the road just to keep it on the road and away from other cars on the road.

———∞———

Two of Nassor's demons had flown out to find out where the two angels had gone and what they were up to. High in the sky, the demons monitored the ground with weary and cautious eyes. They knew Alexander had a lot of help on demand and didn't want to run into them before they were ready. Suddenly, they heard a call for help within the crazy car. The strangled call was from Trainer. There they were. Alexander and Boris played pinball with the car going down the road. Letting Bill die was not a bad thing anyway, and it wasn't going to be stopped by those two especially. It was time to make their move.

The two demons drew fast and hard, pointing their swords directly at the angels. With a screaming hiss, they charged at them. The screaming hiss alerted the angels to what was coming, and a quick nod from the head of Alexander, and the plan was ready.

Both angels drew their swords while ensuring Bill's car remained on the road. The charge kept coming and coming, closer and closer until the arcs from the angels' swords sent the two demons flailing out of control to the side.

—◆◆◆—

Fred knew he needed a plan and had the only plan he could think of in action. "Hey, one thing I did learn was that prayer is always the best plan of action. The total time that we are on the road, along with Bill, the prayer squad is praying for us."

"Faith and trust, is that all it will take?"

Fred could see Uncle Bud was starting to understand. "Faith and trust," Fred confirmed and then added, "watch it work."

"Jesus really is all that someone needs, isn't He?"

The smile on Uncle Bud's face said all that was needed.

—◆◆◆—

The two demons spun and finally got themselves under control. The car was still moving forward and was creating a gap between the angels and themselves. The gap was not long, and it was not time to surrender. The swords steadied, targeted, and they launched into flight. The more they fought, the more wild and erratic the car got. The more the angels hit and bumped the car back on the road, the harder Trainer attacked the inside of Bill's body.

The pounding in his head had been joined by assaulting blows from inside his stomach. Control of the car had become a thing of the past. The car weaved, jerking him around the road, seemingly impossible to stop. No matter how hard he tried to pull his foot off the accelerator, he just couldn't. His hands jerked back and forth on the steering wheel, sending the car careening down the road. With steering and speed out of his control, panic had started to set in. As panic set in, it was accompanied with unrest, fear, and confusion. All together they attacked his mind with a flutter of thoughts.

Fear started subtly, *"Are you aware of all the circumstances that can happen to you?"*

Unrest picked up on that, *"You will not sleep until you know."*

Confusion carried on, *"Can anyone really know anything?"*

Panic tried to finish the task, *"You can't even live through this. Who are you anyway?"*

His heart rate had begun to accelerate, and his breathing was closing in on hyperventilating. The sweat had become pure blood, and it had begun to soak his clothes.

Just relax, this is a simple task to do. No reason to think any different. Bill was desperate to coax himself back down to normal, but it was not working.

Panic answered back, *"You are going to crash this car and die. What are you calling a simple task? The only thing simple about this is dying."*

Fear came in, *"What if you don't die? What if you become a vegetable and can't move a muscle? Who will take care of you and Samuel then? Do you really want to be helpless and lost forever? Choose death. It is better than any other option."*

Unrest rattled blank thoughts around in his head, *"Can't be. Not now. I'm unable to take this burden now."*

Confusion smiled as he spoke into his brain, *"What are you going to do now? Can you stop the car? Do you have a chance against the death you are roaring at? Going top speed to your death again? Why are you doing this?"*

Bill's head and gut pounded intensely with every heartbeat, and his thoughts twisted and turned. Then he realized he really was rolling at top speed with no control of the car and still could not get his foot off the accelerator.

Finally the car spun around into a parking lot, and his foot locked hard on the brake, sending it squealing to a stop. His eyes focused on the sign on the door in front of him; "Law Offices" was all he could read clearly, but he knew that somehow he had made it to the right place.

The angels beside the car had kept the demons at bay with their swords, but their job was far from done.

Ailith was sent to shield young Samuel from the attacks being placed on Bill. Mary had been holding the sleeping Samuel while Henry had been praying over and for all four of them.

———

The pain never relented, and Bill didn't know what he looked like, but he knew he had to get into that office looking like he was in control. The uncontrolled shaking had to stop. Bill closed his eyes, forced his mind empty of thoughts, and counted slowly to ten. He had enough composure to move steadily and gradually through the pain.

Trainer seemed not to be an issue as he stepped out his car and began to walk toward the law firm's door. Step by deliberate step he preceded through the door to the receptionist. Standing tall, he asked for the attorney that he was meeting with. The receptionist made no facial expression of shock or terror at his appearance, so he thought he must not look too bad or she had the best poker face of anyone he had known.

She immediately notified the attorney of his presence and went back to the task she was working on when he walked in. A minute later, the attorney opened the waiting room door and called for Bill to follow him to his office. Still focusing hard on looking his best, he followed him without a word through the hall of half walls into a big corner office with a big round table with four chairs around it. "So you are selling the place on Power Lane. I have checked on all the legalities, and it is yours by inheritance. I took the liberty to get the paperwork drawn up with contracts ready for signatures."

"Good. I don't know what exactly will be going on today, but it is good to be ready." Bill thought about the sale as his death and didn't want to spend months making the transaction. One of the things his father's log had said was to get all the paperwork ready so the sale could go through without complication. Trainer would be punishing mad if he knew he was selling the place.

"You look like you've been beat up by a Mack truck. Are you sure you want to do this?"

"Yes, the quicker it gets done, the easier it is on me."

"Bill, I know you don't want to tell me what is going on, but you look like you have been through the wringer. What is going on?"

Bill thought about his answer and decided the truth would silence his question anyway as it is unbelievable. "I have a demon inside of me called Trainer. The house has been in the family line of Trainer-possessed people for its life. He wants it to stay that way."

The attorney looked puzzled and then asked, "Do you have a Frank Collins in your family line?"

Bill's face exposed the shock that locked up every muscle in it. "Yes, he is my grandfather. He died before I was born."

"Then your father was Joseph. Why didn't he complete the transaction of getting the house in his name?"

Bill looked shocked at that. "He said in his instructions to me about the house that it should have been. He was trying to sell it."

The attorney picked up the phone and punched three numbers and waited for the person on the other end to pick up. He could hear the phone ring from the speaker.

"Hello." The voice on the other end was older and cracking.

"Is the paperwork ready for Bill to sign?"

"Yes, I will be there with it shortly."

"Your father tried this very same thing and never completed it. With the death certificate you gave us at the first meeting, all we had to do was get that paperwork, have you sign it, and your buyer can sign the forms I drew up, and then it is all done but the filing. Once they are filed, the new title will be received in our office in a few weeks. It will all be done but the financial exchange."

The beep of the phone interrupted any further conversation. "Yes," the attorney spoke into the phone.

"Your other party is here. Shall I show them in?" the receptionist asked.

"Please and thank you."

The knock on the door was from the older attorney. "Come in, Dad. We're ready in here."

The older attorney entered and directly behind him entered Fred and Bud. The attorneys went through Bill's dad's paperwork and showed him where Bill needed to sign. The older attorney left with a warning, "Be careful. Get this done quick. Trainer has a bad attitude."

The attorney was left with the client and buyer. "Fred, how much are you willing to pay for the house?"

Fred pulled out the check. "This will have to do for the house and the fees for the involved parties."

The attorney took the check, checked the amount, and figured the amount that would remain for Bill. "Bill, would you consider one hundred forty thousand dollars enough for a cash sale?"

Bill looked at Fred and back to the attorney. "Yes, I would sell the house for that."

The attorney filled in all the appropriate blanks, explained the sale agreement to both parties, and pointed to where each one needed to sign. After all the blanks were signed, the attorney said, "Okay. With this done, Bill, you have sold the house to Fred. I will get this processed. Fred, when the title arrives, I will contact you. Officially and legally, Fred, you are the owner of 5757 Power Lane."

Fred, Bud, and Bill thanked the attorney and left the office. Outside the office, Bill could no longer hold control. He began to shake and wobble at the knees, just managing to keep himself upright. Fred reached out and caught one side, and Bud caught the other. "Are you all right?"

Bill began to sweat as he answered the question, "I am fine. I have to go by the house I just sold and convince Trainer it is still his even though it isn't. When do you plan to go inside?"

Fred looked distressed as he answered, "I'm not sure. Someone in that house doesn't like me. I have never been able to go by the house without feeling hatred and a desire for me to die."

Bill nodded as he was escorted to the Benz. "That is Trainer, as they are known to me. They must be some kind of demon. What they can do to me scares me. Once they know I sold the house, they will try to kill me."

Bill's eyes rolled back in his head; the sweat became pure blood as he went limp in the arms of Fred and Bud.

———

Bill heard Fred praying as a different voice in his head said, "Save me, Jesus. Just say, 'Save me, Jesus.'"

He heard Bud agreeing in prayer with Fred. Bill, unsure of the voice, tried to say, "Can't do that. I can't do that."

The voice assured Bill, "You must. Call on Jesus, and He will save your life."

Bill recognized the name Jesus. He finally decided it was his last chance and said, "Save me, Jesus. Save me."

———

Alexander and Boris immediately prepared for the attack of the demons while the Spirit of the Lord entered into his heart and the very domain of Trainer himself.

Trainer cowered into a corner, seeking a way to get to the tattoo on his right shoulder. The Spirit reached out a hand and firmly grasped Trainer, squeezing him in the grip. Trainer grunted as the life and fight was squeezed out of him. Then with one final word, "Go and come back no more." Trainer was thrown into the tattoo, which immediately became swollen, took the shape of a spaceship, retreating to the house on Power Lane.

The incoming horde were cut off by the host of God's army and sent back to the house.

—⁓—

Fred and Bud were still praying when Bill's body relaxed and started breathing with a more regular pattern. Fred watched as Bill opened his eyes. "Thank you," he said with a faint whisper.

"Bill, is everything all right?"

"I don't know," Bill said. "Is there a tattoo on my right shoulder?"

Fred looked for one and couldn't find one. "Not that I can see. Did you have one put there?"

"No," Bill answered. "That means that Trainer can no longer do me any harm. Jesus saved me and kicked Trainer out."

Fred was confused about what just happened and asked, "What exactly are you talking about?"

Fred tried to understand as Bill explained. "In the attack, I heard a voice tell me to call on Jesus to save me and He would save my life. On my right shoulder was a tattoo. That was the method of transportation of Trainer to get to his host's body and a safe hiding place in the body. You may have been praying with your eyes closed, but if that tattoo is gone, then he or it can no longer reenter my body again."

Fred understood that. "You just accepted Jesus as your Savior. When you did that, you made your heart His home. Where He lives, no demon can live. We have a group that meets every chance they can to pray and study the Bible, the book Jesus wants us to live by. If you want to, you can join us."

Fred was surprised at the excitement in Bill's voice. "You would help me to understand more about Jesus?"

"I sure would. From the way it looks, I will have no other choice but to make that my full-time job pretty soon. With all the complications I have been having, I haven't contacted my boss for a long time. He will most likely fire me because I am not turning in my work on time."

Bud said, "I am picking the other prayer warriors up, and I need someone to transport one person. If you want to follow me, you can bring the closest one to your house with you and I can take the rest."

"Sure thing, that will be fine."

After exchanging information and making the arrangements, they got up. Fred said, "See you there."

"Will do."

As they parted, they went to their vehicles to go to their homes and prepare for their upcoming Bible study.

—∾—

Nassor, Moloch, and Trainer were in the office. Nassor shouted out, "What happened!"

Trainer knew better than to look directly at Master Trainer, so he looked at the floor as he said, "I was kicked out of Bill by God's Holy Spirit. I wasn't given a choice but to leave."

Nassor's anger was restricted, "You were to fight to control him and keep him, surrendering to no one. Why do we no longer have an adult to work with to train Cadet?"

Trainer cowered and said, "I was unaware of what to do because I was not trained. How am I to deal with these things when I am left out in the dark about what I am up against?"

Nassor's anger flared at that, "Moloch, you were responsible to make sure he was trained to do the work he had to do. What is your response to this?"

Moloch looked surprised and shocked, but most of all, terror filled his eyes. "The angels became a barrier, refusing me to get close enough to do the proper training he required. Even with your help, it was impossible to cross that barrier."

Nassor drew his sword with fire arc and said, "I am not the cause of your failure. You will have to answer to the master for that. We have to keep a hold on Samuel or this whole show is over. The master will have all our heads in a basket for that."

22 HELL'S FURY

Nassor, Moloch, and Trainer boarded the ship on the roof. Nassor's fury mixed with fear. Trainer was just a blank slate with no more strength than a regular imp. Now, Bill had been freed, leaving no one to train Cadet. Worse yet, he couldn't come up with a clear location as to where he was. His only hope was that Moloch could take Trainer, find Samuel, and force their hand in his life.

Samuel was approaching three months of age. With the number of Christians surrounding him, finding and taking Samuel would be a task difficult at best. The house needed the entire defense it could get now. They were unsure of who actually owned the house, but they held it by possession. Nassor would hold that property with his very life and the lives of every demon in that house.

Moloch knew that he had no good excuse as to why or how this failure took place. As well, he knew the preparation for Cadet was far from done. The reports said that the young one was worrying about this Jesus already and had no answers to his questions and concerns.

The master would be angry at the least. At the most…he didn't want to think about that. Instead, he put his focus on what he was going to say to the master to even stand a chance at survival. He knew there would be no mercy; that was for sure. Times like this brought back the thought that maybe he should have been loyal to Jesus the first time in heaven. That decision was made a long time ago and could not be taken back.

───∿───

Trainer had been shut out practically since birth. Every attempt to get training had failed ever since the hospital. The logs that were so promising were blank paper; the times to get into the house had been stopped by something or another; the battles were more than any untrained demon could handle. The last battle was not even a fight. His life and fight was squeezed out of him in just a matter of seconds. He didn't even know who he was fighting. How was that a fair fight? His only hope was to cast the blame on someone else and hope it stuck.

The master's voice was clear and distinct, "Exit. Report to me, now!"

The exit was quick as they cleared the ship and knelt facedown, saying in unison, "Master."

"Trainer, stand before me." The master was already not pleased. "Why are you here instead of working on Bill?"

Trainer trembled as he stood and began, "Master, I was working on getting the training from Master Trainer. I was not near him to get it nor was I equipped to fight the fight. I was blindsided by someone beyond my control, so I could not see where the fight was until it was too late. I was offered no help from Master Trainer. The final fight for Bill was fought with a spirit that choked me out and sent me away in seconds."

"Stay here." Satan turned to Moloch. "What do you say to this?"

———✧———

Moloch stood beside him and glared with anger at Trainer then turned to face the charges. "I have been busy trying to keep the prayer squad under attack. Any opportunity to train Trainer has been occupied in the battle against them. Your appointed leader has not given me a chance to do anything but fight his fight."

The master's eyes drifted to Nassor as Moloch continued, "When I was in control, we had training started and Bill under our control. Now I'm afraid that we may have lost Samuel as well."

"Nassor, answer the charges." Moloch felt the anger flaring in his voice, and the red heat of his office had risen in temperature.

Nassor now stood before the master. "I left him and his men to do his work. He was never in a position where it was completely impossible to keep Bill. He has not done his job again. All he wants to do is pass the buck on to me. I sent two of my own demons to help Trainer in the fight. Moloch was not keeping up with his part of the load."

His words burned deep into Moloch's body, "Where is Samuel?"

Moloch, feeling Nassor's glare on him, looked to Trainer, but Trainer looked to an empty space. He knew that Trainer must answer the master or he would suffer the consequences. "I have tried to find him and could not."

The sword slowly pulled out of the sheath of the master. "Who do I cut to ribbons for the failure of all three of you? None of you have completed your job. You, Nassor, were responsible to defend the house alone. You, Moloch, were responsible for training Trainer and helping take out the prayer squad. You, Trainer, had one job: keep Bill in line for the mission. Who did their job?"

Moloch watched as the master's eyes blazed into Nassor. "Did you?"

"Master, we still hold the house." Hoping that was enough.

"Do we? Does Bill still own the house?" master asked, eyes never leaving Nassor.

Moloch felt Nassor's burning, intense glare. The master shouted with fire, "Nassor, you will answer me."

Nassor turned back to the master, "I don't know. My demons were unable to get any information as to what went down at the meeting."

"Moloch, do we still own the property?" The fire turned too quick to him.

Moloch knew the answer to that question was not going to be liked. "I don't know. My men and I were busy on a mission with the prayer squad."

The master's eyes flared at Nassor then quickly turned to Trainer. "Do you know anything?"

He watched Trainer tremble as he said, "I was blinded through the whole meeting. I know nothing of what went on."

The master's sword swung and arced in front them all, sending all three fleeing back and kneeling. "I will not lose this war. You have to do your jobs and make it all right, now!"

"Yes, master."

"Bring my scorpion." The master turned his back on Moloch and Trainer, with nothing more to say to either of them. Moloch was glad to have the master's burning fire finally off from him.

"Nassor, you will make sure Samuel is found and trained. You will go back to the house and keep it under my control, and you will send Trainer and Moloch to find the baby. Once he is found, they both will train him. This fails, and all three of you will be slashed by my sword. Just make it happen."

—◆—

Jesus had joined the celebration in heaven when Bill accepted Him as Savior. Ailith, Alexander, and Boris were celebrating with the rest of the angels as they watched the scene play out.

"Where is Samuel?" Ailith was preparing to protect the child at all cost.

Boris answered, "Samuel is with his in-laws. They are now believers and taken into the fold of the prayer squad."

"Excellent! Who is in line to keep the child safe from the searching party?"

"Until the party leaves for the search, the three angels watching the supervising adults will be enough. After that, we will have to deal with assigning someone to watch the child specifically." Alexander was already aware of the extended workload they were all under.

Ailith looked to the available warriors ready to fight, knowing that Adley and Aaron were already assigned to reach out to him spiritually. "Sakata would be good to protect and hide the child."

Boris looked at Sakata and saw his larger-than-normal size, knew his experience with special missions like this, and understood the wisdom he had in difficult times. "He will have his work cut out for him."

Alexander had seen the same thing and said, "I would rather have an angel like him to help than many others he could choose."

Ailith responded, "Yes, he will have his hands full, but he will not stand alone, and I believe in him to keep the boy safe under all circumstances."

Ailith turned to the crowd of celebrating angels. "Sakata, may I see you?"

With that, Sakata and Jesus came over to where they were. "What do you want to see me about?"

"Young Samuel is now the target of the demonic horde of Power Lane. They are sending Moloch and Trainer to find him and possess him. He can be protected by the adult guardian angels in battle against the horde. We will need your size to blind those two from finding him. Prayers have come up for this, and the prayer strength is strong. Of course, this is only with the Lord's permission."

They turned to face Jesus and waited for his answer. "Sakata, you have your assignment. I will call you back when its need ends."

"Lord, You are Lord of all and all-knowing, what is going to happen?" Boris just felt something bad was going to happen.

Jesus answered, "He must choose whom he will serve. He is in the right place, but not even that will guarantee he makes the right decision."

Boris submitted, saying, "Yes, Lord."

The rest of the angels followed, "Yes, Lord."

———∽∾∾———

The scorpion was bright red and glowed with the flame and fury of Satan himself. Satan raised the tattoo and placed it on the back of the scorpion. The lines of the tattoo were absorbed by the scorpion to make them one entity. "The added power from the scorpion will enhance the control you have over Samuel," he said as he looked at Moloch and the others.

Moloch was silent as he watched and felt the power grow stronger by the second. Moloch thought of the day that he had forced his host to follow or die and knew he did not have that much power then. This for sure would break the backs of the prayer squad, bringing success to their mission. Certainly now, Satan will finally develop a human army to rule the world as an equal to Jesus.

—⁂—

"We will see how the heavenly host deals with this. We will take Samuel while taking out their strength, and you will be lord of all in heaven and earth."

Satan watched as the demons lifted their swords, hissing and laughing with the thought of victory.

"This will be my day. I will live victorious in all heaven and earth."

The witnesses roared and hissed even louder.

Satan looked at the three demons. "Go, take him and kill everyone else."

—⁂—

Nassor led the way, Moloch followed with pride, and Trainer followed behind Moloch. With a shout, the scorpion rose from the office of hell and embraced the mission set before them.

It took the scorpion seemingly seconds to find the house on Power Lane and land. The roof tattoo took on the shape of the scorpion, and Nassor appeared in the office with power.

The scorpion rose off the roof, leaving an indelible mark. Moloch glared with glee. "Let's go get Samuel, and I might just as well kill some heavenly host angels while I'm at it."

Moloch could see the hatred on Trainer's face. Moloch had noticed Trainer seemed stronger, angrier, and more in touch with the plan as he held his sword.

As they took their seats, Moloch saw a large screen light up, and everything on the surface showed on the screen.

———◈◈◈———

The scorpion was in the air and so was Sakata. Sakata bore no visible weapons but stood secure in his task of keeping the scorpion from seeing Samuel or Bill. It took one quick look to see the host of guardian angels already blinding the searching scorpion, swords drawn, knowing this fight would be a long hard fight. The team of angels had surrounded the prayer squad and child, making sure all were protected.

Sakata flew over the prayer squad but under the guardian angels. The fighting angels had taken battle positions against the scorpion before it ever saw them.

———◈◈◈———

Moloch immediately recognized the guardian angels on sight, knowing each one by name. Still Samuel wasn't on the radar. Staying high, not in fear but more of priority, the scorpion kept an eye on the ground, looking for Bill or Samuel. Their orders had been specific: get control of Samuel and kill the prayer squad. Moloch looked one more time at the prayer squad, then at Trainer. "Are you itching for a fight? Are you ready to try out those new wings?"

Trainer said, "Oh yeah. Leave no angel standing."

Moloch swung the scorpion back around in the direction of the angels. Swiftly he parked it, allowing it to settle flat on the ground.

"There they are. Fred and three others are sitting together praying. They won't see what hit them until it is too late." Moloch searched the sky and saw no guardian angels. They must have been lured topside by the scorpion.

"Follow my lead and kill as many as you can in the first pass." Moloch watched Trainer glow with understanding, spreading his wings to fly.

Moloch held the front path and spread his own wings. Silently and swiftly they launched forward at the praying enemies.

As they approached, Moloch watched as Randolph unsheathed his sword from his hiding place and launched toward the two demons. Three more, equally as fast, were flying their way with swords drawn, shooting arcs of light in the sky and cutting at everything in their path.

Moloch and Trainer turned and fled, just getting into the scorpion before the angels got to them. Moloch's fear and panic sent him running, and it would be fear that sent him into battle. He knew what Satan wanted, and he had better get it done. For now, it was time to settle on hunting Bill and Samuel.

The scorpion rose off the ground and into the air to continue the search. After a complete search of the area, it flew on, leaving a trail of red smoke behind it.

———

Randolph looked toward Sakata. "I think he was looking for an easy kill. We now know the scorpion is equipped with two demons. Moloch and the other one we don't know."

Sakata answered, "The one you don't know is Trainer. He has been forced to become a warrior because Bill now belongs to Jesus Christ. I am here to keep the scorpion blinded from finding Bill and Samuel."

"I thought they had no authority to kill those that belong to Jesus?"

"They are ignoring Jesus's orders. Anger is fueling their attacks. You did an excellent job in the surprise defense. You will have to be ready for any and all attacks. They will be personal and deadly. With only one intention remaining on the prayer squad and Bill, they will kill them all." Sakata had been through this before, still remembering the terrible battles before finally defeating the enemy.

Sakata kept his eyes to the sky, looking for the flying scorpion from hell. "Samuel, Bill's son, is the last remaining heir they have to develop their army that will destroy God's rule over heaven and earth as we know it. This would only be another attack in a long line of strategies that have repeatedly failed. Beware, they fight hard."

"We are ready and will fight harder."

Sakata stood unwavering. "You will, I am sure of that."

———

Bill had Samuel resting peacefully in his arms as the four adults raised their heads after saying amen. Bill asked out of sheer curiosity, "How do you plan on taking possession of the house? You know that Trainer will want that house and will certainly fight for it."

"God is going to take the house. Remember, I just serve the Lord. I can't do anything on my own. Just out of curiosity, how much of that land did I buy?"

"The best I can offer, about forty acres. I was willing to sell it cheap for painfully clear reasons."

"God knew what He wanted to do with the property. He is still in control of the circumstances." Bill watched as Fred pointed his index finger in the air to make his point.

"I have to agree with a big AMEN!" Bill was fired up, knowing that God had a plan and he was found worthy to be part of it.

———

As the prayer meeting broke up, Sakata remained over Bill and Samuel. He saw the scorpion returning, continuing the search. He knew that even though the other guardian angels were dispersing, following their prayer team member, they had their eyes to the sky, watching the comet-like tail from the scorpion. They were aware of what the demons inside searched for.

———〜〜〜———

Randolph kept a closer look for the course it was taking. His fear was that the house was its power supply and would be dependent upon it for the power to operate it. There was no way to tell for sure what or where their power came from, but that was not his job. His job was to protect Fred; he planned to do that with everything he had.

As he scoured the area with his ever-watchful eye, he could see the guardian angels huddled on the roof while the prayer squad went on with their daily tasks, obeying God in everything they did, living in constant prayer.

———〜〜〜———

Moloch was frustrated and angry, the feeling of being chided, being held down constantly. They had flown silently for a long time, feeling the overbearing task weigh down on their shoulders.

"Trainer, what have we missed? We have searched the complete prayer squad's locations, Bill's home, and all relatives. Not a single blip of any kind. Where else could Bill possibly try to hide Samuel?"

"I've been thinking about that. We have not tried Bill's in-laws. They have kept the baby often in the past. We should scan there and see what we can come up with."

The scorpion never changed course as it came to settle over the house in question. Moloch stared intently at the blank screen. The only thing on the screen was a circling line with a small tail.

Moloch's anger and frustration flared, "Where is that kid?"

Moloch's stare had proved useless, so he turned to Trainer. "What are you looking at?"

"It looks like a locater for heavenly host angels. Everywhere we have looked, there has always been the same blip on this screen. This may be something to keep in mind."

Moloch jumped up to look at the screen. "That's not locating angels' locations. That is locating demons' locations and marks. We could learn how to isolate one particular mark, then we could pinpoint exactly where Samuel is. This is a great find."

Below the screen was a keyboard not containing letters but symbols. They were unfamiliar to Moloch. As he watched the blips, some moved while others remained stationary. Moloch looked at Trainer. "Let's pick a blip and follow it. It is time to learn what this thing is telling us."

The blip they chose had just begun to move as they made their decision. Moloch took the controls and began maneuvering the scorpion toward the blip. Once the scorpion lined up with the blip, the screen flashed a light on the blip, highlighting it above all the others. Looking down on the ground, they found a walkway with hundreds of people moving both ways. There was nothing that would distinguish any one person from another that they realized.

The second blip they chose was heading in the direction opposite the first. As the scorpion maneuvered again, it found its target. There was only a stray dog walking down the walk. "That's not what we are after."

The third blip chosen had been still, motionless with no other blips near it on the screen. The scorpion maneuvered easily, and the screen indicated the target had been found. A quick look saw nothing out of the ordinary or that they would guess would cause the blip on the screen. They had isolated three blips. Of the three, any number of things from a human to any object was the cause; a dog most likely was the cause for the second; and thirdly, an object of some kind was the most reasonable assumption.

Moloch debated tearing his own head off. Everything he had tried with the equipment at his disposal made it even more difficult to figure it all out. Moloch retrained his eye on the radar, hoping that some sign of Samuel would come on the screen.

—◦◦◦—

Trainer focused on the side screen and ground picture as the blips highlighted; he would attempt to identify what was causing it to activate. Something Trainer had not seen before, each blip had a sign that went with it. When the next blip highlighted, he punched the button with the correlating sign, and a screen lit up showing him exactly what they both wanted to know.

The first blip he tried was that of a young girl walking beside her mother, so he assumed and hit the button. The girl seemed mild-mannered enough until she jerked away from her assumed mother. He watched as she ran off with her back to her, into the street and back to the walkway, hitting whatever was in reach of her hands. Her mother chased her down, grabbed her hand, and began walking beside her again. This time, the mother was lecturing the young girl showing her frustration.

With another blip, he hit the matching button. The screen lit up again. A young woman showed up walking on the walk below. She glanced to her left at the window ahead of her. Her attention had been grabbed by a piece of jewelry. With one quick motion from her hand, the glass shattered and fell. She grabbed the jewelry and ran, knocking people over as the alarm blared out. With incredible speed and power, she disappeared into the mass of people on the walkway.

He grinned evilly as he realized he had figured out the code. At last, they would be able to track Samuel without any more difficulty.

23 THE PREY

Moloch remembered the standard used to search out the first man he possessed that started the Trainer reign. The man had to want a family, desire to teach and train children, and be respectable in the community. Satan desired an army that could walk down the street without raising fear in everyone who knew them. He remembered selecting the young and strong. What he soon discovered was to take caution in his selection because he could never continue the process if the man was not in the world free.

Now looking at the monitor blips, he formulated a plan. "Trainer, we have the freedom to do whatever it takes to get the job done."

"Yes."

"Working with this line of men, we have never accomplished the first task."

"Don't remind me."

"What if I took on a new family line of men while you work in the line of Bill?"

"Could you go and possess another man?"

"Why not? I started the whole line with one man."

"That would double our chances of success and speed up the rate in which the army is produced."

"Yes, but beyond that. There are many more choices that we don't want them to make. We don't want them to allow God in their lives. God has always been the biggest fight."

"Yes, He and His servants are the ones that shut me down so many times with Bill."

"If we don't have that problem," he said as he pointed his bony finger at the screen still full of blips, "then we should have total freedom to rule and reign as well as people to get control of the unruly from the outside. That should prevent some of the other problems as well."

"I see where you're going, like getting Samuel in the hands of a man that would teach him to follow us."

"Certainly. Where Bill will fail us, a God hater will not. I can make him think Samuel is his and put a drive in him to steal him away and hide him forever. Samuel will learn our way from the time he is a baby and not fight us as an adult."

Trainer smiled and said, "Let's put the plan to work. It sounds like a great idea to me."

Moloch smiled as he looked at the screen. "Who would make a good target?"

Both stared at the screen, and then Moloch touched a dot on the screen. The face of a young preteen girl showed on the screen. Attractive in all ways, but she was too young and was the wrong gender. Another dot was touched, and the face changed to an older man, close to retirement age, walking down the sidewalk. Moloch tried again with another dot. The screen changed to a young man with potential, but Moloch knew he would have to verify that he could work with him. "Don't get too excited. I got to this point with several young men the first time never able to get a hold of them. Let's take a look and see."

The scorpion flew down and landed on the young man's shoulder. Information gathered quickly, and it darted off into the air. Moloch knew the data gathered meant the DNA wasn't the correct match and there was a high probability of rejection. Moloch took this as an opportunity to teach Trainer a valuable lesson he may need to know. "Why didn't I choose this young man?"

Trainer looked at the data, and Moloch watched his face as he tried to decipher all the information on the screen.

Moloch went over the data, explaining the implications of everything gathered and what was the best he could get. He returned to the screen, picking dots. The faces appeared one by one, and he had difficulty finding what he was really looking for.

Another young man popped on the screen. He was strong and looked like a good candidate. It was time for data collection. Again the scorpion flew down, gathered the data, and flew off for a better look. The data collected didn't match the person. Further research indicated that person was genetically a female. This made him unworkable for the plan. "Keep going. We will find someone that fits our needs."

"I hope so."

Again the faces appeared and changed as the dots became people. A third young man appeared on the screen. Everything looked right. The scorpion flew down to gather the information, quickly retreated, and jumped to another shoulder. The data on the third young man was complete. The scorpion quickly flew into the air avoiding an attempt to smash it.

"That is a good sign. Alert and aware of our presence, we will have to be quick. Look at the data. He's a cousin of Bill's. This young man went to the same school as Bill, played nose guard on the high school football team. He's still in shape because he's a competitor in fighting."

"Look at this, he also knows Harry and already has a disdain that can be used to get at the prayer squad at the same time." Moloch was proud that Trainer was learning so quickly from him.

"Yes. Here is how we are going to have to handle this. I will get to the rear of the tail. You will have to fly down and whip the tail to strike. I will be sent into him just like the venom of a regular scorpion. You understand the controls and what you have to do?"

"Yes, I do. Be ready."

Moloch went into the tail, and Trainer took the controls.

—◦◦◦—

Gary was walking down the street to find out what this gym that opened up had to offer. He was looking for a place where he and his coach could meet and train. The coach's house was full of people and interruptions that made training difficult, and he wanted to get to the point of serious training to be a professional fighter. He knew it wasn't going to happen there.

Whatever it was that landed on him earlier wasn't getting a second chance. It was hovering like a dragonfly but looked like a scorpion.

He focused on the flying thing while saying, "Stand back. I'm going to send this thing to its death with my foot."

Ray, a smaller man with none of the skills possessed by Gary, stood away and waited. "What is that thing?"

"As best as I can tell, a flying scorpion. It's time for it to die. Come to papa, little bug. I need the speed practice."

Gary watched as the flying scorpion came in a straight path toward him, tail ready to whip. "Time it, Gary. Focus and timing."

The scorpion got into range, and his right foot lifted ever so lightly for the attack. As Gary watched the scorpion close in, he lifted his foot off the ground in a flash, marking his target. His foot slammed hard into the scorpion, sending it into a light pole standing on the edge of the sidewalk. He watched it flip-flop and land hard on the ground. "Want some more, whatever you are?"

The scorpion swung from its back to its feet, and Gary watched the wings retract into it. "This isn't a bug like I've ever seen. You?"

"No way, man. I can't believe it! What is that thing?"

Gary saw the movement as the scorpion came toward him. "Good thing for thick leather boots." As it approached his foot, he waited patiently, timing for the kill. "Time it out. You can do this."

The scorpion was within range as Gary jumped forward, foot smashing into the ground. The scorpion scampered sideways and out of the way. Gary jumped again, trying to take the scorpion out. Again, the scorpion put distance between them. Both were completely still, waiting on the other to move.

Ray interrupted the silence, "Gary, let's back away and leave. We can go around the block the other way."

"Ray, I am not gonna be humiliated by a bug. This will be over soon, or I am running."

Gary watched, trying to bore a hole in the bug with his eyes. "One more round. If you survive, I'll let you be and go. If not, I win."

The scorpion seemed to stare at him and slowly started moving his way. "Watch it, Ray." His right foot propped on its toes, the wings seemed to roll out. "Make your move, little bug."

The wings spread open wide and up the scorpion went. Gary's foot swung around on target, smashing into the scorpion. It locked on his shoe as he continued around and smashed hard on the concrete. Quickly, it ran up his pants' leg, stung him, and retreated into flight away from him. The left foot smashed hard into it, sending it into a trash can along the sidewalk. The scorpion vanished in the trash.

Gary knew it got him, but it was gone too.

—◦◦◦—

"Moloch, Moloch, did you get in?"

Trainer felt the satisfaction as he heard, "In and taking over. Go find Samuel."

—◦◦◦—

Gary's leg hurt, but he was on a mission and didn't need to worry about that until he got to the gym. "Ray, let's go. I want to get this checked out."

"Okay. I can't find that bug anyway."

"Nothing can take two hits of my foot and move much anyway. I'm not worried about it."

"I'm coming," Ray said as he ran to catch up with Gary.

Gary walked on down the road with Ray. He finally saw the sign indicating the gym front door. "Ray, this looks like a big gym. There's an open area for the individual training there. A big plus was more weight equipment to get stronger. The only question left is if they're willing to let me use it and for what price?"

"I don't think they would have a problem with you using it. The problem will be how much."

A little while later, they walked out with a membership and approval to allow his coach in without a fee. He unclipped his phone and punched the numbers in for his coach.

He passed on what he found to his coach and confirmed the upcoming appointment for training.

———✺———

Moloch found his way into the bloodstream and targeted his course. First the brain and set the controls in place. It was definitely a long time since he had done this, but it felt good to be back in the game again.

The bloodstream carried him to the main arteries. The main arteries carried him to the heart. Once in the heart, the receiver was set in the first of the four chambers. From the heart, he moved on to the lungs. In the lungs, he set the receiver in its place. From there he went to the spine. The receivers were set in particular intersections to get pain control to different sections of the body.

Now to get the sending units planted in the brain, and control will be easily gained. The trip to the brain was easy for him. He knew that planting these would be difficult if it took too long. He set himself up to get them planted with speed and location control. He was ready to roll and almost in place; one more push from the heart and plant one, plant two, plant three, plant four. He never stopped until all four was in place.

He allowed the bloodstream to take him to the chamber just below the sternum between the lungs. There he set up the main control systems, connecting him to Gary in all ways. There was no guessing as to how to get the best control this time; he set it up as he knew from experience.

He could see through Gary's eyes, hear through his ears, taste through his tongue, and all the senses came easily on line. Are you ready, Gary? It's time to make the world happen. Moloch rubbed his hands together in anticipation.

"Gary?" Moloch said as he tried to get the communication line up and running.

—⁓—

Gary and Ray were walking back to Gary's house just a few blocks away when he heard in his mind, *"Gary?"*

He turned to Ray and said, "Yeah? What do you want?"

"Huh? What are you talking about?"

From inside, he heard again, *"Gary, it's not Ray. It's Moloch. I now live inside you."*

"This is who? You what? Ray, you know better than to play dumb games with me."

Ray's face was covered with a surprised look. "I'm not playing any games with you. What is going on?"

"Gary, listen. The scorpion that stung you in the leg left a deposit in you. That deposit is me. You must listen to me and stop talking out loud. Just think what you want to say, and we can have our own conversation."

All right, what's going on?

"That's better. You can call me Moloch. I am here to help you, and I want you to help me."

How can you help me, and how can I help you?

"I can help you become the champion fighter you want to be. I will instruct you on the rest."

How can you help me be a champion fighter?

"Trust me on this. No man has beaten me in physical combat. Using men with no fighting experience, I've made wimps of fast street fighters. What can I do with an experienced, trained fighter?"

This sounded too good to be true. My coach has taken me through years of training to get me to this point. *You're saying that you can make a noticeable difference in my skills?*

"Try me. If I can't do what I said, then I will not ask you to help me."

We'll see about that tomorrow at the gym.

"Deal."

24 THE MEETING

Fred was preparing for the lesson to teach at the Bible study. His heart ached as if God was trying to tell him something. He had opened his Bible to Joshua 6 and began to read. As the word of God filled his heart, understanding from the Lord enlightened his soul. The aching in his heart confirmed the message from the scripture.

He read the passage twice to get a better understanding of what he needed to teach. He had gotten in better shape, the best shape of his life actually, from riding his bicycle. Because of this, as long as he allotted enough time, he could ride to the Bible study. The lesson was simple: follow the proven path of obedience.

The time had come for him to leave. The ride had gotten easier in the few weeks he had been forced to do it. It had become a pleasure and a challenge at the same time. The hill just prior to the Power Lane house was long and steep, making it the toughest part of the ride. He had prayed and pedaled for the last thirty minutes. He needed all his energy to get up the hill and past the house. He always stopped at the bottom of the hill, taking a refreshing drink of water before the climb. This day was no different; he had his water bottle in his hand, ready to drink. With everything in its place, he rose on the pedals only and pushed with all his might down on the pedal. Speed and acceleration climbing, the muscles felt the usual burn. The force continued to keep the wheels spinning as he proceeded the climb, struggling for every rotation of the pedals.

His eyes remained focused, never letting them drift from the road. His complaining legs pushed for every bit of speed that could be achieved. Every inch a joy to overcome, the cycle climbed steadily up the hill. He could almost see the demons reaching out for him as he got to the road in front of the house. He continued to push at the pedals hard, making them spin like a windmill, accelerating the cycle by the house.

The demons continued to reach out, trying to get to him. He knew it was Jesus keeping them from getting to him. As his praises to his Lord lifted up to the heavens, the cycle rolled on. He wasn't sure what was different about the house this time; it was as if it knew that something was wrong and seemed to fight harder to get through. The remainder of the ride was uneventful as expected, and he had enough time to shower before the Bible study began.

—◆◆◆—

Nassor saw the rider on the cycle coming and prepared for the attack. Four of the demons were to sit back as a second assault squad was instructed to find the hole and punch through it. All demons waited on the order to attack. Just as the cycle approached the property line, Nassor yelled, "Attack."

All but the four demons flew as a wave at the line of impending angels. The arcs of the angels' swords didn't hold up the demons at all, and the collision came at full force. The wings of the angels had not broken, but they had to rise to hold the demons that were coming in high.

The second wave looked to be coming high but dropped low. Striking low with their swords trying to clear a path, they hit with all their fury. Their swords were across the line but not enough to reach the rider as he rode on past. The firing line tried to slash at the cycle tires. Dropping back just a little and slamming forward at the lower-level protection to get just one more inch of distance, they made a final desperate attempt to stop and kill the cyclist.

All the demons dropped back to the house with a fury. The hissing could be heard in the heavens and in the pit of hell. Nassor's anger was known by all, and the fire coming off the tip of his sword smote at the air, cutting it in half. "What do I have to do? How hard is it to kill one person?"

The other demons fell back as the fire snuffed out at contact with the sheath of the sword. Nassor turned to the other demons. "Find a way to kill him. The sword of my first-in-command will go to the one who can kill him."

——ᴠᴠᴠ——

Fred looked at the group now calling themselves the prayer squad and marveled. Just two months ago it was only four strong, just one week ago it was only eight strong, now the prayer squad stood at twelve. They all had welcomed Bill and his in-laws with open arms into the group. Now they were welcoming Richard and his entire family to the group. He could see God providing not just new members to the group but meeting needs of the group through them.

Fred started this meeting with joy. "Praise God for this tremendous new growth. God is reaching out and providing for all of us in our time of need. Let's praise the Lord in song, with all we have in us, for He is truly God of all gods."

Their voices of song lifted to the heavens, praying that God would find sweetness in their praise of His mighty deeds.

When the time came, the room grew silent, and a tear ran down Fred's cheek. "I have really struggled this week for the lesson. I believe I had more to learn than you do this week. We are going to start in Joshua six." There was a long pause of silence as the pages of Bibles ruffled before they settled for the reading.

"Now the gates of Jericho were tightly shut because the people were afraid of the Israelites..." The reading continued through to the end of the chapter.

"God showed me that the occupants within Power Lane are frightened and desperate. All of the issues we are having is a result of the desperate attacks to weaken our strength. Look at the fear in the citizens of Jericho. The wall was extremely thick and solid, and then there was another equally strong wall separated by a six-foot gap between them. The only way in was through the gates. If we had as strong a security system today, we would trust our most precious valuable within it without a second thought. Yet, something had the people so scared that they shut and locked the gates without being attacked by anyone.

"Folks, God said that I bought that house to make it His. Anyone in it has a right to be afraid. Here is the clincher: God has to take the house for us. We, in our humanness, cannot take that house. The battle for Jericho was not won by a great army charging the walls and overpowering the inhabitants. Rather, it was won by God overtaking the city and giving it to the Israelites.

"The farther I looked into the scriptures, the more I noticed the details coming out. God mapped out the order in which what was to be done, dotting every *i* and crossing every *t*. He left nothing to chance. Let's look at the detailed instructions. First, Joshua and his fighting men were to walk around the city one time every day for six days. Second, seven priests, each carrying a ram's horn, were to walk ahead of the Ark of the Covenant. Third, the priests blew short blasts on the horns while they marched around the wall. This was done daily until the seventh day.

"On the seventh day, the short blasts rang from the horns as all the others. The difference was that they marched around the wall seven times. This was affecting the way the inhabitants thought of the marching army. At first they were frightened and ready to go to battle as they marched around the wall. Most likely, by the third day, that fear had become a time of entertainment. Now, at the seventh day, it was a time to bring a picnic lunch and watch the parade. The only thing lacking was the band needed to change the song." Fred paused to let what he had said soak in.

He continued, hoping some of this was found agreeable to the prayer squad. "After the first time around, they were expected to leave. Instead, they were going around again. More and more of the inhabitants were gathering to see what was going on. The top of the walls were becoming littered with people looking on. Lap two complete, lap three complete, they continued to count until the seventh lap. At the end of lap seven, God's chosen people stopped were they stood, the priests blew a long blast on their ram horns, and the people shouted a long shout. God then collapsed all four walls at once, falling in on them. He had to have shaken up every man, woman, and child looking out from the wall. Can you imagine the shock of all those inside as well as outside as this happened?

"The fighting men of Israel ran in, burned the city, killed every man, woman, and child still alive, leaving no one or no animal alive.

"I began to take a second look at the details of the instructions given to Israel and saw a different picture play out."

Will they see this? Are they ready to see this? He couldn't fret about that now, he still had peace about what was going on and what he knew had to be said. The rest was all up to God to do anyway.

"Instead of the city of Jericho, I saw the house on Power Lane. Instead of Israelites, I saw the twelve of us. We did not have the Ark of the Covenant, but we had other ways to carry God with us."

Scanning the room for any sign that this was already off course ended quickly with John speaking up, "A-a-a-a-amen, go-go fo-fo-for it."

"We walked around the house in this order: I led, John, Harry, and Peter follow, then the newer members of the prayer squad took up the rear. The original four members of the prayer squad lead, praying, while the rest of you sing a praise song to the Lord.

"Before you tell me that I am off my rocker, I am off my rocker for even suggesting such a plan at all. If you guys tell me I am nuts and you won't do it, then I will honor that."

Without asking, the group said in almost complete unison, "Go for it. Let's do it."

Fred asked them for clarity purposes, "You guys want to walk around the house once for six days and on the seventh day walk around it seven times?"

Bill asked in return, "I know I'm the newest member here, but is there a better way than following God in obedience?"

Fred thought about that and answered, "There's never a better way than obeying God."

Peter asked, "Are you thinking that this should start tomorrow?"

"Yes, I am actually. Does anyone have a conflict with that?"

Fred could see God working in their hearts already. Henry said, "I can transport four, and my wife can take another four if someone can get the rest."

The group started arranging transportation with a buzz of excitement that God was giving them the house for them to occupy. Fred looked in shock at the work going on as everyone started to get involved in the project before them. When the group got quiet, Fred said, "We have all agreed to do this. Let's start this out right—with prayer."

They all bowed their heads and prayed out loud one at a time. God's power filled them and stirred them.

The spies still watched as the prayer squad not only gathered together but began to teach and pray. Two of the spies flew back to the house to report.

———

Nassor saw the two spies drop in from the roof. "What is your report?"

"The prayer squad is twelve strong. We found Bill, he is in the prayer squad now. Young Samuel slept while they listened to the teaching and prayed."

Nassor was more than angry. "Where was the scorpion?"

The spies looked confused. "What scorpion?"

Nassor stared ominously at the spies. "What is going on that you can report?"

"They are planning to take the house from us."

That caught Nassor's full attention. "How and when?"

"They said something about walking around the house starting tomorrow."

Nassor's anger turned to confusion. "How can they take the house from us? That will work perfectly for us. We will kill them all while they are walking around the house."

The spies were a little confused but continued, "They have enough vehicles to get everyone here. We aren't sure of anything else."

Nassor smiled a big ugly smile and said, "Well done, we will take care of them on this end here."

—◆—

Jesus said to Ailith, Alexander, and Boris, "They are ready. The battle is Mine to fight. When they march around the house, I want your entire host between them and the attacking demons. Ailith, you are in charge. Keep them safe."

Ailith replied, "Yes, Lord."

Ailith turned to the defending angels. "We already know what to do. Be ready for anything."

———◆◆◆———

Nassor left the house in the hands of his first-in-command and flew to Satan's fiery office. "Master."

"Nassor, what are you doing here?"

"Master, I am here for reinforcements. The prayer squad is planning to attack the house and take it over."

"You can't handle a few people coming into the house?"

"Master, you know they will bring a large portion of the heavenly host with them. When they do that, the fight will be lost to the heavenly host, not to the people."

"So, you are looking for forces to match what you expect the heavenly host to bring." Nassor knew Satan was aware of the consequences of losing this house and was not ready to face that. "We have Samuel in our control again?"

Nassor was not ready to answer that but knew he had better. "No, but he is located, and we will have him shortly."

"You better. I am sending you with whomever you think you need. Do not let the house be taken. This is a command."

"Yes, master."

Nassor gathered the horde support and went back to the house.

———◆◆◆———

The scorpion crawled its way to the top of the trash can. Trainer remembered the fight to get Moloch in Gary. He had checked for damage to the scorpion and found none. He knew the time had come to start the hunt for Samuel. He looked around to see if Gary was still in the area. The street corner was busy, but Gary was gone. The wings straightened out, and the scorpion took flight.

The radar screen lit up with red dots. After poking a hundred of the red dots, getting the pictures, and clearly identifying that they are not Samuel, Trainer decided to go to Power Lane to get help from Nassor.

The trip to the house was uneventful. The scorpion landed smoothly on the roof and settled in, allowing access to the house. Trainer came to the office and bowed before Nassor. "Master, I request your assistance with the scorpion."

"Where is Moloch? He is to teach you what you need to know."

"Moloch left the scorpion and went into Gary to start a second Trainer chain. I am looking for Samuel to take him over."

"What do you need my help with? Didn't Moloch show you the scorpion and how to use it?"

"Moloch showed me all he knew. He himself has not seen it before entering it the first time. We have learned some but are getting a general picture without being able to isolate any particulars." Trainer wanted the help without further angering Nassor. He knew what that anger led to.

"Come with me to the scorpion. I will show you how to isolate and penetrate your target."

They went to the scorpion together. Nassor went immediately to the radar screen, and Trainer watched as he looked at the brightly lit keypad, with many pictures selected. "This will never do. You have too many targets to choose from."

"That's the problem I'm having."

"Listen to me. You can push any of these buttons and isolate a group. Let's look at this group." Trainer watched as Nassor pushed the button with the two circles and three lines dividing the *x* in half. "This is Trainer's mark. This will isolate all Trainer implants."

Trainer watched the screen as all but four of the red dots vanished. "The radar is still picking you up in the scorpion. You're right here. Power Lane is here too. This one," he continued as he touched the red dot, "is the other chain started at the same time as Moloch. It has struggled to get going too."

"Moloch said he was alone when he went out."

"Moloch told you what he knew. Why do you think I was sent out after Moloch's failure?"

"I thought it was to get rid of the prayer squad."

"That was the part that everyone knows. The other part was to combine the two original chains to make one. Now this one is Moloch starting over again. No matter how much I agree or disagree, it is done already."

"Is it good or bad that Moloch possessed Gary?"

"We will have to see."

"There are two other buttons you need to know. This one"—Trainer's eyes went to the button with the picture of a single circle with the same three lines over it—"is all the help Trainer will need to accomplish his task. You can speak to them by pushing the dot and talking into the mike right here." Trainer looked where he pointed above the screen to a small section with what looked like a speaker in it. "This," he further explained, "will remove all red dots and replace them with all of those who have accepted Christ as their Savior."

Trainer reached out his finger and pushed it. The screen went blank; then slowly, blue dots started appearing on the outskirts of the screen.

"Be careful at fighting directly. It is easier and quicker to poke at them from the side and run. You have learned that from working with Bill."

"Yes, yes, I have."

"Now armed with this information, you can use the scorpion to find Samuel, accomplishing your task easily."

Nassor slid out of the scorpion, and Trainer ascended in to the sky with the blue dots on the radar. "Time to go find Samuel." He pushed Trainer's mark on the keypad and watched the four dots appear.

After hunting all day, Trainer decided to go over the house and rest for the night. The hunt could easily resume from there tomorrow.

25 THE HOUSE

Three cars pulled up to a stop by the road in front of the house. Just then a bicyclist rode up and stopped in front of the line of the cars. Fred and the others took their places in the line, and with the first word of prayer from Fred, they began to march. As they marched, the others started singing praises to God.

———∿∿———

The angels knew what had to be done. They formed a perimeter that was solid, waiting for the attack of the horde. They heard the hissing and waited for the order to attack. On the first step, the horde flew to kill, swords drawn and flaming. The angels' swords arced bright with light, cutting the air and locking into a defensive position. The horde flew at all sides of the house looking for a weakness in the angelic line—for one place to break through to kill the prayer squad.

The angelic line held, the low line hit first, slashing at the demons attacking. The swords sparked as they collided and crashed into the line. The archangels caught the high wave. Each of the demons' swords swung striking the angels' swords being pulled away while the second sword slashed the demons, quickly pushing the demons back. Some had severe cuts across different parts of their bodies. Others fell to the line to be slashed and dissipated.

The squad marched around the house, prayed, and sang. They got in their respective transportation and went home. Their individual guardian angels marveled at how the line held against the horde. The fear felt by the horde drove them hard.

The angelic line suffered minor slashes and stab wounds but held strong. Ailith was deeply concerned about the new strength of the horde. Only with their Lord's strength would they hold against it.

———∞———

Jesus saw the ensuing battle and the strength of the demon horde. He met Ailith at the gate. "How are you going to do against the horde?"

Ailith shook his head. "Without their obedience in prayer and praise, we will not only falter, but the prayer squad will all be killed in the walk." Jesus was glad to know that they were aware of where their strength came from.

"Take care of the wounded. They will need strength for tomorrow. I need to contact some praying friends to get their help with this fight."

Ailith looked to Jesus. "I could smell the fear on the horde. They are being driven by it. I'm not sure if they would rather die fighting than facing the master after failure."

Jesus looked knowingly. "They would as they are already promised death for failure. Your death will be quick and gracious, the other death long and hard."

———✿✿✿———

Nassor was in the office seething. "We lost! This is round one. We have to win and get at least one of the prayer squad in round two."

The two other demons in the office stood away, silent, ready to leave in a hurry if needed. Nassor was not in a mood to play, wanting to eliminate the fight or war altogether. He needed to pronounce his victory badly. The fire against the prayer squad burned hot and deep. "They will die if every demon has to die to get them."

Each of the four team leaders was called into the office. The four demons came quickly. "Yes, master."

"Our strategy we used failed. We need a new strategy, one that will surprise the angelic host and break a hole in the line, allowing us to get to the prayer squad. Any suggestions?"

Team leader one said, "What if we concentrated our forces on one side? When the other side comes for reinforcements, a secondary attack squad breaks through and kills the prayer team as they approach the holes made in the line?"

Nassor asked the rest, "What do you think about this idea?"

The other team leaders looked, nodded in agreement, and team leader 2 said, "That may work. It would weaken the line on the other three sides, allowing a small squad to be able to break the line."

They all agreed. Nassor concentrated on the four leaders. "It is a go for tomorrow. Lead your teams with that plan."

"Yes, master," they all said in unison.

———

The blond lady in the church had been a prayer warrior for a long time. Tonight was a night she had been through many times before. Something was going on in God's kingdom, and God needed her to pray for whoever or whatever it was. This night, she had not been able to sleep well or get out of prayer. She could see a house, a small group of people walking around it, and a dizzying blur of motion in between. She had been praying all day on and off. Now, the pain in her knees was great, but she knew she had to stay on her knees for these people.

———

The young man in his youth, known to all in the church as a warrior of God, suddenly felt a burden beyond what he had felt before. All he knew or felt was that a small group of people were walking around a house and in need of prayer support. He was with three faithful friends, all ready to pray at any time with him. Together, they knelt to their knees and prayed, seeking God in this matter.

———

The pastoral staff meeting had started with prayer. The staff had all gathered to put together the day's agenda, setting the course for God's work for the day. Just before breaking up to get the work done, one of the secretaries said, "Before we all start our morning task, I feel like we need to pray for a group of people as they are walking around a house."

The senior pastor looked at her. "Do you know these people?"

"No, but we have prayed for many people we don't know because we feel God has said to. Is this really any different?" The secretary had a point that was inescapable.

The pastor conceded and bowed his head to pray. The entire pastoral staff prayed for the duration of an hour.

The youth pastor got the group's attention. "Anyone really want to have a day off?"

They all said a resounding, "Yes!"

He returned, "Does anyone else feel like we should all meet at this time every day for the next six days to pray like this for these people?"

Three of the staff members stood up, saying, "Yes, I do."

The four of them looked at the others in the meeting as to say, "Are you with us or against us?"

One by one the group stood agreeing until all were standing. Making the commitment to come and pray for these strangers every day for a total of seven days.

—◦◦◦—

Jesus was smiling as thousands of people were put in place to pray every day for the next six days for a group of strangers walking around a house. Not one of them knew any more than that, but all were obedient and serving the same Lord and Master that the prayer squad was actively obeying.

—◦◦◦—

Ailith called the defending angels to him, "The prayer squad is getting ready to walk again. You angels are their front line of defense. The strategy of the demons will change daily. The prayer squad will pray, plus there are one thousand prayer warriors that God has placed a burden in their hearts to pray for this situation. You will have the strength to withstand whatever they throw against you."

Boris looked worried. "Commander, we have faced injuries the first day. We are severely outnumbered. Is there anything that can break this prayer strength that we had at the first battle?"

Ailith looked at Boris. "Your fear is clear. You worry about the prayer squad rightly. Know this, God is in charge and providing what is absolutely necessary to make his plans happen. When they are obedient and pray, you will not be defeated."

Boris said, "Yes, commander. All is understood."

—◦◦◦—

The next morning, the cars and bicycle were parked in the same spots. The demons in the house were anxious and fidgety, drawing their swords half out of the sheaths just to replace them back in. The four commanders were doing all they could to keep the fight reserved for the angelic line.

The one thousand prayer warriors' hearts burned again to pray, seeking God for this group of people. They were kneeling, lying, standing, hands raised in the air, praying for people completely unknown to them.

The angelic line descended and formed just as it had the day before, swords drawn and ready. Ailith took the high watch, ready to make the necessary orders and adjustments.

The prayer squad had knelt together and prayed prior to getting in their marching positions.

—◊◊◊—

The scorpion rose up from the roof of the house, flew over the praying prayer squad, and began to search for the child Samuel. Trainer might have been new to wings but was ready to make a move to Cadet. The radar had shown no evidence that the prayer squad was even there. Trainer looked at the screen, pushed the cross button, and watched and waited as the blue dots appeared. "We can still locate Bill by locating the Christians. Now, to figure out how to locate Samuel."

All of a sudden, the screen filled with a bright light; directly in the center, there was a tip or focus point that was clearly the cause of the bright screen. As the screen cleared, he no longer saw Bill but the face of one of the guardian angels. His mouth moved clearly forming the words, "Leave now."

The scorpion backed off to safe distance. Bill was now walking around the house on the screen, but the entire body of the guardian angel was still centered on the screen.

———✍———

All but a few of the demons flew at the front line, attacking the angelic line with a great commotion. Ailith shouted out the command, "Line one support to front."

The three other lines on the sides and back flew, attacking from the back. With all the attention to the front, the demons that had held back flew out to the back line and hurled themselves through the line. The frontline demons were trying to draw back but were forced into a fight from the angels behind them. The demons attacking the rear were quickly cut to ribbons by the archangels and dissipated. The fight to get into the house was almost as furious as the fight at the line. Finally the demons shot straight up and went flying straight down through the roof.

"Lines, reform."

Quickly all the angels took their original fighting places and watched.

———✍———

The demons remaining that could fight were not enough to accomplish anything, so they remained in the house, hissing and looking edgy, ready to fight. Some of the demons had started working on the injured while others were just trying to rest.

"Conference, now!" the voice was clearly Nassor's.

The four leaders flew quickly into the office and knelt, saying, "Master."

"What went wrong with this plan?" Nassor breathed heavily, and anger rolled out with every exhale like smoke.

Team leader 1 broke the long silence, "It didn't account for the second line or the impossible strength they had on the line."

Nassor's breath came as fire, "I want no more excuses. What will it take to get through this line to the prayer squad?"

Team leader 2 said, "This might work."

"What might work? Tell the rest of us." Nassor was ready for a good idea.

"Divide the sides in two. The fist wave is divided in half—half hit low, half hit high against the wall. This occupies the two layers already in fighting. The second wave flies over the wall, diving after the prayer squad."

Nassor looked deep in thought as the smile formed on his face. "A plan with lots of potential. It is about time someone thought for a resolution."

The smoke and fire from his breathing had gone, seemingly as quickly as it came. "All right, we know the plan. We know what to do. Let's make it happen."

The four leading demons went to work, getting the fighting demons up to speed.

—◦◦◦—

The thousand praying had all said amen and were going about their regular chores of the day. Though some still had a heavy heart, the prayers had gone up, while God had taken care of whatever was going on.

Jesus was still watching as the prayer squad was just finishing the march of day 2.

—◦◦◦—

Looking in the windows, Bill thought it was like an ordinary empty house, but he had been in the basement, seen the green glowing thing that called himself Master Trainer. He knew the best he could do was to understand that God wanted to win this battle and had it in His control.

—◦◦◦—

They had not attracted a crowd of people like the press or a group that had come for a short parade. What he didn't know was what had been brewing across the street. They had not noticed the swelling of the ground or the scorpion settling into it, waiting for the time to get to Cadet.

—◦◦◦—

Ailith gathered the company in for instruction. "Good job down there. You should be starting to feel your strength grow. As that happens, you will experience more and more strong challenges. The saints assigned to do the work are doing it well. The saints praying are obeying with perfection."

The angels bowed, saying, "Yes, commander."

———✧———

At the end of day 2, Fred wasn't sure what he might have felt but knew that something was fighting at the house. Wasn't it Harry that had said he could feel tension or something worse while they walked around the house? If he felt what Harry felt, it was more than just tension? This was a feeling of stress, anger, and hatred resulting from a major conflict.

John had told him earlier that the house would fight, struggling against all odds. The fight would not be against flesh and blood, but against Satan's power in control of the house. The demons would need it and want it badly—beyond any normal comprehension they could come up with.

Do I doubt God's capability to defeat this demonic possession? How can I know what to feel when I am walking around the house? If there is really this much of a demonic battle going on now, what can we expect going on toward day 7? God, what have I gotten this group into? Fred's mind reeled with nonstop thoughts, so much that it made it impossible to be still and listen.

Somewhere, in the mist of those thoughts, John's earlier words about the house came through. "You need to know that God will take the house. The battle will be His. Remember to obey, and God will take care of the rest."

Fred fell to his knees. "Oh, God, how can I do this? I'm already over my head. All I have left to do is obey You, acting on the faith that You will take care of Your end. Give me the grace to carry me through this."

He wasn't sure if he felt better yet, but he had gotten the burden off his chest, and giving it to God was better than any other option he knew of. The time had come to sleep, and he fell into bed, hoping sleep would overpower his nerves to carry him away. As his breathing smoothed out, sleep did overtake him, carrying him in dreamland.

—☙—

The next morning, the ride was harder than normal. He felt the weight of the leadership on his shoulders, but was filled with the doubt of a simple follower.

—☙—

Harry saw the fear and doubt in his eyes. Pulling him aside, he said, "Fred, you are feeling the battle around you. Don't start doubting now. You have always led us to be obedient to God in all circumstances. This is a circumstance that we all need to be in strong faith without doubt. You are the leader God elected because God knows that you will stand strong."

Fred looked at Harry. "God knows exactly what I need to hear, doesn't He?"

"He sure does. He has the people to keep you going in the right direction as well."

The two had joined the others for the Morning Prayer; Fred led like the man he had always been. The doubt and fear had melted; the first step started confident and strong. The tension and fear came quickly, but with it came understanding that it was already defeated by Jesus Christ.

———✺———

The demons knew the plan, waited for the command, and anxiously targeted their prospective targets. "Attack."

The demons' first flight group took off, locked on target, attacking the angelic line. Seconds later, the second wave attacked with fire, trying to create holes in the line. A few seconds later, a third wave shot up at a forty-five-degree angle to go over the angelic wall. Suddenly, one angel for each of the attacking demons on the third wave interfered and blocked the top.

The scorpion flew in, whipping his tail at the prayer squad with no success. The guardian angels whipped, slashed, and cut at the scorpion. Avoiding the pinching claws and the tail, the guardian angels' swords began to penetrate the thick skin of the scorpion. The scorpion was forced to retreat and watch, still unable to find Cadet. Was he in the group walking around the house? They had to know, but the guardian angels were keeping them from seeing or knowing what was going on.

———✺———

The marching team continued around the house through the thick tension and fear seemingly coming from inside and outside the house. Their eyes could not see anything to cause concern, but they all began to feel it.

The prayers and the praises rang in the ears of God. God's protection was in full force through the highest intensity of the battle. God watched as the demons flew back into the house without touching one hair of the prayer squad.

—◦◦◦—

Nassor screamed in anger, "Conference, now!"

The four leaders flew quickly to the office. "Master."

"What happened?" If the leaders had any thoughts, they weren't sharing them with him.

Nassor was fuming, "What are they doing that we cannot get to them?"

There was still no answer from the four leaders. Nassor threw his arms up in disgust. "Have these guys ever done anything other than walk around the house?"

Leader 3 broke their silence, "All they have done is walk."

"Then why are we fighting, weakening our forces while they are trying to entertain us with a parade?"

The shock of the four leaders showed brilliantly on their faces. "What are you saying, entertain us with a parade?"

Nassor could see more than shock on their faces; confusion had slapped its impression on each of them. "Not one of them is going to get in this house by walking around it. Instead of fighting, causing our forces to get weaker, we can watch from the outside while resting the horde. Then we are ready for the battle when they bring it to us."

Understanding swept over the faces of the demons. The four leaders hissed and roared with excitement.

Nassor's mind began to wander. *What is it that they really want anyway? Can't they get them alone to kill them?*

The leaders and Nassor agreed and set the plan into action.

———

Ailith gathered the angels together, weak and haggard from battle. "You are standing strong and winning the battles. The prayer squad is protected. They have approached us in three different ways. We don't know how they will attack tomorrow. We know this. The battle will come, and we have to be ready for it. Rest, prepare, and be ready to stand strong and defend again another day."

The angels in chorus said, "Yes, commander."

———

Fred requested that the prayer squad gather together. He hoped that Harry and John were receiving something special from God. The fear had spread to the new members of the prayer squad. What could he say to the new members to keep them obedient through the hard times? They were all looking at him for something that he did not have: answers to their fears.

"I felt the fear while walking around the house. You may have felt it yourself. I am here to assure you, this is the way God has told us to take possession of the house. God has protected us through all this and will not allow anything to happen to us unless He intends to turn it into something better. I know how you feel because I have been going through this for the past two days. Obeying God is always the best way no matter what the circumstances come out to be."

Silently Fred prayed, "Thank you, God."

———

Bill not only felt the fear but felt Trainer near, knowing that Samuel would be there. "Trainer is most likely hunting for Samuel. I felt him trying to get to Samuel today. He somehow has found me, and therefore has found him. I know God is protecting him, but I am scared and don't want to see Trainer take Samuel like he had me. What can I do?"

Bill could feel the concern of Harry and the others. Harry replied, "Bill, I am sensing that God knows your fear and is promising you that He has Samuel in His plans. He must work with the choices Samuel makes, the same as He worked with you as you made your own choices.

"God is going to allow things to happen so that Trainer can be ultimately defeated. You have all of us on your side and angels working around the clock to keep Samuel safe. Trust God to do the work, and He will take care of Samuel. Don't forget to pray for Samuel every day. God is listening."

Bill wasn't sure if that made him feel better, but it did give him something to stand on and instruction at the same time.

———

Fred knew that it would be difficult and could only hope that the pressure would relax. He was filled with doubt that it was going to get any easier. He sensed the prayer squad seemed to feel more secure to remain obedient to God.

———∽∾∽———

Day 4 lurked about with the rising sun. Had the statement brought about enough peace to get the squad together? Did something more need to be said? Fred had spent hours in prayer and still couldn't be sure until they all got the house. The only thing that helped was the feeling of peace under the feeling of concern. Deep down, he knew that God was in control and already knew all the circumstance with every life involved.

The two cars were already moving toward the house. His answer would come soon enough. It was now time to sit and wait on the results of the prayer.

With anticipation and excitement, all the rest of the prayer squad slid out of the cars, walked to him, and said, "We are ready to walk. God is in control and will protect us."

"Thank you, God." Fred knew of nothing else to say.

———∽∾∽———

The angelic line formed around the house, hands on swords ready, waiting for the ensuing attack. The prayer squad lined up in the usual line, preparing to march. The horde inside saw this, stepped outside the house, hands grasped on the handle of their swords, and took a defensive stance around the house.

The march around the house was uneventful for the prayer squad. The angelic line, on the other hand, stood watch, expecting the horde to fly over in attack. The horde kept their hands on their swords until the prayer squad walked by, and then they raised their hands in applause. When they had passed, their hands grasped back down on their sword's handle.

In anticipation of trouble, one of the guardian angels wrapped both hands on his sword. With that, the demon across from him drew his sword, slashing fire in an arc. The guardian angel immediately drew with a full arc of light. Nassor quickly bound between them; one look, and the demon put away his sword. The guardian angel followed suit, eyes staring at each other; Nassor held his hand out in a silent command. The demon kept his sword away though he was still itching for a good fight.

Nassor obviously controlled the horde, though he desired to kill Ailith while he was so close to him. The plan had been formed: make them attack, then use their own force to kill them. That meant waiting and holding the force under control.

The walk around the house lasted too long for the demons. Their own excitement hard to hold in, they managed to force themselves into control. Nassor knew he had to get them to relax and watch. For the fourth day in a row, they had walked around the house, making no attempt to do anything. Even the scorpion had stayed back as told.

Nothing—no fear, no anger—nothing was felt by anyone in the prayer squad. It seemed excitement, anticipation, and rest buzzed around the house that day. This made the walk easier but unnerved Fred. He tried to hide his feelings from the others but feared they were showing throughout his whole body.

He allowed the others to lead the way in this meeting with their comments. Their excitement could not be denied or agreed with by Fred. He was glad that the torture seemed to end, but it made no sense; it just made no sense. This led him to try to understand something that was not for him to understand. In the end, he knew the only answer was to give it to God and accept what it is for what it is.

Ailith looked confused. In front of the whole team of angels, he asked Jesus, "Why would Nassor take the fight out of the horde? This bodes to our advantage. Why would he want to do that?"

It was not a question that anyone could answer. Ailith and all the angels looked to Jesus for the answer and saw a smile on his face. "Be ready for My command. Just be ready."

Nassor flew over the horde in the main room. "We are celebrating, not fighting. For the fourth day in a row, they have done nothing to actually enter the house. Until you see the tip of their sword, you're to stay put. We want them to relax, let the angels get off guard. As long as they are on guard, we have not been able to punch through the line. If the line relaxes, the holes will form from surprise. All will die in one battle. Are these instructions clear?"

In unison, the horde said, "Yes, master."

—*∿*—

The fifth day started as any other day, the overriding emotion coming from the house was happiness and laughter. The horde had already started dancing and clapping to the music from the parade. The angelic host was shocked but accepting of the attitude of the horde. By the end of day 6, the horde was in a party mode, celebrating and dancing to the praises to God.

26 THE PRAYER

Bill scanned through the list of names and addresses of those that attended the funeral. His eye stopped at Rebeca's name. He picked up his phone, dialed her number, and paused. *Is it too soon? Certainly she would take a phone call from me.* He pushed the talk button and listened to the line ring.

She answered on the third ring, "Hello."

"Hello, Rebeca. How are you today?"

The excitement in her voice pronounced every word, "Much better now. How are you?"

"Doing better. I decided I need help with all these thank-you notes. Do you have a little time to help me?"

"I have all day. I can be over there anytime you want me to today."

"I was going to get it over with. I need to get it done anyway."

"I will be over in ten minutes. Do you need me to bring anything?"

"No, I have everything here including all the food an army could eat for a month."

"Okay. I'll be right over."

Before he had a chance to say good-bye, he heard the click. *Am I ready to for her to come over?* The house was clean. The few toys on the floor lay around Samuel, and he saw no reason to move those. He looked at his clothes. *This will never do.* He was wearing the shorts he slept in and an old T-shirt he put on to get breakfast. She was already on her way. He took the steps two at a time and darted to his room to get changed.

He grabbed the top pair of clean jeans and a pullover shirt, took them into the bathroom, and checked his face in the mirror. The shadow covering his face would have to go as well. He shaved and dressed as quickly as he could. *She will be coming soon.* He splashed a little cologne on, hoping that would be enough. He hurried down the stairs and back to the couch so he would be working on the thank-you notes when she arrived.

———

Rebeca just hung up the phone, grabbed her car keys, and made a quick check to make sure she was ready. She stopped cold, dropped her keys. *Hurry up, girl, you gotta get dressed.*

She was wearing her bed clothes and had not changed at all this morning. There was no reason until the phone call.

She darted into her bedroom and grabbed a pair of blue jeans and a shirt. She stopped as she glanced at the shirt, put it back, and looked through the rest of her shirts and blouses. *I need to look good, not hurried.* She looked back at the jeans in her hand. *What blouse would go with these? All of them, Rebeca, get one and go.* She grabbed her favorite plain pullover shirt and hurried into the bathroom. She cleaned up and dressed quickly, decided she was ready to go and went.

By the time she got on the road, she was already five minutes later than she said she would be. She drove over quickly, wanting to see him. *Goodness, girl, what is wrong with you? He just lost his wife who is your best friend! You gotta get a grip on it.*

———

Bill was used to waiting on Saundra, and this he figured was no different. He sat there addressing envelopes that never seemed to end. The stack looked untouched as he continued writing, trying not to think about anything. Then he heard the car pull in the driveway. He got up and went to the door. He opened the front door as she got out of the car. The smile on her face told Bill what he wanted to know. She dressed in jeans and a pullover shirt just as he had. She allowed her natural beauty to shine through without the mask of makeup. Bill always liked the natural look. Bill could only see an angel walking toward him.

"Hey there, glad you could make it. Come on in."

She smiled at him as she walked in past him. Bill said, "We'll be more comfortable at the dining room table." On the way, he gathered the stuff off the couch and carried it to the table. After setting the stuff on the table, he pulled out the chair. "This is Saundra's chair."

"You know, Bill, Saundra said you gave it away that you liked her."

"How did I do that?"

"Just the way you acted around her. The look on your face and body language was warm and caring."

"What do my actions tell you?"

"That you don't know what to do. You want to like me but don't want to go too fast."

"You got all that from me pulling out your chair?"

"No, I got all that from the lunch. What I got from today was no more than confirmation of that."

"I guess I'm not much of a mystery."

"It's not the mystery that makes you so likable. It is you that could be seen every day with all your mistakes that is so likable."

"Is that what Saundra told you?"

"In her words, you are the best man to be with because you were intended for her."

Bill didn't know what to say. He put a stack of thank-you cards in front of her. "That doesn't explain your excitement on the phone a few minutes ago."

"I'll leave that for you to figure out." She took the first thank-you card and wrote out the note, walked over to the computer, put the paper in to be fed, put the note in the scanner copier, and hit the copy button. When she returned to the table, she said, "Let's work on those envelopes together."

"Okay. Where did you learn that trick?"

"From your techno wife. She had shortcuts that she used all the time."

While they worked on the envelopes, they continued talking about techno tricks Saundra taught her. "Bill, why did you really invite me here?"

Bill formulated his answer carefully, "Because you were correct, and I don't know if it's too soon to feel the way I feel. What do you think?"

———

Patty wasn't hiding anything from her family, and her brother's ribbing was never-ending. Her lack of trust had her running to the phone every time it rang. That brought more teasing, but she could face that over the harassment she would get if Richard had to get her to the phone. The one time she was getting in the bathroom, the phone rang.

She could hear Richard say, "Hello."

She listened closely and couldn't hear anything else and hoped it was for someone else. Then she heard, "Cool, see you tonight. Let me get Patty for you."

"Don't say it, Richard." She was clearly through the phone line. "I'll be out in a minute."

Speaking intentionally loud, "She is getting dolled up to talk to you. She will be here in a minute."

She ripped the phone out of his hand. "Ha-ha. You're funny. You just wait. I'll get even with you." She put the phone to her ear. "Hello, Peter."

Peter's reply came back, "Is this the normal, Patty?"

"Yes, I'll get him when he starts calling the girls. Girls know what to say."

"Do you want a ride to the prayer meeting, or are you riding with the rest of the family?"

"I would love a ride. When do I need to be ready?"

"The van is on its way. You won't believe what happened."

"I'm ready. When are you getting here?"

"Ten to fifteen minutes. I'll knock on the door for you."

The van stopped fifteen minutes later. Peter jumped out and ran to the door.

She looked at Peter. "Run to the van, let's go."

They ran at a full sprint and got in the van. "What was all that about?"

"He hasn't left me alone since we left the Bible study yesterday. He will pick on me until someone pulls me out of the house."

"Maybe you need to make it where it is not so fun."

"How?"

"I was asked earlier today by some of the prayer squad if you liked me. Just tell him we're dating now, so you better start playing catch-up."

"Do you mean that?"

"If you want to, the choice is yours."

She wrapped her arms around him. "Thank you. Revenge is going to be sweet."

"Sit down, lovebirds," came from the driver's seat. "Ladies in the seat. Peter, on the floor and hide, you're overload."

Everyone cooperated, and Peter said, "Let's go."

Patty said to the driver, "I could sit on his lap."

The driver retorted, "One per seatbelt, driver's rules."

The noise of the van overran the rest of the conversation, but Patty's eyes never left Peter.

She whispered in Peter's ear, "Where are we going on our first date?"

Gary arrived at the gym before the coach. He checked in and told the girl at the desk where to send the coach. He went to check out the aerobics room and realized the mats he brought would be needed. The wood floor would become slippery when sweat got on it. The space was big enough to get the movement drills done easily. Coach would like that.

Gary thought about what he heard from Moloch and decided to see if Moloch really was there, or if all of it was a figment of his imagination.

Moloch.

"I'm here, Master."

You'd better impress me. If you don't, whatever you want done will not get done by me.

"I am confident—'impressed' will be the wrong word. I'll bet you'll be amazed."

We'll see if you can back that up.

"Try me with something simple, like stretches."

He got down both legs straight out. With his back straight, he started to slide his hands down his leg. His back bent until his hands were extended beyond his toes and his nose was buried in his knees.

I should not be down here on this stretch.

"I told you. Your speed and height will be dramatically increased as well."

You still have to impress the coach.

"You just do your workout, and I'll take care of the coach."

He continued stretching by spreading his legs straight sideways from his body. Again, running both arms down his legs until his nose hit the floor. Exhaling slowly, in just seconds, he could actually kiss the floor. I've never been this limber in my life.

After about twenty seconds, he raised up slowly. He rolled over and ran both hands down his left leg. His nose again lay beside his knee. The same happened when he did his right leg.

I don't know how you are doing this, but you can keep on going. This is great. It would take me years to get here on my own if I ever did.

"You are starting to be impressed. I have much more to show you today."

Gary just relaxed, took in a deep breath, and went back down into the center into the deep muscle stretch. The whole time he spent stretching, he was amazed at how limber he was all the way around.

—◈—

Coach Hogan entered the room and stopped. He was amazed at what he saw Gary doing. He just watched as Gary got up and turned to get the workout mats. "You are more limber today than I have ever seen you. That is good. Maybe we need to get you kicking higher, maybe taking the top of the head with your heel. You've never done that to me before."

"Today is a new day, coach. Shall we see if I can impress you?"

"Impress me, son. The more you show me you can do, the more I will make you do. You want to be a champion? Let's work to make you the best on the planet."

—◈—

Coach was a big man and knew what it was to be in a fighting ring. He was a winner with a "no excuses" attitude. He expected your all, every workout and every fight. He was willing to make you so exhausted that you were carried out because of the workout. "I see you have already done the stretches. Lay out the mats, champ."

Gary grabbed the mats and laid them all out lengthwise.

"Good. Up, drop, five each, pushups. End to end, this is an endurance test. You will do this twenty minutes or until you drop. And don't you dare quit too early or you will do it again."

Gary took a deep breath and waited for the go.

"Go."

Gary launched to the end of the mat and dropped like it was easy. He did the pushups and kept moving fast. For twenty minutes, it seemed he never slowed down. He did well over two hundred pushups without even looking like it hurt.

"Good. Quick move on those sit-ups. Get into position."

Immediately he responded to the words of the coach and got to where he needed to be.

"Up, down, left, right," he called the pattern for two hundred sit-ups, and Gary kept up all the way. "Good. Up on your feet. Mat sprints, go."

Gary took off, hit the floor, turned back, and ran back out over and over again. After an hour of that, Coach Hogan handed him a water bottle. "Hydrate. You are working harder and doing more than I have seen you do. What is the difference?"

"Desire, coach." Gary shouted more like a Marine than a fighter.

"Good. Lay me out the floor."

The time came for the aerobics class, so the floor was laid out in another open area. In a minute, the floor was out. "Gary, keep good form and keep up the energy. I know what a five-minute round feels like, now you are going to experience a five-minute round."

A moment of silence as he let the water absorb and Gary's breathing become more relaxed. "Are you ready?"

"Yes, coach."

"Gear up. Light contact, five minutes, I'm your opponent."

Gary and Coach Hogan entered the ring with protective gear on and prepared to spar. "Let's warm up first. Give me a chance to get my muscles moving."

"One." Gary threw out a sidekick easily blocked by the coach, and the counter was allowed. "Two." Coach threw out a roundhouse that was easily blocked and countered. "Three." Gary spun with a back kick that was easily blocked and countered. "Okay. You should feel better too. Ready?"

A nod was enough.

"Fight."

The kicks and punches flew, blocks and counters just as rapidly. He never slowed down through the five minutes of sparring. The coach held him off throughout.

"You have improved. Remember that every fighter has someone that will beat him no matter how good he is. You're not watching your timing. Focus and timing will win you more fights than the fastest hands and feet. Let's hit the weights."

On the weights, Gary was so much stronger than the last time.

The coach's expression was becoming more and more filled with anger. He picked up his towel. "I don't coach cheaters.

You have been taking steroids against my word. I won't be back to coach you."

"Coach?"

"What?" the anger in his voice still prominent.

"I haven't taken any steroids. You have to believe me."

"Prove it. Everything I see here today proves you have."

"What can I do?"

—⁓—

John sat and watched as Patty and Peter made their attraction clear. Anger flushed in his heart. He didn't know what to think. He knew God wasn't being fair to him. First killing his relatives and not Fred's, now he is separating him from his prayer warrior on the prayer squad. If he only knew why God wanted him alone and abandoned by the prayer squad. A decision was made. If he had to be alone, he would make the best of it. He wasn't giving Peter anything to gloat about. He got Patty; he would not get his help with prayers.

27 THE CONQUEST

The angelic line formed around the house, the horde took their defensive line with big toothy grins glowing on their faces; day 7 was about to start. The prayer squad parked in the normal fashion, prayed for the mission, then took their places in the line.

The one thousand that had been praying the previous days had become two thousand. Simple urging from the Holy Spirit led them to pray and would keep them praying throughout the day.

The party started with the first note from the singers. The prayers flowed uninhibited from the front of the line. One thousand angels, with swords drawn, waited high overhead for the call.

The prayer squad completed the first time around to the disappointment of the horde. Their surprise overflowed when the prayer squad was going around again. The praises and prayers continued on as well as the dancing from the defensive line.

—❧—

Starting around the second time, the scorpion rose from the ground, whipped the tail around to battle stance, and flew at the prayer squad from outside the defensive line. Sakata and the guardian angels drew their swords, flashing the arcs in the direction of the scorpion.

Trainer worked on shrinking the scorpion in size to seize Samuel. Trainer worked on the offensive attack. The comet tail of fire behind the scorpion burned with revenge and hatred.

The praises rang from the back of the marching line. The strike just seconds away as the scorpion approached with speed and determination. The guardian angels and Sakata wrote their intention on their faces, their swords ready with determination to keep Samuel from this attacking bug.

Sakata caught and deflected the first blow from the scorpion's stinger while evading the claw. The sword's strike hit the claw with enough force that it yielded back, flaring sparks all around. The tail whipped around and struck at the protection on the side. Randolph felt the tail cut into his shoulder, injecting hate like a poison. Randolph's sword cut at the tip of the tail and dislodged from his shoulder. With a quick second strike, the tip of the tail fell to the ground.

Out of nowhere, the scorpion began to shrink. It got smaller and smaller and smaller until it reached the size of a gnat in the air. The only thing visibly clear from the scorpion was the fiery tail trailing off indicating its course. The swords blocked the path to all the extent the angels could. Until the scorpion vanished, they fought it. The scorpion found its way to the tattoo, settled over it, and struck Samuel with its tail.

A wail of pain screamed out of Samuel. Tears welled up in his eyes. The pain shot up and immediately subsided. The scorpion diminished into a two-dimensional tattoo on his shoulder.

———

The end of lap 5 rolled around when Samuel's scream broke the praise chorus ringing out. Bill assured the baby with a loving pat on the back. He quieted right down and fell back asleep. The singing and prayer continued on as they continued walking. The clapping and dancing of the horde went uninterrupted by the scream of Samuel.

———

The last lap around, they came to the place they had always started, stopped, turned to face the house, and fell silent. The horde made enough noise that they never noticed anything until they heard, "PRAISE GOD!"

At the sound of the call, the angels' swords in unison whipped out as they flew with a fury at the demons. The angels hidden high above did the same. The demons flipped, dodged, and fled, pulling out their own swords.

Suddenly, the dodging demons were attacked from above by the thousands coming in strong. The horde was slashed and cut to ribbons, dissipating in a cloud of red smoke rising then being pulled into the pit of hell.

———∾∾∾———

Ailith appeared in front of the prayer squad. They all trembled, stepping back from the sight. "Fear not, I am a servant of the Lord Most High. He sends you this message. Go in and take all of Trainer's property out of the house, put it in the barn, and burn it to the ground."

Just as quickly as he appeared, he vanished, leaving them to the task set before them by God.

———∾∾∾———

Led by Fred, they sang praises of thanks and love to God as they walked into the house free of spirits in all ways.

Rejoicing, they pulled Trainer's property out to the barn and said, "This is it. There is nothing else that belongs to Trainer."

Bill broke in, "There is something you don't know about. Follow me."

Bill walked directly to the basement that had been cleared, went to a loose brick in the bottom of an interior wall, and pulled it out. "Here is the key to the secret room." He crawled in and began pulling out books and boxes of stuff until finally he removed the last box, crawled out himself, and said, "That is all. Let's light that barn up."

The barn door opened up easily enough, the sight was astonishing. The cars, tractors, attachments, every mechanical thing ever owned by a man possessed by Trainer was there waiting for Bill to take it. "Bill, it's all yours."

"No, Fred, it's all Trainer's. Burn it all. You don't want it. It will only draw you away from God into disobedience."

The expression on Fred's face changed as he realized the seriousness in Bill's voice. Without walking in the barn, Bill and Fred together struck a match, let the flame cover the tip, and threw it in the barn. As the door closed, the amber of fire glowed through the door. The fire consumed all that represented Trainer with the exception of Trainer's log taken out by Bill.

—⁂—

While changing Samuel, Bill took off his shirt and noticed the tattoo on his son's shoulder. He lay on the bed kicking and talking like any other three-month-old baby. Bill's eyes said it all. He was expecting the spaceship, but what he found had claws and a tail. He knew Trainer had not only found him, but had somehow entered him as well. Trainer was gone from the house and from him, but the remnant would still have to be fought.

Bill finished changing his diaper, called in the others, and wept as he held his son tight, knowing the battle was just beginning—again.

CPSIA information can be obtained
at www.ICGtesting.com
Printed in the USA
LVOW04s2054120816
500060LV00016B/194/P